PACIFIC RISING

Nathan Naismith

Prologue

5th August 1945, Okinawa

The war-weary and aged battleship, *USS Redmaine*, silently left the still-smoking carcass that was the island of Okinawa, its landscape now pockmarked with craters, trees standing alight like candles honoring the dead.

The men onboard the battleship were unsure of what was to come. They had left their comrades behind on the battered island under the cover of the moonlight to pursue their ever-elusive prey.

The Americans had capitalized on the Japanese retreat, advancing through the islands with all the vigor they could muster. No one had expected the Japanese to have stood their ground and fought with such ferocity. Each side had an agenda in the fight: the Americans passionate and fiery over the unwarranted attack on Pearl Harbor, the Japanese adopting a radicalized notion that they would rule all the corners of the earth under one shogun. Each side would claim their cause was just, like so many before them, extending far back to the Crusades in the Holy Land.

The American battleship had left under strict orders from Admiral Nimitz, sailing for the Philippine Sea and eventually its target: Tokyo. On the bridge, Captain John Barker stood silently, his hands clasped behind his back. His men watched quietly and waited.

Despite Japanese naval losses, Barker felt they still had some fight in them. With the war almost won in Europe, his enemy was more dangerous than ever. What drove him on was his nationalistic zeal in what he was doing. He felt it among all his men as he looked away from the endless darkness and stepped out onto the bridge wings, joining one of the young lookouts who kept a steady watch. He hoped that zeal was enough to keep them all going.

Barker had received the mission orders by private communication in his cabin. The industrial section of Tokyo was the primary target. Secondary targets weren't considered due to what he carried onboard. He was to maintain full speed under the cover of darkness. If he was lucky, he would beat the other ships who were briefed on their part in the mission. He had been down to the weapons room, inspected the contents, and spoken to the lieutenant in charge. He shivered at the thought of the untold destruction he was about to cause. Barker couldn't easily take a life, but to save his country. That was different.

"Anything on the distant horizon, son?" he asked the young watch man beside him. He noted the shaking hands holding the binoculars. The lookout, who looked no more than twenty, jumped in fright at the captain's voice.

"No sir, nothing in my sights." The young man hesitated before continuing. "Where are we off to, sir?"

The captain sighed, taking off his cap and scratching his salt and pepper hair. He had lived a fulfilling life, and had done his part for the country, ageing him more than his years suggested. He was only forty, but he felt seventy.

"We will know soon enough. Keep an eye toward the northeast. I don't want anything leaping out at us from the darkness." The captain looked at the young man.

"Fuller, isn't it?"

The watch man nodded nervously.

"Good work so far, son," said a smiling Barker, before he stepped back inside.

His lieutenant, Carter Yates, stepped out of the radar room, saluted, then whispered in his ear.

Barker studied Yates for a moment. The man's normally fiery temper was tempered, and a weariness had gathered around his eyes.

"Are you sure, Yates?"

The lieutenant nodded. "Positive, sir. Just came down from the Admiralty."

Barker grimaced. The thought of men far away from the battlefield playing general irked him immensely, but he didn't want to show his disdain standing in a room with men who relied on him to keep an open and cool mind.

"Right you are, Yates. Get back downstairs and keep an eye on our package. We arrive at…" Barker checked his stainless-steel watch, "… approximately 2300 hours."

Yates saluted again and slunk off into the bowels of the ship without another word.

Barker looked out through the stained and grimy windows of the bridge. He issued a command, following the Admiralty orders Yates had just delivered to him. They would arrive at their destination in four hours. His men were battle ready and so was he. As tired as he was, he wanted to be with them when their enemy was in sight. There was time enough for sleep later.

* * *

Three hours later, Fuller, the watch man Barker had spoken to earlier, sounded off. The men on the bridge stood to attention at the sound.

"We have landfall," Fuller announced. "Looks to be an island, about thirty miles off our starboard bow."

Barker grabbed Fuller's binoculars. "Sheer rock walls. No sign of a beach anywhere."

Yates stepped out of the radar room, "What do you think, Captain?"

"It could be just another island, could be an early warning radar station," Barker replied.

"We can't see much in this infernal darkness and fog. I say we slip right past them," Yates said.

"I'm with Yates on this one, continue on course." Barker replied.

Barker was confident that they were out of radar range, and no enemy ships had been sighted. Their mission was all but assured. He approached the helmsman and issued adjustments to the course.

One of the kitchen staff brought coffee and sandwiches for the crew on the bridge. Most of the men felt Japan had used up everything they had. With Okinawa taken, the next step was the mainland. With the ship's engines running hot, they didn't see the tiny speck above them, hiding far up in the cloud cover. Barker and Yates were oblivious to the next few minutes that spelled their doom.

* * *

Japanese pilot Taki Mimora saw the outline of a lone ship sailing in the Philippine Sea far below him. He dived his Zero and moved in for a closer inspection, using the cloud cover and smoke from the ship below to hide his movements. There was no question. The design wasn't theirs. With Okinawa taken, that meant it was an American battleship. He didn't hesitate in calling it in. Taki was a young and inexperienced pilot. He didn't know he was part of the final days of Japan. Part of Japan's policy to train anyone who desired to defend their country, young and old, in a last-ditch attempt to survive.

Brought up on traditional teachings by his family, he would gladly give his life to the emperor and his people. It was why he signed up when the call came. His parents understood what he wanted to do, not arguing with him when he left that day. He lived in the city of Hiroshima, a city far away from the war. He figured Tokyo would be the target for the Americans when they come.

He reached for his radio and relayed what he had seen to the hidden radar station on Tor-shim Island.

Just out of radar range, a Japanese cruiser responded to the radio communication sent by Taki. The captain onboard had no hesitation in closing in on the battleship, sending it to join the graves of the Americans who had dared attack his homeland.

Within torpedo range, the Japanese captain issued the order to fire.

* * *

The young watchman on the left-wing bridge sipped his coffee, blissfully unaware of the torpedo's trajectory toward the *USS Redmaine.* He put the cup down and raised his binoculars, spotting the torpedo moving through the water. Its only identification was the foam arc from its mini propellor as it jettisoned through the water.

"Fish in the water," the young watchman cried. Barker and Yates reacted in surprise. They hadn't expected to be seen, moving as silently as they could, maintaining radio silence.

Yates ran to the wing bridge as Barker began screaming orders to turn the ship away from the incoming torpedo. It was too late.

Yates looked on in horror as the torpedo slammed home into the side of the *Redmaine.* The explosion lit up the night sky and the sea around it in a miasma of yellows and reds. The ship's hull peeled back like a can of sardines. Oil poured through the hole in the hull and into the engine room, flooding it as men called for help. Some sailors were crushed under fallen pipes. Others desperately tried to escape, but the ship's structure had warped from the explosion. The entrance door inside was useless, cutting off their escape, and spelling their doom.

Yates was thrown back into the bridge, colliding with other men before he climbed to his feet.

"Captain Barker," said Yates. "We have to release the bombs now, or we will go under in a force to be reckoned with." The once-cool captain's demeanor had gone, replaced by a shadow of his former self, unable to think, let alone issue orders. Yates knew he had to take command.

With the *Redmaine* engine room flooded, oil seeping outward, it was only a matter of time before an idle spark sent them all sky high. Even if they went under, Yates was determined to finish the job. As the alarm sounded, he ordered all onboard to evacuate the ship..

Grabbing the receiver from the phone swinging from its cradle, he dialed the weapons room below. Yates hoped the men in the torpedo room had not left yet.

No answer. *Damn it,* he thought. He ran down the stairs, past men in orange life jackets heading topside. He would finish this himself.

Reaching the engine room, he climbed inside, his feet sloshing in water as the *Redmaine* tilted heavily on its side. The prototype torpedoes had already been loaded. He waded through the water, fighting against the raging torrent as he grabbed the swinging trigger and checked the red lights on both. *Red means ready to fire.* He pressed the first button. Nothing happened. He pressed the second button with the same result. White faced; Yates smashed the buttons with his fist.

"Fire, damn you, fire, you, useless piece of—" A cavernous groan sounded throughout the ship, drowning out the voices of the men who remained onboard.

Yates didn't get a chance to think as the upper level gave way, sending a loosened steam pipe crashing into him. The *USS Redmaine,* so close to achieving its goal to test the secret prototype weapon developed with New Zealand scientists, groaned as it was pulled under by the Pacific, an ocean more power than any battleship. Waves surged over the stricken vessel and pulled it below the surface.

* * *

Taki Mimura watched as the explosion claimed the lives of most onboard. He knew the Japanese cruiser would finish off anyone who survived the cold waters. He circled as the Japanese cruiser arrived, not seeing the crew on the edge of the railings gun down the hapless survivors, Captain John Barker among them.

As the *Redmaine* drifted down into the depths of the Pacific, a mission in an airfield far away in an undisclosed location was being prepared. A B-29 called *Enola Gay* was being loaded with another devastating weapon. Its target: Hiroshima.

The *Redmaine* sank without anyone alive to tell the tale, its mission an absolute failure. The cold water claimed hundreds of souls and brought them down to the seabed. For the Americans, it was a mission that would be buried deep within red tape and bureaucracy for countless decades to come.

Part One:
Old Enemies, New Friends

Chapter 1

2023. North Korea.

Commander Connor Evans rested the stock of his assault rifle against his shoulder and breathed slowly. Clearing his senses, he looked through the rifle's scope and triggered the built-in night vision.

The greenish hue of his optic sight outlined the huge prison compound of Kaechon Concentration Camp, North Korea. Its presence felt ominous under the pale moonlight. The camp stood two and a half kilometers southeast of Kaechon City, its twinkling lights like fireflies in the darkness. Evans couldn't help wondering if the morbid nature of the camp kept the local population in line. His speculations would have to wait. He returned his focus to the concrete and metal structures below.

Initial scans by drone had shown the collection of buildings were set out in neat rows, which lent a certain deathly pall to the normally pleasant vista around it. Rolling emerald hills were visible by day, but they were obscured now by darkness and low fog.

The buildings were demountable, raised on concrete stilts to avoid seasonal flooding. Evans thought the roofs might be aluminum, though with only a little moonlight, and the green wash of the night vision to rely on, it was only a guess. He swept his sights across the buildings, noting corridors of green grass and concrete interspersed between them. It wasn't the environment or the gloomy surrounds that concerned him. It was the fact he hadn't seen a single patrolling guard.

He shifted his sights to the outlying fence and the thirteen feet high wall topped with razor wire that ran its three-hundred-meter length. He grimaced.

Evans couldn't see a way over the top, at least not one that wouldn't attract attention. His strategy so far had been by the book, and stealthy. However, his eagle-eyed recon specialist, Janus, had flipped that initial plan on its head. The former Latvian special forces commando, skilled in the art of concealment and surprise, made short work of beating the compound's security arrangements, surpassing any records from previous missions. Janus had spotted the cameras first. Nestled in eaves, and situated on poles positioned at regular intervals, the cameras commanded a broad view of the grounds, ensuring any covert entrance would need to be a matter of timing and precision.

A voice crackled in his ear. "Janus to Evans, do you read?"

"Go ahead Janus," he replied.

"I am in position. Had a small scuffle with two stray guards out for a midnight stroll. Safe to say, they are tucked in nice and tight now."

Evans smiled. Janus was a piece of work. He was glad he was on their side.

He shifted his gaze to the closest gateway, one of two on site, according to his team's report. Though it looked peaceful, Evans knew it was anything but. It was reminiscent of the concentration camps of Nazi Germany, this time nestled within mountains a far throw from the snow-covered Alps.

Flicking a switch on his gun, he turned on his thermal optic and began a sweep of the two corner towers on the perimeter of the camp. The closest tower revealed a lone guard, pacing. The furthest displayed two guards playing cards. *Hell of a job,* Evans thought. He looked at his watch. It would soon be dawn. It was now or never.

He only had one shot to get what they came for. Shouldering his rifle, he gazed down at the infamous prison compound. Its official name was called Kaechon Concentration Camp, but to those confined within, it was hell on earth.

Connor Evans was a former SAS soldier, Commander of Darke Company, and Captain of the floating headquarters, *Serenity.* Contractually, Darke Company offered their services to the governments of the world and the highest bidder, but Connor would never accept a contract without the input of his team, something he believed set them apart from other mercenaries.

Although his arrival had been less than an hour ago, two other members of Darke Company, Tori Winter, and William Southgate, had scouted ahead to ensure Connor's plan would go like clockwork. Their quarry was a political prisoner held inside. A man known only as 'Chi', an informant for the CIA. Their objective was clear. Snatch and Grab. Once they had their man, they were to take him to a small inlet down the coastline, far from prying eyes. They had positioned a zodiac to bring him to *Serenity* as quickly as they could. That was Plan A. They had a Plan B. Connor just hoped he wouldn't have to use it.

Speaking into his neck mic, he instructed his team to sync their watches. *20mins.* That was all he could risk before their window of opportunity disappeared.

"Connor to team, lock and load, use of lethal force is permitted, but only where necessary. We do not want to take out any other prisoners if the going gets rough. William, be on standby for break and enter on the western fence line on my go."

He looked behind him at the tree line and opened the duffel lying nearby in the bushes. He had sent Southgate to plant it earlier that day. The former British SAS operative was only too happy to oblige. Bundled inside was a coiled metal cable complete with a carabiner clip. Since stealth was crucial, any use of their air propelled grapple guns would give away their positions. Keeping it old school, he moved quickly, selected the largest of the trees as his base, and threw the cable around it, cinching it with the carabineer. A hard pull indicated it would hold.

He moved to the edge, peeking over into a dark void. He licked his dry lips and felt his heart quicken. Despite his training, Connor wasn't a fan of heights, preferring wherever possible to keep his feet on the ground. This, unfortunately, wasn't one of those times. Clipping the other end of the rope onto a harness within the duffel, he slid into it and moved into position. He took a sharp inhalation and dropped down the cliffside.

Connor abseiled down the jagged cliff face in less than a minute, arriving at the bottom with practiced ease. He unclipped himself and climbed out of the harness, tucking it behind some rocks to ensure it wouldn't be found. Moving toward the nearest trees, he watched the fence for any sign he had been seen by the guards. Nothing. The distance he'd estimated from above had now changed significantly. It looked like he was set to run the length of three football fields, if his estimate was correct.

He felt a presence behind him, turning and raising his rifle. Too late.

"If I was an enemy, you'd have been dead already." The female whisper didn't hide her Australian accent. Her rifle was pointed at Connor's chest.

Evans smiled. It was Tori Winter, a member of his team. He could see her hazel eyes in the moonlight, flickering with excitement for what was to come.

"Maybe so, but I'm not. You ready on my go?" Connor asked.

He saw her nod in the semi-darkness, revealing a set of white teeth as she moved closer.

"Alright, Janus, keep an eagle eye, we make our move in… *three, two, one.*"

Without a word, Connor began moving across the field, aware of Tori close behind. He shot a glance toward the moon. It was hidden behind cloud cover, but he knew that at any point the moonlight could turn into a natural spotlight working against them.

Covering the distance with relative ease, his fears proved unfounded. They reached the fence without a sound, Connor and Tori dropping to a knee at its base. He kept a close eye on his thermal sight as Tori went to work. A former soldier and demolitions expert, Connor favored her on break and enter missions that involved finesse or required loud distractions. He only needed one of those skills now. She removed two items from her back: a furled carbon fiber cloth, and a closed hook and grapple. Tori threw the device over the fence. The grapple's rubber coating deadened any sound it might make. She pulled, feeling it grip, then nodded at Connor, satisfied it would hold.

He placed a hand on her arm, and they counted down from ten. There were no alarms, no ear-splitting klaxons, and no shouts from unseen patrolling guards. Satisfied, Connor took the lead safe in the knowledge Tori was right behind him. He grabbed the cloth, threw it over his shoulders, and began to climb the wall. At the top, gripping the rope, he unfurled the cloth and laid it over the wire. Silently, he pulled himself over and climbed down. He waited for a moment, observing his surroundings. Satisfied they were still ghosts, he tugged on the rope to signal Tori to join him. Minutes later, they made short work of both the exterior and interior fence that lay three and a half meters apart.

"Janus, report. Anything changed?" Connor kept his voice low, kneeling in the darkness.

"Negative, Boss, still no movement. Seems a bit too quiet if you ask me."

It was too quiet, but Connor decided to take full advantage of it. With Tori in tow, he moved toward one of the demountable buildings and peered down at the miniature screen to check their route on his. The small LED screen barely registered any light, ensuring they would not be seen.

He nudged Tori, pointing at his wrist. "The main office is located toward the northwestern corner. We are near the vehicle maintenance shed. The northeastern corner is where the prisoners are housed. William would've got in by now. We'll intercept him."

"Heads up, Boss." Janus's voice, calm as always. "You have movement. Two guards heading your way from the southeast. Let me know if you want me to drop them."

Peering around the edge of the building, he registered no movement at first. Then two figures glided out of the fog. Prison guards on a routine patrol.

He turned to Tori, indicating that their planned route would not work unless the guards moved on. Connor shifted to the opposite corner. Plan B would put them within shooting distance of the closest watch tower if things went south, and it added more time to their already shortening window of opportunity. It was a risk, but he wasn't their commander for his ability to talk the talk.

He looked behind, gave the 'ok' gesture with his fingers, and he and Tori moved in unison. Keeping to the shadows kept them out of the camera's sweeping views. A single wrong move would be disastrous as they snaked through the buildings, reaching the centre of the camp with relative ease. A large, square building marked in Korean as 'workshops.' They were at the heart of the compound.

About to move out of the shadows, Evans halted as the voice of Janus once more broke into his earpiece. Two sets of guards. The first two moved freely on patrol, but the other two were standing still, according to Janus. A small flash of orange light revealed the location of the nearest two. A cigarette break. *Damn.*

The guards were blocking the most direct route to the housing blocks. Connor couldn't afford to delay much longer.

Connor racked his brain, then a yell shook him from his thoughts. Pressing himself into the wall, he watched as the two guards stared in his direction. The guard with the cigarette flicked it away and they moved toward Evans and Tori's position, guns held ready. Connor was about to issue the order for Janus to eliminate them, when they turned off their path, entering one of the buildings.

Tori exhaled. Realizing he too was holding his breath, Connor slowly released it, blood pounding in his ears. He allowed his racing heart to slow. *So far, so good.*

Chapter 2

Devising the strategy to break into the prison had been the easy part, but finding a political prisoner surrounded by many others was like trying to find a needle in a haystack

Evans had ordered his second in command, Tori's sister Kelly, an expert hacker in a previous life, to do what she could to find the location of the informant. Her search had turned up nothing but his prison and dental records. His precise location would have to come from another of his team.

Evans keyed his neck mic. "William, you inside yet?"

No response. Evans started to try again, then Will's voice came through.

"Almost got myself in a bit of a bind there, but I think I'm alright. Picked a nice night for a quiet break in, Boss."

William Southgate was a former British SAS soldier who couldn't help but crack wise, even when under pressure. Connor figured it came down to nerves when on mission.

"How close are you to the mainframe server?" Connor asked.

"Inside the administration building now, Boss, moving into position in thirty seconds. Standby.,"

Evans looked at his watch. It had been almost ten minutes, and time was running out. He looked at Tori. They had to move and move fast.

A sliver of moon broke through the cloud cover. As the seconds ticked by, Evans listened to the sounds around him, amazed at how quiet it was.

"Got it, Boss. Block 4A, the prison blocks."

Evans moved quickly, Tori following as they threaded between the buildings toward the blocks. They reached their destination, a painted

4A emblazoned on the side of one building. Evans looked around, as Tori stepped up to the nearest doorway and kneeled. She used a small screwdriver to remove the security panel. Tori cut two wires, installing a small bypass connection between them. The door clicked. Evans, not wasting time, toed the door open, and moved inside alone.

Flashes of his high school history lessons flashed into his mind as he took in the squalor within. Though not as horrific as the concentration camps of Nazi Germany, this came close.

Evans slid on his prototype night vision glasses, and moved quietly among the bunk beds, careful not to bump any feet or stray legs of the sleeping prisoners. The flimsy wooden bunks squeaked as one prisoner moved in his sleep, making Evans pause. He listened, but all he heard was snoring.

Then he saw their target. Evans moved to the prisoner's bedside and pulled a small syringe out of his waist band, unstopping and plunging it into the man's neck. Chi's eyes flew open, but Connor's hand over his mouth ensured he made no sound. Chi stared at Evans, then his eyes rolled into the back of his head.

The tranquilizer took effect immediately but, as a precaution, Evans waited. After twenty seconds, Evans called it, grabbing one of the man's arms. As quietly as he could, he heaved him onto his shoulders. It would be up to Toro to cover him as they moved to their escape route.

With Chi's weight on his shoulders, he checked his map and made for the door, maneuvering around the sleeping men. When he reached Tori, she leaned into whisper.

"No sign of the guards that appeared before, but I saw lights toward the workshop. We may have to resort to Plan B sooner than expected."

Evans nodded, "Right, let's move. The sooner we get out of here, the better."

They had just begun to move across the grass toward the next prison block when the alarms sounded.

"Shit, we're sprung," Tori cursed.

"Plan B now!" said Connor. "Will, if you haven't already, get the hell out of there."

The piercing klaxon echoed around the valley, which amplified it further. Tori took point as they ran past the workshops, any attempt at stealth now abandoned. Evans knew he didn't have to tell his team how to do their jobs, and he was certain Will would've already made his exit.

Janus's voice interrupted his thoughts.

"Boss, overwatch report. Multiple guards moving. You are going to be surrounded real soon."

Evans issued his orders. "Think you can remove a few of them?"

"Loud and clear, Boss, the fireworks have already begun." Evans couldn't hear the shots over the alarm but as they rounded a corner, they came face to face with two guards, guns raised. Tori raised her own a fraction too late, but two rapid shots from Janus removed both guards from the equation.

Spotlights from the guard towers flashed on, as Evans, Tori, and the unconscious prisoner moved across the compound. They ducked behind a building, shielding them from the nearest patrolling light.

"What do we do now?" Tori hissed, peering around the corner.

Evans thought fast. "Overwatch, how well guarded is the vehicle maintenance bay?"

"Scant at best, Boss. Are you thinking of creating a bit of shock and awe?"

Evans didn't reply, but the smile that lined his face said it all.

Moments later, Tori kicked open the door and they moved inside the vehicle bay. Inside, the lingering smell of petrol and grease stung their nostrils as they eyed two jeeps. Evans threw open the back door of one, and bundled Chi into the backseat, as Tori climbed into the driver's seat.

Evans slammed the rear door and joined her in the front, clicking a button on the dash. The building's door began to open, but not fast enough.

"Punch it," he said, looking over his shoulder, before adding, "But I would duck if I were you."

Tori threw the jeep into reverse, the tires squealing before finding traction and plowing into the sheet metal door behind them. The roller door came off with a deafening screech along with the rear half of the jeep's roof, removing it as cleanly as a can opener.

Tori immediately pulled the handbrake and, using the grass beneath them, pivoted the jeep in a full three sixty. The pair were thrown around unceremoniously in the front seats. As she accelerated again, Connor looked into the back, taking stock of Chi's peaceful demeanor, still unconscious, and unaware of the chaos that surrounded them.

"I say we have woken the hive. Don't you think?" Connor said, taking in the commotion around them.

Tori gave him a look as a chorus of bullets thudded against the exterior of the jeep. According to the map on Connor's wrist, they were heading for the southern gate. There were two exit gates between them and freedom. The first they would be able to punch through, but the second would surely stop them their momentum wouldn't be enough to punch through the second reinforced gate. A section of field beside them exploded, sending dirt and grass cascading across what remained of the jeep's roof. Evans grabbed Tori's silenced assault rifle. Holding an arm over his eyes, he used the stock to smash the window before leaning out and firing back at the guards. He saw through the smoke and spotlights that they had regrouped far quicker than he expected. Two jeeps bounced along the grass and barreled toward them.

"Gates fast approaching, Boss. You sure we can make it?" Though she was militarily trained, he could hear the note of doubt in her voice.

Evans leaned back. Plan B didn't involve being chased by guards and half of the camp. He looked through the damaged windscreen and got an idea. It was reckless as they come, but it was better than nothing. Tori caught his eye, and she saw the look on his face.

"No. No way, Boss. There must be another way."

"Keep the guards busy as long as you can. You'll have your exit soon enough." Without another word, Evans kicked open the door and threw himself out into the darkness.

Chapter 3

Evans figured the grass would cushion his fall. It didn't. His shoulder nearly blew out as he rolled across the grass, gritting his teeth as he tumbled to a stop. Without pausing, though his body rippled with pain, he climbed to his feet and took off at a run, a hail of gunfire following where he had been moments before. He threw open the door of the closest guard tower and thudded up the metal steps two at a time. A prison guard coming downstairs went for his gun. Evans grabbed it, bashing the barrel against the railing, the shock making the guard let go. Connor threw a straight punch into the man's throat. He ripped the gun from the gasping man's hands, shouldered past him, turned and kicked him down the stairs. He didn't look back when he heard the thud of the body below.

Reaching the top of the tower, he threw open the door, startling the two card playing guards. One swung the spotlight, the other unleashed a burst of fire at Evans. Diving to the side, he placed two shots into the man's knees, sending him to the ground screaming. *He won't be walking anytime soon,* he thought, shifting his aim to the other guard who fumbled for his pistol.

"Drop it. Now!" Evans yelled as the man managed to pull it out of his holster. Though he had a defiant look on his face, the guard dropped the pistol and kicked it over to Evans. Keeping his own gun trained on the man, Evans kneeled and picked it up, tucking it into his waistband.

"Now lay on the ground and place your hands on the back of your head." The guard did as he was told as Evans spotted what he had hoped to find. Crossing the room, he fired at the locker door. When the door sagged open, his eyes sparkled at what lay inside.

* * *

Tori threw the car hard into the corner, feeling like a hooligan drifting at a set of lights, doing donuts to escape the police. Their original plan was concrete, but Evans always had a second up his sleeve. He had never let them down, always taking point on every operation. A whizzing bullet made her turn her head, but not fast enough. It sliced across her cheek, and she felt warmth rise on the left side of her face. *Where are you Connor?* She rounded the corner for what felt like the tenth time and headed once again for the rear gates. Her time was almost up as she squeezed the wheel harder, accelerating past the workshops and into the road that led directly to the gates.

With perfect timing, the first gate went up in an explosion of fire and metal, guards fleeing for cover as shards rained down on them. She threw the jeep into top gear and barreled forward. She knew only Evans could think of something so off the cuff, as she saw the second gate follow suit. Unlike the first, the second had two parked jeeps nearby that exploded simultaneously, eliminating half the section of wall giving her a clear way through.

"You did it, Boss," she called into the radio. The only reply was static.

* * *

Evans threw down the rocket propelled grenade launcher and began to move quickly. He wasn't sure what had happened, but his communication device produced only static. He tapped it again, as two more guards appeared from the stairwell. He fired at the open doorway, using the temporary respite to spy his method of escape: a satellite cable that led to the top of the tower, and an adjoining cable leading to the spotlight. He grabbed them and, without a thought, hurled himself over the edge of the tower, baselining down away from the camp and onto the ground. Shots followed him as he looked for the red lights of the jeep in the distance.

As he ran, his mic came alive. "Conn- Conn- wh-are-you?" Tori's voice broke through the static, and Evans heard garbled replies from the rest of his team in response.

Not sure if they could hear him, he said,

"I'll meet you at the rendezvous point. Connor out."

He ran to the tree line as the klaxon continued ringing in the valley, guards spreading out to track him, likely with dogs to catch his scent. At the sound of jeep engines, he threw himself to the ground, hoping the longer grass would hide him. His main concern was the convoy of vehicles chasing Tori. Once the jeeps moved on, he climbed to his feet and kept running, knowing his best bet would be to reach the equipment he had left behind.

"Connor, it's Kelly, can you hear me?" Her shrill voice made him grit his teeth.

"I'm here, but things have changed," he said. "Tori has our package en-route. I will find other means to reach you. Focus on the mission at hand."

"Connor, I can send Kurt out with the chopper, he can meet you—".

"It's too risky. The whole prison, hell, the whole area, will be on high alert at this point. Call this one Plan C. It's one for the books. Let me know when the package is safely onboard."

He heard another engine heading his way, and he crouched in the trees and darkness. It was one of the patrol jeeps moving slowly across the dirt road, a guard sweeping his torch among the trees. Connor shrunk further behind one. He had found his Plan C.

The sound of the jeep's engine dropping to an idle, followed by the sound of the door opening, made Connor pause. He didn't think it was coincidence. The guard was reacting to something that had drawn his attention. He moved closer to Connor's position and brought a radio to his lips. Silent as a shadow, Connor threw an arm around the man's neck and cut the air off slowly until the man passed out. *That should keep him quiet for a few hours.* A voice came over the radio in Korean. Connor knew no response would mean a certain investigation. He wouldn't get by with his basic Korean. and opted to ignore it. He frisked the guard quickly for anything of use and dragged him further into the brush. It would give him much-needed time, as he made a dash for the jeep. Climbing in, he drove away.

He didn't get far before two pairs of headlights appeared over the crest of the hill behind him. He looked in the rear vision mirror as a volley of gunfire made him duck. One shot blew the mirror clean off. *The chase is on now...*

Chapter 4

Tori continued to accelerate as fast as she could through the winding mountain roads. Her target was a coastal beach where a small, decrepit boatshed housed their means of escape. The boatshed's owner had rubbed his hands with glee at the pittance they paid him to store their getaway craft there on short notice.

The jeeps behind her were gaining as she upshifted, planting her foot to the floor.

"Kelly, I am coming up on the boatshed, but I have two bogies following. I may have to shake them first."

She glanced into the mirror and saw one move in front of the other, a move she was familiar with. The second jeep would use the draft from the other to slingshot alongside her. The team had employed this maneuver themselves multiple times. Fortunately, Tori knew how to counter it. She waited with bated breath as the jeep went to make its move.

* * *

Connor threw his jeep wildly into the corners, knowing he had to catch the guards chasing Tori. It wouldn't be long until the local police and army were after them if they kept drawing attention to themselves.

"Kelly, what's the status report of the team?" he asked. He threw the jeep into another corner, forgetting to drop a gear, sending it into a tailspin he barely corrected.

"Janus and Will are making their own arrangements to get back onboard. So far, we have had no issues with their departure. You and Tori, on the other hand, have caused hell for a simple prison breakout."

He smiled at that. "Standard procedure, wouldn't you say?" He crested the hill, seeing lights far in the distance, followed by two others dangerously close. "Tell Tori to do her best to hold them off, and that I am on my way."

"I wouldn't call it standard procedure—" she replied.

He paid no attention to her, as he noticed the sloping descent to his left. Opting for the path of least resistance, he turned the wheel and drove down the steep slope.

Connor had the advantage then, as he saw Tori's vehicle sweep from side to side, preventing the jeeps from sliding up alongside her. He had the advantage as he closed up behind the closest jeep. Using the front bumper, he drove into the rear of the jeep tailgating Tori. The stunned driver yelled at his passengers to open fire as Connor ducked behind the dash, shots raking the windshield. It was then he remembered the two sets of lights chasing him. In total, four jeeps were taking potshots at them both.

Connor knew they had to level the playing field. He continued to push the jeep in front, as he brought the stolen pistol up and fired rounds into the rear passenger. He knew that inside were lethal rounds, but the situation wasn't in his enemy's favor. He saw all three guards lurch, as he opened the jeep door and leaned out, one hand on the wheel, keeping his foot on the accelerator while firing two shots into the rear left tire. He was hoping for a miracle. He pressed his bumper into their bumper and used the momentum to spin the jeep around, overtaking it. The two jeeps behind bore down on him as the vehicle in front careened and caught the side of the road. At the speed they were going, more than ninety kilometers per hour, the jeep flipped and began to roll. The driver and its occupants were flung around like ragdolls as the jeeps behind did their best to avoid the vehicular missile. The guards' reactions were their undoing, as they turned into one another, desperately trying to flee in panic.

Connor watched in his rear vision mirror as all three went up in a billowing cloud of smoke and fire. He raised his eyebrows, surprised by the sudden explosion. He didn't celebrate for long as the last jeep came alongside Tori despite her best efforts to weave across its path.

Connor knew they were close to their destination, but also that they were going way too fast for the sharp corner coming up meters ahead.

"Tori, you're going too fast, repeat, you are going too fast. Hit the brakes. I'll take care of the jeep alongside you. You need to slow down."

"Negative, Connor, I got this, you have to trust me."

Connor shook his head, though she couldn't see it. "There's no time, do as I say, I need you to brake now. That's an order."

He saw the red taillights light up, as he threw his jeep to the right, watching as Tori and Chi's vehicle left a trail of burnt rubber and smoke behind it. He hadn't planned for this, but once more the guards turned and fired. He ducked behind the dash.

The first rays of the rising sun crested the horizon, blinding all on the road as Connor hit the jeep ahead, planted both feet on the brakes and turned the wheel hard. He had shut his eyes a fraction too late and had dancing grey spots obscuring his vision. The rammed jeep ahead careened in front of him, sailed through the steel barrier, and flew off the cliff.

Connor felt his own luck had run out as his own jeep failed to stop in time, despite his efforts, continuing its trajectory until it too met the same fate, falling over the edge down onto the rocks below.

* * *

Tori threw open the door of the jeep, smelling rubber and petrol. She glanced into the backseat at Chi, who still dozed peacefully, unaware of the destruction around him. Bottling up her worst fears, she grabbed her gun from the passenger seat and ran to the cliffside barrier, looking at the twisted metal where Connor had taken a dive to save her.

Chapter 5

God help me, Joshua Davidson thought as his surrounding began to shake and rattle. His knuckles whitened as he clutched the armrests. *I hate flying.* He looked at his aide, Stephen, sitting beside him calmly scrolling through his phone. The rattling eased, and the turbulence tapered off. He sighed heavily.

"Everything alright, sir?" Laura Goddard asked. The bright young woman had been looking out one of the oval windows at the passing cloud, its wispy formations like cotton candy. She looked at him now, her bright green eyes meeting his.

Joshua smiled, pulling out a handkerchief and dabbing his forehead, feeling pinpricks of perspiration not only on his forehead but also inside his suit. He wished he was anywhere else but a thousand miles up in the sky, travelling to Tokyo on a diplomatic mission.

"I'm fine Laura. Flying's never been one of my favourite things in the world. I feel much safer on the ground. Nothing can happen to me there."

Joshua Davidson was tall, tanned, and handsome. He had silvery flecks in his dark hair and the beginnings of crow's feet etching his skin either side of his eyes. He had spent the last few weeks back home in Australia until the call came for him to return to Japan on urgent business. It was obvious what the reasons were to him and the rest of his consular group on the plane. They had all accompanied him back to Australia to see loved ones and family. The return trip of six thousand, eight hundred and twenty-one kilometres felt like stretching a rubber band with their hearts attached.

"We should be over the South China Sea soon. Let's hope we don't have any trouble on the way," Laura muttered.

"The sooner the better. I don't like being cooped up for too long," he replied, hearing the tremble in his own voice.

The plane began to shake once more as they hit another patch of turbulence. The check seatbelt sign blinked on above them, and they tightened their belts. Joshua gripped the handles harder this time around, gritting his teeth for added measure.

Two things happened at once that no one onboard could have foreseen. First, the plane veered sharply left, throwing all onboard hard against their seats. Second, the flight attendant onboard the government Gulfstream screamed from the far end of the plane. The angle of the turn was so sharp, Joshua couldn't pull himself back to look down the aisle. The jet veered right, drawing further grunts from Joshua and his team. All at once, the aircraft corrected itself. Joshua warily let go of the armrests, taking a moment to peer down the aisle as the pilot's voice came overhead.

"Ladies and gentlemen, I want to apologise for the sudden manoeuvre we had to perform. An unidentified jet of unknown flew right at us. The co-pilot and I initiated evasive manoeuvres to compensate for such a risky overflight. We should now be safe to continue. We will contact the local authorities for immediate investigation."

Joshua dabbed his forehead with the now wet handkerchief.

"What in the blazes was that? A risky overflight? You can bet it's China flexing its muscles once more. One of these days—". The aide didn't get to finish as Joshua raised a hand.

He didn't want to encourage Stephen's sentiment. He was already on edge as it was, and that would only add to it. Joshua looked away from Stephen at his female assistant, Laura Goddard. She was no more than two years older than Stephen, both in their early thirties. Joshua was in his early sixties, but he felt age creeping up on him like a cloud on a sunny day. He believed what Stephen was saying, and he couldn't deny the risky pass by the unknown aircraft was alarming. He was about to ask Laura's opinion when the pilot's voice came over the intercom.

"Ladies and gentlemen, we have a critical situation now. We are currently being tailed by two jets of unidentified origin. We have yet to establish radio communication. We will continue to hail them and remind them they are shadowing a government flight from Australia."

Steven was the first to react. "It's them, I told you. They must know we are on our way to Japan, they must. We need to land now and report this." He unclipped his belt and leaped to his feet as the plane veered right once more. The manoeuvre sent Stephen backwards into the overhead compartment bay before dropping him sprawling on the ground near Laura and Joshua. Joshua unclipped his belt and leaned down to help the poor man to his feet. Stephen had suffered a small cut on his head and was rubbing what was already showing to be a small purplish bruise on his cheek.

Joshua glanced at Laura. She had taken off her belt and now kneeled on her seat, looking out of the window at one of the unknown military jets. It carried no distinguishable markings that she could see and was hovering off their left wing.

"Sir, I don't know what's going on out there, but unless they are tasked to provide some sort of security, I would say we have a diplomatic situation on our hands," she said, trying to hide the tremble in her voice.

Joshua joined her at the window. "Laura, we must stop this now. We are on a diplomatic flight to Tokyo. We present no clear threat. We need to hail a nearby country for assistance. Find out where that flight attendant is with our drinks, I need something to calm my nerves. Make it a double when you find her."

Laura nodded, watching as Joshua walked up front, knocked on the cabin door, and let himself in.

She walked to the rear of the small gulf stream jet, the curtain at the back pulled shut. She had heard the attendant scream during the turbulence but attributed the sound to the manoeuvre that had jammed them against their seats. Reaching the curtain, she pulled it back without a care.

* * *

Laura had believed today would be just like any other. She couldn't have been more wrong. Standing before her were two males, dressed head to toe in black combat fatigues and combat boots. It wasn't what they wore that had drawn her attention, rather their headwear. Both faces were concealed behind *mengu* masks, traditional samurai face coverings embellished with demon horns and black pits where their eyes were positioned.

One of the men had his gloved hand close to the terrified attendant, whose bright blue eyes shimmered with tears. Laura saw the silenced pistol pressed to her skull. The other male levelled his pistol at her without comment. Both men said nothing, nor could she see the faces behind their grotesque masks. At first, she couldn't say anything as all moisture appeared to have evaporated from her mouth. Finally, she spoke.

"Who are you, and what do you want?"

As clichéd as it was, it was the only question she could ask, given her situation. The flight had been swept clean before they were cleared to taxi, and she hadn't seen either of these men on the plane. The only people cleared for this flight were herself, Joshua, and Stephen. The other clearances were reserved for the security team and attendants, as well as the two pilots onboard. She couldn't figure how these men got onboard Her observation didn't change the fact she was looking down the barrel of a gun pointed at her forehead. She knew that if she screamed for help, she was likely dead, but then again, whatever these men wanted, she doubted they would leave them all alive.

The masked man pointing the gun at her grabbed her arm and turned her around sharply, placing his gun to her head. She felt the coolness of the muzzle against her skull as she was marched down the aisle. If she wanted to get out of this alive, she couldn't let her own fear control her. Everyone onboard was now a hostage.

Laura could only watch when Steven looked up from his phone as she was pushed down the aisle, his other hand nursing a napkin to his head to stem the bleeding.

"What the—" was all he managed before the masked male shot him in the calf.

The silenced shot was muted but the young man went down screaming and holding his leg. The cockpit door opened immediately.

Joshua stood in the doorway, lost for words. When Laura tried to move, the male pushed the gun harder against her hard. Laura watched Joshua raised his hands, sweat lining his forehead. Her only hope now was the pilots. Everyone onboard was trained for a hostage situation, but they never thought it would happen. Laura didn't need to mouth to the co-pilot for help. The co-pilot ad already reacted, unclipping his belt and rising with a pistol in hand, taken from its place underneath the flight controls. The masked male holding Laura sent two silenced rounds down the length of the plane dropping the co-pilot without a second thought. The other pilot, stricken by fear behind his aviators, looked over at his dead co-pilot. He chose not to be a hero, and turned back to the controls.

"You bastard," said Laura, "you know we are being tracked—".

Her words cut off as she was swung around and made to watch the other male bring his gun down heavily on the back of the flight attendant's head. The young woman's eyes rolled back. She crumpled, and her attacker thrust her into the nearest seat like a sack of potatoes, where she lay, unmoving. The masked male holding Laura spoke for the first time as tried to fight back. His voice was muffled by a bandana. Laura's mind reeled at a thousand miles an hour and she could not get it to translate what she had heard.

The second masked male, after dumping the attendant, marched down the aisle to the front, directing his attention to Joshua. Laura watched helplessly as he was thrown to the floor in front of her, lying beside the whimpering form of Stephen.

Leaving the man who held the gun to Laura to keep an eye on them, the quieter masked male marched into the cockpit and pointed the gun at the pilot. She could hear the man telling the pilot something but could not make it out. The plane veered away from their present course. Their flight destination had been changed. She looked down at Joshua who, like her, carried a fear in his eyes of what was to become of them.

Chapter 6

A kaleidoscope of colours flickered across the glass panes rising tall into the night. A mixture of orange and yellows mostly swept across their reflective glossy surface headlights mingling with the white flashes of screens as people walked along the footpaths near the neon lights of restaurants. The smell of oriental food rose high into the air, creating a thin aroma that mixed with the close press of bodies throughout the streets. The city of Tokyo was considered an exotic location by many, sitting within the shadow cast by Mount Fuji that rose like a giant in the background, as tourists got lost within the rat maze of towers, stores, and smaller buildings. Seen from above, it looked like a colony of ants as people moved about. At least that's what the lone figure in the helicopter thought as the aircraft thundered through the sky toward one of the taller city centre towers. As the helicopter began its descent, the figure could make out a mixture of air conditioning units, heaters, as well as a few rooftop gardens. One verdant space stood out more than most, the helipad sitting within the confines of a lavish garden interspersed with frangipanis and other exotic flowers. The figure looked at the garden and made a face; he didn't care much for it. His father had told him that gardening meant giving something back, that it was a way to escape the ways of the world and become one with nature. He didn't care much for the nonsense his father spouted; he had long stopped listening. The helicopter came to rest on the pad. A man in a white oriental suit walked toward the helicopter as its blades slowed. He pulled open the door, bowing toward the helicopter's passenger in respect. The man climbed out, acknowledged the bow, and nodded toward him.

As the door slid shut behind him, the lights that lit up the garden illuminated his reflection in the black glass. Colonel Kenji Toyotami was only in his early thirties, but had seen a great deal; he had travelled to places many could only dream of on their small salaries, and he had seen things that even the most seasoned travellers might stare at in awe. But he still wanted more. That's where this visit came in. He was secretly hoping that the time was near, that the inevitable was about to become very real.

He walked quickly across the concrete pavers from the helipad to the twin doors leading to the lower levels. The heels of his expensive Marlowe's smacked noisily on the slabs underfoot. On pressing the button, the door opened with a gentle pinging sound, the customary elevator music within a familiar comfort. He pressed the button for the floor three storeys below.

The doors opened into a lavish reception area of Toyotami Industries, a large conglomerate and weapons maker founded by his father General Hideyoshi Toyotami. A large canvas print of his father resplendent in military attire adorned the large wall. Below the portrait, a beautiful Japanese woman, her black hair pulled away from her face, rose from behind the desk and bowed toward him before sitting once more. She wore a simple white blouse and dress pants complete with heels adding to her five-foot height. Kenji looked at her like he looked at a piece of meat. With the power he felt he had in one hand, it would be almost too easy, but he sated this lust in other ways. There was time enough for that later, and no doubt she knew it, since a trace of recognition flickered in her almond eyes as Kenji moved away from her.

Two cedar doors positioned at the end of the long hallway led to his personal office. Positioned on the floor below his father's, he felt belittled and not equal to his parent, something he often fixated on. The office was large and spacious, modern, and fresh looking. Kenji walked toward one of the tall windows, draping his dinner jacket over the nearest lounge chair in front of a desk at the side of the room. He exhaled, his eyes absorbing the city before him. How the world had changed. He looked at the companies that surrounded his own. Kenji could only feel a level of contempt toward them. *Sell outs… Traitors.* The time would come soon enough to pay for this betrayal.

A knock at the door broke his thoughts, as the young receptionist peered inside.

"Mr Toyotami, a man named Jiro is on the line for you. Shall I put him through?"

He smiled at her. *Fate.*

"I'll take the call, put it through to me."

He moved toward his desk and clicked a button underneath the wooden frame. The nearest wall slid away to reveal a large collection of monitors, several displaying the stock market, or the local and international news. The middle screen displayed the face of a man he trusted more than anyone in the world.

"Jiro, I trust you are well. How goes our acquisition?"

The man on screen gave a smile that reminded Kenji of a shark.

"Very well, sir. We expect delivery shortly."

"Good, I expected nothing but results from you. With such good news, however, I feel I am missing something. It's not procedure for you to contact me otherwise."

Jiro hesitated. The reaction was not lost on Kenji, despite the lack of physical presence.

"What is it? Tell me now," he snapped, leaning forward in his chair.

"There has been a… disturbance in North Korea. I can take care of it, but it may pose a problem."

Kenji shook his head. He didn't like bad news.

"What disturbance? Speak plainly or I'll find someone else to answer such a simple question."

Jiro nodded, his smile gone. He was familiar with Kenji's violent outbursts.

"A breakout attempt was made by a team of unknown origin. Reports suggest they removed a political prisoner from the camp, and that the prison guards gave chase."

"Casualties?"

Jiro nodded again. "Several. So far, the only reported casualties were on the Korean side."

"Who was the prisoner?"

"They are keeping tight lipped about that one. Rest assured my source will let me know as soon as we hear anything."

Kenji kept his temper in check, reflecting on Jiro's words.

"Keep me updated. For now, make sure the acquisition continues smoothly. I will be with you shortly after I take care of a personal affair."

Jiro bowed his head as Kenji hit a button to end the call. He saw his own reflection in the large screen, and his mood soured. He rose from his chair and began pacing in the middle of the room, thinking on the matter.

A breakout means nothing to me. My timetable is set, the pieces are moving. Nothing can stop me now. The world is mine.

He pressed a button on top of his desk, revealing yet another hidden detail in the room: a small elevator built into the other wall, hidden behind a bookcase. He walked inside and, seconds after pressing a button, he reached his destination, stepping out and walking along the tiled floor.

Kenji stopped suddenly, standing in the semi-darkness, the light of the elevator casting a glow over the scene. He raised a hand and clicked his fingers. Like magic, lights came on, revealing a scene out of a horror movie.

A man sat before him, bound to a wooden chair. He was bleeding from a large gash on the side of his head. Smaller cuts dotted his body. Below him, dried blood caked the floor around a central drain.

Four men stood guard around the corners of the six metres by six metres soundproofed room. The water soaking the floor was evidence of the work in progress before he arrived.

Kenji bent over to look at the man's features, grabbing a handful of hair to raise the lolling head to his own level.

"Loyalty. Almost a foreign concept in this world. Honour. A long-forgotten Japanese tradition. I expect both qualities from those within my organisation. What I don't expect is for funds to be siphoned by one of my own. For this, payment is to be made."

The man barely registered the words, his head swaying in what appeared to be a feeble attempt at begging forgiveness.

"Please…" he whimpered.

Kenji rose, pushing the man's head back roughly with a force that rocked the chair, causing an echo around the room.

"I trusted you. You know what must be done."

Kenji was certain the man only saw his expensive shoes. If the traitor raised his head, he would see what was coming.

Kenji stood before the man, whispering.

"This doesn't end with you, my brother. Your wife and daughter come next."

The man tried to plead again, as two of the guards approached, slicing the bonds that held him. He fell forward. One guard caught him, the other pushed the man onto his knees.

"I'll give you one chance, brother, to die with honour." A loud crash followed as a scabbard with a small sword called a *tanto* was thrown within an arm's length of the man.

Kenji watched with pleasure, expecting the man to reach for it. His displeasure was severe when the man disregarded it entirely. Without a word, Kenji strode toward him, pulled a katana from a scabbard proffered to him by another guard, and, in one clean movement, finished what he'd started.

Straightening his tie, he passed the blade back to the guard, handle first.

"Clean that mess up and get it out of my sight," he said to the other guards.

If you can't trust family, who can you trust… he thought, without a backward glance, as he returned to the elevator.

He had work to do. In forty-eight hours, the world would be recast as it should've been decades ago.

Chapter 7

"Plan C? I knew you were crazy, Boss, but I didn't think you were that crazy," Tori said, her face a mixture of admiration and concern.

A metre below Tori, hanging by his fingertips, was Connor.

"Can we talk later? I'm hanging to see where this conversation goes."

Tori smiled, ran to the jeep, and yanked open the trunk. She took the only equipment she could use, a thick extension cable, and raced back to Connor.

After throwing it down, Tori braced herself with one foot against the twisted steel barrier, then pulled Connor up. He clutched onto the silicon cord with both hands, reaching the top and hauling himself over onto his back, as Tori collapsed backward with a grunt onto the asphalt.

"Guess we are even now," Connor said looking up at the sky, chest heaving from the climb.

"You know it," she replied, getting to her feet and dusting off her pants.

They knew they had little time till the Korean guards caught up. Without another word, Connor got up and climbed into the jeep, continuing the descent as fast as the corners allowed.

"How's our guy?" he said, as the jeep bounced along the roads.

"Still sleeping with the fairies."

"Good, we still have a way to go," he said without looking at her. "*Serenity*, this is Connor, come in, enroute to rendezvous now. ETA ten minutes."

"You know one day, Boss, heroics like that might get you killed."

"Maybe, but that day isn't today." He looked out the window watching the oranges and yellows of the new day shimmer across the horizon. He didn't want to admit it, but he knew she was right.

Twenty minutes after Connor was hauled to safety, the black zodiac pulled alongside his prized possession and gift from his late father: *Serenity*

The *Serenity* was a top-of-the-line luxury war craft possessing hidden weaponry in its sleek lines, from machine guns built into its fins, both front and back, to hidden missile tubes hidden along its fore-and-aft lines. Evans had spared no expense on the weaponry of both yachts within the organisation. The *Serenity* also possessed the latest in intelligence gathering, communications, and recon. The vessel could scramble any wavelength within the area, or shift its signature to a different location, allowing it to slip away quietly both day and night unless seen by the naked eye.

Onboard, he was met with the none-too-pleased expression of Kelly Winter, Tori's sister. She stood above him on a gantry, arms crossed, a frustrated expression etched on her face.

"Something I said?" he said, grinning.

She shook her head, a single strand falling onto her forehead despite having her hair pulled back in a ponytail. "No, something you did. Risks like that will see us looking for a new commander soon."

"Relax, Kell, I am in one piece, as always. We don't take unnecessary risks. It's the name of the game."

She went to respond, decided against it, flicked the hair out of her face, and pulled out her signature tablet. Tall and lithe, Kelly was a track star at school who harboured a secret. She was an expert hacker and computer whiz, never without her tablet. She climbed down a small set of stairs to be level with him, the tablet tucked under her arm. Her blue eyes searched his.

"Just don't do that again, please. You had me worried."

"We can continue this conversation later," he said, smiling. "Let's put as much distance between us and Korea as we can."

He gestured for Kelly to follow as he walked down one of the passageways running along the side of the ship toward the communications room. The *Serenity* was designed to be as covert as possible. Disguised on its upper levels to appear as close to a luxury yacht as possible, with no expense spared. The crew had full use of its facilities until they pulled into port, when they settled into their quarters hidden in the yacht's depths ensuring all onboard knew only what secrets it contained behind its false walls. This illusion, Connor's most ingenious design for the yacht, would have the harbour masters of the world guessing as they travelled from its native homeland, Australia, to ports around the world.

"Should we be worried about eyewitnesses to the breakout?" Kelly asked as they walked side by side.

"It's something to consider, but they would only have the jeeps we stole to go on. No one would've spied us this far out unless they put two and two together. I can't imagine too many people pointing at a yacht as a means of escape, can you?"

Kelly frowned; a clear sign she had a point to make.

"Speak up, I'm all ears," he said.

They arrived at a door hidden behind a wall panel that led to what they all called the 'Hub'. The epicentre and social commune area of the yacht, and central control room of Darke Company. He had founded the organisation after his father's death, a family legacy. Several years later, Connor had kept his word to his father, ensuring that the organisation had flourished over time.

"It's just… something doesn't feel right about this," said Kelly. "Once we pass Chi over to the Americans, we can leave this all behind."

Kelly left him with that thought, and moved toward her centre console, issuing commands to the crew inside to prepare for immediate departure. In total, eight crew controlled all aspects of the yacht. Connor respected them enough to know that if one crew member fell short, another of his own trained crew would take their place, a greased cog in a well-oiled machine. He knew the value of teamwork from his days in the SAS, where relying on someone else might just save your life. He had never forgotten that, and instilled that the same value in his team and crew.

As Connor cast his mind back to the past, William appeared from behind, startling him.

"Hey Boss, just thought I'd give you a heads up. Janus is back onboard at the range, and Chi is tucked away in the medical bay. The doctor suggests letting him rest."

"After what we've been through, we need it more, I think," Connor replied. "What do you think of all this, Will? What makes Chi so valuable to the Americans?"

William nodded. "I wondered the same thing. It wasn't like any normal job we have carried out for our patriotic friends. So far, we haven't been able to find anything on the system. Best to leave that to Kelly, her background in intelligence gathering is second to none."

Connor smiled, fighting a yawn. "Either way, he is out of here this time tomorrow. I'm starving. I'm going to grab a bite to eat, you in?"

William nodded again. "Is that your Plan D?" he teased.

Connor laughed. "I can't believe this, is everyone going to give me a hard time on my heroics? It worked, didn't it?"

Leaving William and Kelly to their own devices, he made his way to his cabin, two thoughts in his mind, a third probing. The first two were sleep and a hot meal. The third was what concerned him the most. What did Chi know that made the Americans want him so badly? Hours later with little sleep and his mind still focused on the connection between Chi and the Americans, he figured the only way he was going to take his mind off things was to head down to the onboard gym. A place he usually reserved for times just like this.

Chapter 8

Kelly's phone beside her console rang, the caller id showing up as private number. The phone had been designed to display such calls, until she had installed a software program to decrypt numbers and display their location. What she hadn't expected was a call flashing up the Australian government's ID. She answered, listening carefully. Kelly tapped a few keys on the keyboard, scanning dozens of sites, and transferring videos onto a larger screen for all to see, as the caller continued speaking. National news headlines blared across the screen: *Ambassador Davidson missing, presumed dead over South China Sea.*

She hung up the phone and hit another key, tracing Connor's location onboard, then made her way to the upper deck.

The toxic smell of sweat and dirty rubber hit her first, making her instinctively gag as she stepped into the large room. Kelly avoided the gym as much as she could. Most of her time was spent in the 'Hub' since she became Darke Company's second in charge. The day to day running of the yacht and the crew kept her busy enough. She spied Connor working out away from the other military crew members, keeping to himself, bringing a barbell crashing against the rack, weight plates rattling with it.

"You used to be able to lift heavier. Age catching up to you?" she asked, standing over him. Connor looked up at her, a smile dancing in his grey blue eyes, before sitting up and pulling out his earphones.

"Something wrong?" he said raising one eyebrow, his smile fading at her expression.

"We have a problem. Actually, it's the Australian government's problem," she replied.

Connor wiped the sweat off his face with a towel. "Walk and talk," he said.

Out of earshot of the gym, Kelly continued. "I just received a call from George Daniels, our contact in the government."

Connor paused midstride. "He wouldn't contact us unless he had absolutely no choice and wanted something done off the books."

"My thoughts exactly," said Kelly. "It's an evolving situation. Daniels told me the ambassador to Japan, Joshua Davidson, didn't arrive at a scheduled meeting between his counterpart in Tokyo. News outlets somehow have their hands on the story already, and it's been reported his plane went down somewhere in the South China Sea."

"It's no small problem, then. What does he want us to do?"

"I think it's better if he explains all this to you, Connor. This doesn't sound like your run of the mill kidnapping. From everything Daniels told me, the ambassador and his staff simply disappeared."

"No ransom demands, no one claiming responsibility?"

Kelly shook her head. "Nothing at all. I would normally say give it time, but the last time this kind of thing happened with consulate members…" she let the thought hang.

"Get everyone to the conference room on the double. Doesn't look like anyone will be getting much rest now."

Connor checked his watch. The planned rendezvous with the Americans was in three hours. After the handover, he could turn his attention to the missing ambassador. The South China Sea was their next destination.

The conference room was located beyond the 'Hub', accessed by a hand scanner hidden behind a painting. Connor spared no expense on security, and only senior members of his crew could access the room.

He placed his hand on the scanner and walked inside. A large, circular table dominated the middle of the room, and almost every seat was occupied. The atmosphere was very different to the quiet of the gym. Scanning the room, Connor smiled at the team he had assembled; a mixture of former spec ops soldiers, former intelligence analysts and other titles that made his own as commander feel obsolete.

He sat down, thumbing the keypad on the glass-topped table. On the built-in screen, Connor called up the most recent report sent to Kelly sent by Daniels. He clicked a few buttons, sending a notification to the communications team in the Hub to patch him through to George Daniels.

"Glad to have you back in the fold, Commander Evans. How was your holiday in North Korea?" Chapman asked sitting diagonally from him at the table. Though he asked in his distinctive gravelly tone, he did so with a smile plastered on his face. Chapman was a medical rescue pilot for the Australian Navy, he earnt his nickname 'Chatty' from how much he talked when his nerves got the best of him on a mission. Even now, Connor knew he was barely keeping a lid on it, almost certain that news of the mission would set him off.

"Can't complain. The usual buzzing hornets, abhorrent heat, and the occasional damsel in distress," he said, with a wink to Tori, who responded with a middle finger across the table.

"What's got the lot of us together?" Chapman asked.

His question was answered by the appearance on screen at the end of the room of the large, ruddy face of George Daniels. The big man looked every bit the politician Evans expected him to be.

"Mr Daniels, it's a pleasure," said Connor. "We don't often hear from one of our own unless something grave has occurred. The local news and my second, Kelly, informed me you need assistance locating a missing jet." Evans didn't say this in a smug way, but, when dealing with politicians, he knew confidence was key.

"Commander Evans, your reputation precedes you. To answer your question, you're quite correct. No more than twenty-four hours ago, one of our jets enroute to Tokyo disappeared. At this stage, no communications or demands have been received by our side. Daniels hesitated before continuing, "I don't mean to be tentative, but we in the government suspect foul play. We may have our northern neighbours to thank for this."

Evans was familiar with the political dissent stemming from how China dealt its hand around the seas that shared its name. It seemed to him that the world was on the brink of war for about the tenth time that year. Although he didn't brush it off comments made by leaders in the pacific, especially China, he felt that amounted to no more than empty threats and chest beating.

"What makes you think that, Daniels?" Evans asked, eager to see whether the politician would have any views not biased against their Asiatic neighbours, or if he had genuine concerns. Surprisingly, it was the latter.

"The situation, Commander, is since that plane disappeared, we have been liaising with Japanese and Taiwanese authorities to search the seas and locate it. Of course, we must be careful not to disturb the sleeping giant nearby, but we have a grid reference before our plane blip disappeared.

"May I ask who was onboard?" Evans wanted to double check that Kelly had heard right.

"Onboard was Joshua Davidson, our ambassador to Japan, his colleagues, Laura Goddard and Steven Robertson, and the flight crew.

Evans wasn't familiar with the other names, but he would get his team to run background checks against the government's wishes, looking for possible motive, considering the only one they had now was what he suspected everyone in the room was thinking.

"Was the ambassador flying back to Tokyo on business or pleasure?" Evans asked

"Ambassador Davidson was flying home to see family and friends for some well-deserved time off, we then sent him back to Japan as part of his job, Commander. He was scheduled to meet the prime minister and defence minister over the affairs in the eastern seas, but he never made it."

"What was the meeting about, Daniels?" Evans knew he might be probing too deep, but when investigating, sometimes he needed to ask the hard questions. Also, he got a kick watching Daniels get more and more put off.

"That's none of your concern, Evans. I need you to locate the plane without causing a political scene. We will deny all involvement if you do."

"We will find the missing jet, Daniels. We have dealt with your government before, so I can expect an increased payment this time, non-taxed, of course?"

Daniels bristled at being spoken to this way, but he wouldn't have come to Evans if he wasn't desperate.

"Sure, Commander, I will follow up and deliver payment when the jet is found, and not before. Try not to embroil yourselves in some political scandal when you are over there. The government, particularly the prime minister, wants this to be dealt with under the table, you understand?"

Evans nodded, smiling at the politician. He knew the game; he played it and he had won, as always. "Don't have to tell us twice. Pleasure doing business with you, Daniels. Expect to hear from us soon."

The call ended, and the screen went black, Evans clicking it to display a live image of the sea taken from cameras mounted on the hull.

Everyone at the table had been listening intently. They turned to Evans, who rubbed his chin, feeling the beginnings of stubble.

"What do you all think of this? Do we point fingers at the most likely culprit, or do we factor in foul play from other countries, or someone else entirely?

"Missile testing has taken place again in North Korea recently. I doubt the Koreans would consider political espionage or kidnapping as part of their regular routine," said William.

"What about Japan?" Tori suggested. "What if they are somehow involved?"

Evans hadn't ruled out foul play by their allies, but he found it hard to believe they would kidnap the ambassador mid-flight, knowing he was coming to Tokyo.

He let the question stand, though no one added anything. Time was now against them, so Evans instructed them to plan a return to their base to unload Chi, then immediate preparations for the next mission. The last to leave the room, he tapped the remote on the desk to switch off everything, the door sliding shut behind him.

Chapter 9

The light of the moon floating in the night sky did not give away the vessel's position. Its darkened hull was cast in shadowy black as it glided purposefully through the water.

It had no portholes, no decks, or any sign of life onboard. It was a ghost ship.

Waves lapped against her hull as it wound to a stop.

Inside the dark hull, Jiro Ikeda marvelled at the array of technology before him. Kenji had spared no expense on decking out the state-of-the-art vessel. Jiro looked around at the skeleton crew. Twelve people ran the inner workings. He was deeply impressed.

One of the crew members leaning over a console, deep in discussion with another, turned to face him, throwing a salute. He disregarded the gesture, nodding instead.

"Sir, our deep-sea radar has discovered the wreck. Should we prepare to dive?"

"Show me what you have found," he asked, ignoring the man's question.

The man nodded and gestured to the radar screen.

Jiro looked at the screen. "Send the underwater drone down. I want a visual before we commit any manpower to this thing."

The crew member saluted, moving to another console, as Jiro turned and watched through the glass behind him which overlooked the ghost ship's interior.

The ship's layout comprised of spanning bridges running parallel to one another with one passing over the middle. Below this bridge hung the underwater submersible on a conveyer belt that rotated with three further submersibles attached to it. The small drone at the front of the belt lowered itself into what looked like an empty Olympic sized swimming pool on the ship's hull. Without warning, the sides of the pool exposed small culverts that began gushing water. The pool filled, and Jiro marvelled at the drone as it sank into the dark deep.

He turned away from the glass and moved to the monitor, standing beside a senior crewman. He watched expectantly as the drone submerged further. What little light it put out with its high-powered LEDs was swallowed up by the water that compressed its structure.

The minutes ticked by as the submersible moved closer to the signature the radar had initially pinged. Jiro gazed at the screen solemnly, the minutes ticking by. The senior crewman broke the silence first.

"Sir, other than sharks it should be safe for the divers to begin their descent.,"

Jiro watched the footage being relayed from the drone as it moved along the outside of the hull. Kenji had not told him the name of the battleship they were after, only that a great prize sat onboard: a weapon that would change the fortunes of Japan. Jiro, not one to question Kenji, kept to himself the thought that such a prize wouldn't already have been salvaged was highly unlikely. Looking at the drone footage on the console screen, he imagined there were still many secrets hidden underneath the surface of the Pacific.

* * *

At the same time, in international waters far off the coast of South Korea, Connor stood on the deck of the *Serenity*, looking across the vast ocean meeting the smattering stars like two old friends. He inhaled, letting the salty sea air linger in his nostrils as he waited. A quick glance at his watch made him wonder where the Americans were.

He moved toward the starboard railing, peering down as the inky black water began to boil. A conning tower rose from the darkness, dripping water, and continued to rise, the submarine cresting the surface, water drained away from its metal surface. Connor looked at the behemoth before him, knowing that what he saw was only half of the monstrosity that sat below. He pulled out a walkie talkie.

"Will, please bring our man to the upper deck, I believe his taxi has just arrived."

Evans looked down at the *USS Reagan* submarine, hearing the bellowing call of its captain from the conning tower.

"Commander, we are ready to receive the package."

The elevator behind Connor opened. William and another of his crew helped Chi to the portside railing.

Connor didn't want to show off any of the yacht's modifications, so they had to transfer their passenger the old school way, using the dinghy located at the stern. It floated gently in the waves as William climbed in first, balancing himself before bringing Chi onboard.

Connor didn't move as William motored over to the waiting submarine. After two minutes the roar of the dinghy's engine announced its return.

Connor spoke into the walkie talkie.

"Kelly, the package has been transferred. Get us moving again on a straight run to the South China Sea."

William pulled back alongside the rear of the yacht, as the *Serenity's* engines powered up. William threw the mooring line to the waiting crewman who, in practiced strokes, tied it fast.

William climbed out of the boat and back on the wooden deck,

"Well, that was easier said than done, but at least the Americans can deal with him now. Where we off to, Connor?"

Connor didn't look at William as the *Reagan* dived, spray erupting from its ballast tanks as the conning tower and the rest of the hull sank swiftly under the water. Connor couldn't hide his own amazement at how something so large left nothing but a few small ripples in the water.

"I couldn't imagine spending most of my life on one of those monstrosities," said William.

"Each to their own, Will. I knew a few people in the military who said they enjoyed the quiet. Some liked the money. Either way, I know where I would want to be if a nuclear war ever erupted."

Connor left Will with that thought as he headed down to the Hub

"Kelly, get us to the last known location Daniels sent us of the plane. Have Chapman prep to leave with Janus as soon as possible. They can scout the area." Chapman was a medical rescue pilot for the Australian Navy, he earnt his nickname 'Chatty' from how much he talked when his nerves got the best of him on a mission. Despite this, he remained remarkably calm at times, even though Connor knew Janus would say otherwise. He knew the pairing would set the grizzled sniper off, but he couldn't think of anyone better to get the lay of the land quicker.

"No problem, Connor. ETA is three hours."

<u>Chapter 10</u>

Joshua Davidson could only see through one undamaged eye as the punch came at him, sinking into his stomach with such explosive force, he could only imagine what his organs must look like afterwards.

His assailant had introduced himself as the 'Gomon-Sha' Davidson understood enough Japanese to know that meant 'Torturer'. He spat blood and saliva as he thought about what this man had already done to him.

So far, he had endured an hour of beatings, sometimes blindfolded so he couldn't prepare himself for what came next. The man's brutality was something Joshua had never witnessed before. The torturer evidently took pleasure in his work. Davidson was almost convinced this man saw it as a form of art. He surmised this when the man stopped, stepping back to admire his handiwork.

Davidson tried to sit up straight, attempting to loosen the ropes that bound him to the chair. He was blindfolded once more, but not for long as a rough tug brought the fabric down around his neck.

He had never met his father but knew he had been a veteran of the Pacific Wars. Growing up, he heard tales of his father's exploits with the indigenous locals who helped the Australian and New Zealander troops through their homeland of Papua New Guinea during the Japanese occupation. He was told by his father's friends that his old man was a mean son of a gun. Now, he felt he channelled his father's strength, though for how much longer he wasn't sure.

He looked at the man who paced before him, delaying the next onslaught. Davidson still wore the suit he wore on the plane before it was diverted and made to land on a remote island in the Pacific.

From his one good eye, his surroundings gave him little hope. The clinical room was white, and harsh light splayed across the cinderblock walls. The only colour in the room was the pool of blood around his feet. The sound of a door made him, and his torturer turn. Two men entered, weapons slung casually over their shoulders. One approached and muttered in the torturer's ear. Davidson tried in vain to listen but couldn't make out what was being said.

The torturer looked at him, "If you still won't tell me what I want to hear, then maybe you need a bit of… encouragement."

Davidson began to violently jerk with what strength he had left, fighting the restraints as one of the guards returned with Laura Goddard in his arms. The torturer looked at Davidson and smiled cruelly.

"Tell me what I want to know, and she won't suffer the same fate as you. For every answer you deflect, she receives what you should. Do you understand?"

Davidson nodded weakly.

"Good. Your name is Joshua Davidson, special envoy between Japan and Australia."

He nodded.

"See? this is easy," the torturer said, getting up close to Davidson, swinging a nearby chair around and straddling it as he stared at him.

"What is the purpose of your visit, Ambassador?" he asked with a sneer.

"You should already know, you bastard," Davidson responded, spitting at the man.

The executioner stood and turned striding over to Laura, raising his hand and bringing it across her face. The smack on her skin echoed through the room.

"Leave her alone!" Davidson yelled, making the man slap Laura once more.

"That's for your defiance. I ask the questions, you provide answers. What part of that was not clear?'

Davidson went to reply, as once more the man's fist connected with his face, making his teeth vibrate. "Now answer the question. Your purpose."

"I am here to see my Japanese counterpart in continuing Japan's stance on nuclear weapons. The world has seen enough violence in the past century to last a lifetime. My aim is to see peace last a little bit longer this time."

"Fine, next question. Who else knows you are here?"

Davidson looked over at Laura, who stood weakly, drugged by the look of it. Tear streaks had smeared her mascara, and she was barefoot. Her blouse was torn, along with a section of her skirt.

"Only those in the Australian government, who will come for me."

The man laughed and brought his face level with Davidson's.

"You are replaceable, Mr Ambassador, no one will come for you. No one knows where you are. You will die here. Alone."

Davidson took the words to heart like cuts to his skin, believing the torturer was right. He couldn't see any way out of this. Gazing over at Laura, seeing the look of despair in her eyes, he knew she too thought the situation was hopeless.

"Tie the woman up and leave her in here with him," said the torturer. "Check on them in a few hours. Maybe they will soon realise the only way I will be merciful enough to grant them a quick death will be once I have the answers I need."

The men wrestled with Laura, who fought and kicked back before being slapped hard across the face, tied up, and dropped on the cold, tiled floor.

The executioner left, the guards following him. They felt confident leaving their injured hostages in a state of despair and misery. They never thought that one person in that room was not what they seemed.

* * *

Both of Laura Goddard's cheeks throbbed from the punishment she had taken from the torturer. When the door closed, she began weakening the restraints around her wrists, rotating them back and forth to stretch the rope. She focused on teasing out a single strand, then brought it to her teeth, pulling the strand and loosening the ropes enough for them to drop. Davidson had blacked out. She rubbed her wrists before untying the ropes around her feet. Not wasting any time, she placed two fingers on Davidson's neck. There was a faint pulse, but it was barely noticeable. Joshua Davidson was in his sixties, and though spritely, he couldn't take this kind of beating for long.

Laura couldn't deny he'd put up a tough battle, but his captors didn't know about his waning health. The assignment to Japan was to be one of his last before his retirement in six months.

His eyes opened slightly, though one was badly bruised, "How did you…?"

"I'm here, Joshua. Do you think you can walk if I untie you?"

He nodded, and, once she'd released him, took two paces before stumbling. Laura barely prevented him falling, underestimating the weight of the ambassador. He was six-three, weighing over ninety kilos, meaning she was carrying almost twice her body weight as she helped him back into the chair.

"It's no good, Laura, you need to get out of here, get help. Even if they are looking for us, they don't know where to look."

Laura shook her head. "Not without you. Let's wait a few minutes and try again, shall we?"

Davidson nodded, but she could see he wasn't convinced. She felt groggy from the drugs they had injected her with, but she could stand and walk, though how she would fare in a fist fight remained to be seen.

"It's time I told you the truth, Josh. I am not just your assigned assistant within the government. I work for Australian Security Intelligence, a field operative to keep an eye on you outside of your usual security. My cover was not to be blown unless necessary. We don't know if they are listening in, but if you think I am going to make a run without you, you have another think coming."

Joshua, trying to smile, winced. "I figured there was something off about you, but then again, I never was a good judge of character. My last marriage…" She silenced him.

"I am going to scope out where we are, and I will come back for you."

Joshua didn't reply. She checked his breathing, then made her decision. She went to the door. Locked.

Laura had trained for times like this. She knew if she was ever captured, they would remove most of her personal items. A small consolation was that they didn't take all her clothes, so she still had one trick up her sleeve, literally. She reached under her shirt and, with a yank, removed the underwire from her bra. She had learnt the trick from a former operative. Instead of using hair clips, easily lost, the wire sewn in her bra was sharpened and ready in times of need. This was one of those times.

She went to work, picking the lock quickly and sliding the wire into the lining of her skirt. She moved into a low crouch, though her muscles protested, and moved stealthily down the hallway.

Soon, she reached an intersection. They were in a facility of some kind. She heard voices from the hallway on her right. Moving away from them, Laura quickened her pace past uniform white walls that soon became dizzying. She wished she could have left a trail of wool behind her like the mythical Theseus. The absence of windows, and a heaviness in the air made her surmise she was underground. A thought that made the walls feel even closer than they were already.

Laura had kept an eye out as she moved throughout the hallways and the lack of surveillance cameras and patrolling guards meant that wherever she was, the facility's location made the torturer feel secure.

Not wanting to waste time on speculation, she kept going until she reached a door marked *stairwell*, written in Japanese, also indicating an emergency exit. She paused before pushing the door. If it was alarmed, she was done for, Risk versus reward. She had no choice. She pushed.

No alarm sounded, and the flight of stairs ahead gave Laura a momentary glimmer of hope. She leaned on the bottom of the rail and looked at what appeared to be an endless flight of stairs above her. She thought of Joshua, of Steven, Joshua's personal aide, wherever he was being kept, and of her family back home in Canberra. Those thoughts buoyed her hopeful feeling as she made the climb.

At the top, a single door waited. She wiped the sweat off her forehead and reached for the wire tucked into her skirt lining. She tested the handle, finding it turned easily. She kept the wire clutched in her hand, knowing it was her only weapon outside of her own combat training.

She opened the door and, keeping low, found her method of escape. She moved deeper into the garage, shocked to find it empty of anyone. Since she had left Joshua, she had yet to see a single soul. She considered returning to him as she stared at the button nearest the aluminium door that led to the outside world and freedom.

Laura found a small office off to the side where two all-terrain vehicles sat, beckoning to her to climb on and leave this hell hole. She found two sets of keys in the office. A quick search of the room turned up nothing about her current whereabouts. She pocketed one set of keys, before grabbing the other, knowing they would likely chase her down, any delay would benefit her greatly till she figured out where the hell she was.

She moved to the door and clicked the button, hurrying back to the ATV. She looked to the left, knowing that as long as it remained roadworthy it could be used to chase her down. On a workbench, she found an inch long flat head screwdriver, and a hammer. She used them to rupture both rear tyre walls.

Laura turned the ignition, clicking a button on the ATV handlebars that activated the large steel shutter in front of her, its rattling sound making her look back toward the doorway, her nerves already on edge, hoping that the sound would not carry until she left the vehicle bay. The shutter rattled till it reached its full opening and looked out at the wind-ripped rain, the weather conditions perfect for her to lose any pursuers. It would allow her to escape unnoticed for a time. One thought crossed her mind as she accelerated out of the door,

I'm sorry, Joshua, I will come back for you.

Laura shot out into the grim weather, the darkness of the unknown swallowing her up.

Part Two:
Out of the Frying Pan...

Chapter 11

Janus Polkowski stood on the deck of the Taiwanese coastguard boat, looking across the water, his mind adrift until a female voice brought him back to reality.

"Janus, did you see the latest?" He turned and nodded at Tori. The scar that rippled along the side of his cheek whitened as he clenched his jaw, preventing himself from firing off expletives at her for catching him unawares.

Tori kneeled and surveyed the pieces Janus had already inspected. In total, there were thirty-six pieces of glossy white hull sitting on the foam-spattered deck. Another section of the boat held smaller items, such as a wheel, a piece of landing gear, and what might be part of a flight seat.

"The Taiwanese did their job, but without diving, we won't know for sure where the plane went down."

"That's because it didn't go down," Janus replied coolly as he looked at Tori over the top of his aviators.

"What do you mean, it didn't go down? The plane was reported to be a Gulfstream jet and, so far, we have recovered enough here to safely say the ambassador and his crew are likely underneath the sea."

"That's what they want you to think," Janus replied.

"Stop playing games and tell me what is going through that blasted mind of yours," she demanded.

"Clearly, you didn't read the memo provided to us enroute to meet with the Taiwanese. Come. I will show you."

He picked up the nearest piece of the jet's hull that had been fished out of the water. Hefting it to waist height, Janus pointed to the stainless-steel side. "See here? The dossier sent to us came with photos of the plane, and the location of its serial numbers. Check out this edge. No plane crash can remove all serial numbers from metal. They are punched in or lasered into the metal. Someone has doctored this piece to make it look like the original hull."

Tori stood, curious for Janus to continue. "And look here," he said. "The serial number is poorly printed. The numbers don't match up. Frankly, they did a pretty piss-poor job. I'd say whoever planted this was thinking no one would investigate it any further. This screams cover up. Question is, where is the real plane?"

Understanding rocked Tori. "You're telling me there is a real chance the ambassador is alive?"

Janus replaced the piece of hull down. "I'd put good money on it that he is alive and kicking. Where is anyone's guess."

"Let's get Evans on the phone and let him know," she said, frustrated at another roadblock in their mission to locate the ambassador.

* * *

With Janus and Tori on the hunt for the plane with the authorities, Connor figured it was time to head underground and any talk on the grapevine about the kidnapping or the whereabouts of the consular staff.

He took for the short trip to his destination. After paying the driver, Connor watched until he was out of sight. He stared up at the old warehouse, its façade rusted and aged. It had stood the test of time, now it would stand another. Connor had promised his father he wouldn't look up any of his old army buddies unless he had no choice. Though Connor still had options, he felt it was an opportunity he could not pass up given what his father had told him of his former colleagues.

He approached the chain link fence and guard post. The warehouse guard, unfazed by the appearance of Connor, looked over the newspaper he was reading before folding it and pulling a clipboard from a hook on the wall beside him. He asked for Connor's name. Connor didn't provide it, instead pulling out a small coin and holding it against the window.

The guard looked at it, reached for the telephone and dialled a number, a quick discussion ensued as waited only seconds. The guard only grunted at him, ending the call as Connor watched the gate roll back, courtesy of the phone call.

"I knew there would come a day when the son of Harold Evans would come calling," came a voice across the open compound.

Frank "Frankie' Sanderson strode toward Connor with his hand already outstretched. The two men shook hands, Connor's caught in the vice-like grip of the big man.

"Dad always had a story or two about you. Guess I owe him an apology now," Connor said, smiling, "Commander Connor Evans."

"Your father didn't lie. He had his flaws, but lying wasn't one of them. As for me, I'm an open book, and I've been waiting for you to drop by. Frank Sanderson, though your father called me Frankie."

Connor remembered his father describing Sanderson as a bull in a China shop, they had worked deep cover operations in Iraq with the Americans as part of a joint government operation, off the books of course, but for all the right reasons. Connor didn't have to imagine why, now he'd seen the man in the flesh.

Sanderson invited Connor into a small outbuilding to the side of the warehouse. Its interior was lit by a single lightbulb and the windows were boarded up, making Connor wonder what the man got up to in his spare time.

Connor sat in the proffered chair before a wooden desk. Sanderson sat across from him. Sanderson had silver grey hair. He wore a sleeveless shirt, and khaki pants reminiscent of his military days. A pair of dog tags still hung around his neck, and a long scar ran from the right side of his mouth down the length of his neck. Connor's father once told him the scar was from shrapnel that Sanderson took for him during the later years of the Vietnam War.

"Now, Connor, let's get down to brass tacks. You dropped off the radar years ago. No one knew where you'd got to. One minute you're a decorated special forces soldier, the next you disappear into thin air. Tell me what you are doing here, son."

"Dad told me to look you up, said if ever needed some information, you were the man to go to."

"You're not thinking of turning to my line of work, are you?" Sanderson said, raising his eyebrows in disbelief.

Connor shook his head, "No, but I need some information on the whereabouts of a missing consular aircraft that dropped off the radar. You hear anything?"

Sanderson stood, and moved around from behind the desk, leaning against its front edge, folding his arms.

"I have heard… rumours. Mutterings, from a few sources, of a jet going missing in the area. Now, as you know Connor, in my backyard things go missing all the time. People, property. It's the name of the game. It's how I make my living now, arms dealing and private security. I wouldn't have done it but you well our native homeland takes care of its own veterans." he scoffed. But when I heard talk of this jet… well, I didn't think you would come knocking."

Connor sat straighter in his chair, the boarded windows making sense now. "What do you know?"

"I know a Gulfstream jet was seen flying over a particular island chain north of here. Not in our neck of the woods, but further afield. There was no mention of who was onboard or anything like that, and, before you ask, I won't reveal the source."

"Why not?" Connor asked.

"Because that's not what you are here for. You said it yourself, you just want information on the missing plane, not to cause trouble with my sources. If I told you the name, you'd likely go gung-ho like your father."

Connor moved to the laptop sitting beside Sanderson and plugged an encrypted thumb drive into the side of it. Before Sanderson could say anything, the grid plot that Daniels provided to Connor and his team appeared on the display.

Connor pointed to the grid, "Where does your source think the plane has landed?"

Sanderson studied the plot for a few seconds, pointing at a section high on the north-eastern side.

"Around that area. The problem is that's contested territory, you know the drill. But the island is in the East China Sea. If you don't mind me asking, where did you get this information?"

Connor looked at the man his father called a friend, before grabbing his collar and slamming his frame onto the desk, hissing in his ear.

"You admitted it before. You work both sides of the fence, Sanderson. I know when someone is trying to pull the wool over my eyes, and this won't be one of those times. Australian lives are at stake. What else aren't you telling me?

Sanderson struggled against Connor to no avail.

"Alright, alright, I'll tell you," He wheezed. "Let me go."

Connor let him sit back, but not before pulling the hidden pistol from Sanderson's waistband and, walking around the desk, keeping it pointed square between the man's eyes.

"I don't know who trained you, boy, but your strength defies your build, I'll give you that."

Connor didn't budge, his aim unflinching.

"The island chain that I pointed to is owned by Toyotami Industries. A weapons manufacturer who made their money during the wars. If your plane went down there, who knows what happened to it? I am only telling you what I know, Connor. I owe it to your old man."

Connor dropped his arm, and popped the ammo clip out of the pistol, racking it and letting the stray casing fall to the floor. He tossed the empty pistol onto the desk.

"Anything else?" Connor asked.

"Actually, yeah. One more thing. The father, Hiroto Toyotami, may have a few screws loose, but his son, Kenji is a whole other kettle of fish. Kid has his own private security force, so I heard, works with some guy called Shinigami. Real piece of work."

He was certain he had heard everything he needed to hear. It was sad to see a decorated veteran reliving the glory days by selling weapons to the highest bidder. It wasn't uncommon for them to be hung out to dry by their own country. He was glad his father hadn't lived to see what happened to the man that saved his life. He could only hope that Sanderson would find something better to do with his life.

Connor left the compound and hailed down a cab on the way back to the Taipei City. His phone rang in the cab. It was Janus with an update. Connor's mind remained clouded as he listened. What had him on edge wasn't what Sanderson had told him about the plane's whereabouts, it was the flicker of fear he saw in the man's eyes when he mentioned someone called Shinigami.

Chapter 12

Kenji Toyotami loved power.

The son of a Japanese General hailing from a dynasty that stretched back to Shogunate heritage had never been lost on him. He had not realised how much he loved power until he completed his education in the United Kingdom. He had studied at Cambridge and Oxford. His education represented an attempt by his father to make him more pliant in the democratic discussions with the western world. Every doctrine and every policy he read not only taught him the power of language, but also the power of physical strength. He had made friends at university, discussed political theory, and engaged in discussions regarding the future of warfare and overpopulation. He viewed the literature with general distrust, a product of his upbringing. Kenji's early education in Japan centred around a phrase uttered by the first emperor of his country- *eight corners of the world under one roof.* His father had taught him that. Unlike his father, he believed as a descendant of the emperor that it was his divine mission to rebuild what was once lost. At first, it was only a dream, until he stumbled across the 'bible' of the Japanese people from 1941 hidden in his father's study underneath several philosophy books on warfare. *The Way of the Subjects,* a book published six months before World War Two broke out. It outlined Japan's conquest of the Pacific and beyond.

Kenji harboured anger toward his father for taking on mistresses after the war. To be educated by western universities to ensure he would be submissive to a greater western world was the final straw. As a colonel in the Japanese Imperial Army, he met Jiro Ikeda. To Kenji, Jiro was a staunch advocate of the imperial regime, of the emperor being a descendant of a god. This meant that

Jiro perceived Kenji as a god. His devout sense of honour and loyalty from cradle to adulthood meant he would follow Kenji to the grave.

Kenji stood in the facility looking down through the glass at the two missiles of destruction that, at one point, were destined to be used against his own country. Now, they would be used against those who struck them down half a century ago. He possessed the power to change the world, and he relished the feeling.

"I suppose you have an explanation as to why I am standing in your office, Jiro," he said, turning from the glass and locking eyes with his second-in-charge, who stood to attention.

Jiro saluted his superior and walked toward his own desk, "I did not think…"

"That's your problem Jiro, you don't think. You were supposed to keep them all locked up. Kept away from my father. Kept away from the world. They were to be left to rot in a hole somewhere, unable to escape.

Jiro stood stock still, his mouth firmly shut.

"Was the female the only one?" Kenji asked, glaring.

Jiro nodded, remaining mute.

"I want you to sweep everywhere the prisoner may have gone. I want you to block off all port entrances and stop all transport to and from the island, you got that?"

"Of course, Kenji-san. I believe the female didn't see anything on her way to the surface. She left the ambassador behind."

Kenji massaged his temples, his head throbbing at Jiro's stupidity. Despite being educated at the finest western universities, his accent remained.

"The female was found to be part of an Australian spy agency called ASIO. She is no mere assistant. She is trained to escape detection, escape captivation," Kenji said.

"She wouldn't have survived the island, sir. The weather was one of a kind that night. It tore down trees, blocked off roads, and caused landslides. If she made it through that, she would've been caught by the dock workers or guards."

"You don't think she would hide somewhere on the island to plan her escape, given the wild weather conditions?"

"We found an ATV in a ditch off the side of one of the goat tracks into the mountains… we figured she went down with it," he said confidently.

"The body… did you find a body in the wreckage?" Kenji asked, his head throbbing from Jiro's stupidity.

Jiro's expression said it all. "I'm sorry I didn't…"

"Think… did you, Jiro? You mean to tell me you assumed she died in the crash without checking?

Jiro dropped his head., "I'm sorry, sir."

"When she escaped from her cell, did you check the cameras?"

Jiro looked up, nodding, "The first order I gave. Laura Goddard was caught on several cameras hidden throughout the facility, but she didn't go anywhere near the laboratories or armouries."

"You didn't think to stop her, or the guards didn't think to stop her?" Kenji asked.

Jiro looked away once more. "The two guards posted were with the torturer, Han Wei. We are running a skeleton staff, Kenji-san. The cameras don't have motion detection, and most of my men are posted elsewhere on your orders."

"I want the recordings myself. Have them sent to my home office. I want the two guards killed who let this happen," Kenji replied, ignoring the excuses.

Though he wished he could shoot the man as well, Jiro still had his uses

Jiro walked toward the desk where Kenji sat and picked up the phone. He spoke quickly, then hung up.

"It is done, sir. They will be sent to your personal account immediately. The guards, I will take care of myself."

"I want the body of that woman, dead or alive, understand?"

Jiro swallowed and nodded, his Adam's apple bobbing. He understood the gravity of the situation, realising Kenji had let him off the hook this once.

"Where is the ambassador now?" Kenji asked.

Jiro tapped a small remote on the desk, changing his computer monitor to show the feed from a camera hidden in the cell where Davidson huddled in a corner on a dirty straw mattress. The walls were bare, the cell no more than a metre wide. A single chain hung from the northern wall, keeping both his arms above his head, unable to eat or drink, unless he was hand fed.

Kenji looked at the pitiful sight of the man who had threatened his power, locked up in cell far from civilisation. He would die there. Kenji would make sure of it.

"Keep him barely alive, I want him to suffer. Tell Han Wei, or Shinigami, as he wants to be known, that if he fails me again, he too will suffer the fates of the two guards."

There was a knock at the door. Han Wei strode in, focusing on Jiro near his desk. His eyes were ablaze as he shifted from Jiro to the other man in the room. As he locked onto the visitor, the fire within was extinguished instantly, changed to one of fear.

"Colonel Kenji, to what do I owe this pleasure?" Shinigami asked, a stammer in his voice.

"I was made aware that you released the hostage video, complete with the detonators. They are set for the time we discussed?"

Shinigami nodded. "They are. By midnight tomorrow, the world's sins will be washed away along with western filth."

Kenji beamed at the man's answer, before he glared once more at Jiro.

"I take it everything is moving into position as we speak?" Kenji enquired.

Jiro moved to a section of the wall. He pulled back a framed painting of Mt Fuji and tapped in a numerical sequence on a keypad. The safe popped open and Jiro pulled out a manila folder. He handed it to Kenji, who flicked through it. It contained a list of names, ships, and schedules, as well as biographies of crew members. To anyone not clued into Kenji's master plan it would mean nothing. Not even the two men in the room knew the full extent of Kenji's had plan. Jiro and Wei were each given a separate file, giving each half the information. It meant both men knew something but not everything. Just how Kenji wanted it to be. He checked the dates on the schedule. They were on time.

"Put it back," Kenji said handing it back to Jiro. "Make sure it remains hidden."

Kenji looked at both men, "Do not let me down. Find the female spy fast. What of the other who was onboard?"

Shinigami smiled cruelly. "He sleeps with the sharks, Colonel."

Kenji looked at his watch, unperturbed. He would soon be running late for a meeting, He needed to keep up appearances so that his father would be none the wiser. *Still, he hates late comers.* Kenji left the two men in the office, heading to his helicopter. It barely registered that Shinigami had fed a human male to sharks for fun.

Chapter 13

Connor stood on the sun deck of *Serenity*, staring at a flock of seabirds moving with the winds as the yacht sailed smoothly toward their next port of call. With the information obtained from both Sanderson and Janus, their stop was Toyotami Industries in Tokyo.

In the distance, the city of Tokyo rose, its prominent landmarks visible as *Serenity* came to a halt outside the port limits. Mt Fuji sat peacefully in the distance, a silent watcher of ancient origins. Connor had already tasked his crew with reaching out to harbour master to guide them into the port. With no response, Connor had halted the *Serenity* outside the port limits and waited.

He heard footstep on the deck behind him, and Kelly's cheery voice.

"I did some digging on the information you were after, and I came across something I think you will find quite interesting."

Connor turned his back to the city,

"What have you got?"

"Toyotami Industries is a huge conglomerate, owned and named after its founder, Hiroto Toyotami. General Toyotami, to be exact. A Fortune 500 company producing handheld weapons and missiles. His son, Kenji Toyotami, is currently a colonel in the Japanese Imperial Army. He doesn't have a specific role in the company. Media outlets report that the father-son relationship is strained. Based on some of the articles I translated, some point to a modern approach to weapons manufacturing. Others speculate Hiroto has taken a few mistresses in his time, despite being married."

Connor nodded in thought.

"Your father cheating on your mother," he said. "That might make you hot under the collar. What about the island chains they lay claim to a large majority of?"

"That's the first interesting part. The chain your father's friend is referring to is Ogasawara Islands. The island chain contains only two permanently inhabited islands and covers over eighty-four square kilometres. I've got one of the crew doing a rundown on each of the thirty islands for anywhere you could hide a jet. I will keep you posted." Kelly tapped on the tablet that never left her side.

"Sanderson seemed to fear these guys. Did your research give any indication as to why?" Connor asked, looking back at Tokyo once more.

"When you are a small times arms dealer, you don't want to awaken a sleeping giant once again, if you catch my drift?" she replied.

Connor understood what she meant but was surprised at the jest.

"Unless Sanderson was trying to warn me not to meddle in their affairs, that gives me reason enough to want to see what they might be hiding. Evidence suggests the plane disappeared near an island chain they own. Did you find anything on someone called 'Shinigami'?"

Kelly stood beside Connor at the railing, shielding her tablet from the glare. As she did, Connor caught her scent on a trailing breeze. He liked it, and it suited her.

"Shinigami, also known as death gods, or creatures of darkness, come from Japanese folklore. That's what a general web search found, so I tried tapping into the Toyotami servers. I got nowhere with that. Their servers are Fort Knox level security, leaving me with just the local police database. Whoever this person is, they are a ghost. If he or she uses this name, its likely they are Japanese themselves. I'll keep digging in the meantime," she said.

Leaving Connor to stare at the city, she headed to the bridge.

Connor locked his attention onto one towering skyscraper. Toyotami Industries. He had already formed a plan, and he had just the man for the job.

Heading to the hidden lower sections of the yacht, he took the elevator onboard to a vast room, divided into various sections. The other sections consisted of three bunked rooms along the far side, four split share beds to each. The rest of the room held two ground vehicles, two zodiac inflatables, and a sizeable armoury at the back. Two men stood shoulder to shoulder in the armoury, loading and unloading each of the various guns, ensuring they were maintained and oiled when they were needed. To Connor's immediate left was a sprawling gymnasium, and to his right was the firing range.

He found Janus there with his favourite sniper rifle, his Barrett 50. Calibre was enough to wake the dead, making Connor wince. Heading on past Janus to another section of the range, he found Kurt in the yacht's armoury.

"Figured you'd be here. I have a job for you."

Kurt put down the pistol he was cleaning and looked at Connor with deep brown eyes.

"What's the mission?" he asked.

"I need you to put your ears to the ground, reach out to your contacts in the area. I need to know more about a man by the name of Shinigami."

Kurt placed the pistol in the twin holster under his jacket and stood. Standing just under six feet, he possessed the average height of his Asian heritage. Possessing an innate ability for languages and multiple fighting styles, he grew up in the streets until he joined the CIA, becoming a deep cover agent in the Yakuza before Connor recruited him to Darke Company. Off the street and away from the Japanese underworld, he changed his name to Kurt from his birth name, Takeshi. Able to adopt a new identity, he didn't waste a moment training himself further in his skills, making him an asset for missions like the one Connor had in mind.

"I want to know everything about Shinigami. I want to know their connection to Toyotami Industries, and what they are capable of."

Connor knew Kurt would get the job done. It was now up to him to investigate Toyotami personally.

Kelly's voice came over the internal intercom, echoing in the vast metal area around them.

"Connor, I need you at the Hub. We have a bit of a situation."

Without a backward glance at Kurt, he headed for the Hub. He didn't like the tone of Kelly's voice.

He arrived as the Hub's main screen played what looked like a live feed of the ambassador with someone standing behind him, a katana held to his throat.

"The western world's decadence is their own downfall," said the reluctant Davidson. "Once more, the eastern world will rise again. In forty-eight hours, a new empire will rise, a new pacific dawn. A terrible weapon will be unleashed, capable of washing away the sins of the west and creating a new ring of fire."

The video cut to a digital timer, the red digits counting down.

The feed cut off. Connor and the rest of his team stared at the screen. "We need to move now," said Connor. "Kelly, I need you to trace that feed, find out where it came from. Get exact coordinates or a location. I need all hands-on deck for this. Get Kurt and Janus to the helipad. Find Tori, she can work with you to run down those island chains and, most of all, find out who Shinigami is. No doubt, that's who we just saw onscreen."

He left the room. His timetable would have to be moved up. It wasn't just Australian lives at stake now.

Chapter 14

Kurt couldn't remember the last time he was surrounded by the sights and sounds of Tokyo's underbelly.

He was a foreigner in his own country, but it was always going to be that way. He had turned against his own. In a former life, he had been a deep cover agent among the Yakuza, forced to do unimaginable things to ensure his cover was not blown. The intelligence he gathered buried more than a few of the upper echelons, but his cover was finally blown when he got too close to a woman. A woman with a secret as old as time. She was not only working for the local police force in Tokyo but was also the mistress of a Triad leader's son.

Now, Kurt kept his head swivelling, eyes checking every exit and every entrance. He had to remind himself he was after information, nothing more.

He weaved through the hustle and bustle and located the alley he had been looking for. It led to an entrance he had used as a former safehouse. Reaching the door, he went to unlock it when he noticed it was slightly ajar. If Kurt had approached from the other direction, he might not have noticed, instead opening it to whatever waited behind.

He drew one of the pistols in his twin holster and pulled a silencer from a pocket. He screwed it on the pistol's muzzle and pointed it at the opening. Placing his body against the door, he pushed it open with his right foot and threw himself to the side as a volley of bullets targeted where he had been only moments before. The room was dark, but the neon lighting from outside lit up enough of it to see two men in suits in the corner.

Kurt knew exactly who he was looking at. *Yakuza...*

He shot twice at both men standing in the corner as another door to his left exploded open, leading to a bathroom. More bullets followed as another of the Triad hit crew unloaded a submachine gun at Kurt. A bullet skimmed past, tearing through his jacket. The room was decked out like any living room, the furniture just as Kurt had left it. He threw himself over the nearby couch, hearing the thump of the bullets punching into the fabric. He reloaded his pistol and fired two wild shots over the top. The gunfire stopped briefly. A *reload*. He only had seconds, but then he saw it out of the corner of his eye. He smiled. *Perfect.*

Two new voices joined the Triad hidden in the bathroom on the other side of the lounge. Kurt moved toward the nearby fire extinguisher mounted on the wall. Grabbing it, and hurling it behind him, he kneeled and placed two shots in its metal casing, turning his head as the extinguisher exploded, filling the room with a white powder cloud.

Kurt hurtled through the open doorway, making the most of the momentary distraction. Men coughed behind him as further shots rang out in the alleyway. He shot with perfect accuracy at a chain holding a nearby dumpster open, bringing the lid down as he jumped on it and grabbed the ladder hanging down from a fire escape. Using every ounce of his body strength, he climbed hand over hand to the top, then ran up the sets of stairs. He heard voices below, and further shots ricocheted off the metal stairs and railings as he climbed. Reaching the top of the building, he allowed himself a chance to take a breath.

The Yakuza kicked open the rooftop access door to the building Kurt was standing on as he took a deep breath to clear his lungs. Heart pounding, he gauged the distance to the next rooftop, as it might be his only hope. He launched himself across the gap, rolling at the last second to lessen the load on his body, not looking back at whether the Yakuza were following.

The chaos caused by Kurt's arrival was felt at ground level. Civilians scattered like ants below him, as he went to climb down the nearest fire escape. A car stopped, and the passenger shot at Kurt, who only just managed to pull his head back in time.

Damn. He needed to get off the roof and back to street level. He knew the Yakuza would hunt him down if he ever showed his face again. he just didn't think they would remember it after all those years. The next rooftop was too far to jump. With no fire escapes nearby, he whipped out a small combat knife from his boot and cut the cord of a nearby washing line. Using the thin cord, hoping it would support his bodyweight, he swung across the gap, clothes thrashing in the wind. He crashed through glass bifold doors on the far side's balcony. Glass shards shredded his jacket and skin as he climbed to his feet and sprinted down the stairwell, leaping down steps two at a time before pushing through a fire exit door. Kurt ran down a sidewalk, dodging through the crowd as best as he could.

He noted the shredded parts of his jacket, and walked past a stall, bumping into a pedestrian balancing baskets of produce on either side of his bicycle. The movement caught the man off balance, sending much of it across the nearby road, halting traffic as people scrambled to help. The commotion allowed Kurt to pull his jacket off, grabbing another from a nearby stall whose owner had gone to help. He walked down an alley, unsure of where he was. He opened a dumpster and deposited his prized jacket inside. Closing the lid, he considered his options. With the Yakuza on the prowl, it was time for him to disappear once more, but not until he found the intelligence he needed.

Once he found his bearings, Kurt headed to a location he knew well. Not only because it had been used numerous times as a CIA drop, but the because it was located below the towering Tokyo tower. Its façade like any other street within the city of Tokyo, lines strung above him, pedestrians moving among vehicles. The smell of fresh seafood making his stomach growl. He opened the shop door and walked inside. A shopkeeper with deep wrinkles stood behind the counter bowing, asking Kurt if he needed help. Kurt uttered a single word: *Chi.*

The man paused. This time Kurt didn't ask again, instead pushing past the shopkeeper to pull open the thick red curtain divider that separated the two rooms. Behind the curtain was a storage room. Kurt scanned the space, before throwing back the oriental carpet rug on the floor. Underneath it was a wooden door. Pulling it open, he unholstered his pistol and pointed it inside.

Chi raised his hands, looking squarely at Kurt as his eyes widened in recognition.

"You could only hide for so long since we busted you out of that godforsaken place."

Chi swallowed, his mouth suddenly dry.

"You have no idea of the hell I faced in there," he replied.

Kurt's expression remained unchanged.

"We have both been through our own hells, yours isn't any different. I want information, and you hear things that the Yakuza and other gangs could only dream of."

Chi climbed out of the door and sat on a barrel in the storage room. The shopkeeper pulled the curtain back once more. It left both in the unconventional meeting space.

Kurt rose to his full height. "I want to know about a person called Shinigami, and his connection to Toyotami Industries."

Chi's almond eyes widened once more, before he nodded slowly.

"I've heard talk of Shinigami. He runs a private security force called the Honourable Ones. The same security force moves in the same circles as Colonel Kenji Toyotami. Whether the two see eye to eye remains to be seen. I would say Kenji is the financier, and Shinigami the muscle. Nothing I have heard mentions the father, Hiroto, in any way."

Kurt leaned against a nearby wall. "Where does Shinigami operate, and how can I find him?"

"There is talk that Shinigami operates out of an island in the chain south of Tokyo Bay. He recruits from the locals around the islands. Anytime the DEA or CIA try and infiltrate the Yakuza, well those agents normally come in with the morning tide, parts of them anyway," he said grimly. A lot of the Yakuza have joined his side. Those that don't? Well, he has methods to make them see his way. As for where you can find him, you don't. He finds you."

A commotion from the front of the shop had both Chi and Kurt on alert.

"Quick, down here," Chi said, pointing to the hole. Kurt didn't hesitate, climbing down with Chi following.

The dank room that Chi stood in was small, with radios, listening devices, and all manner of technology strung around him.

Chi moved to a small file archive sitting in a corner. He pushed it aside to reveal a small hole. "This will take you into the sewers. Go one hundred metres and there will be a ladder. Climb it, and it will bring you to another storeroom. Good luck."

Kurt didn't need telling twice. Chi passed him a flashlight before pushing the cabinet back into place. Everything went dark. Kurt clicked on the light, scattering two rats who were feeding on a piece of meat.

Following Chi's directions, he found the ladder and left through a back-alley door when he reached the top. He made his way out of the alley and beelined toward the nearest phone stand. He purchased a disposable phone and made his way into a crowded restaurant. He ordered a beer from the waitress and dialled a number reserved for emergencies.

Connor answered on the third ring. "How did it go?"

"Pretty rough, Boss. I got what I could out of Chi. He told me Shinigami operates out of one of the islands in the chain. He also doesn't believe Kenji and him are connected in their ideals. He couldn't say for certain. No mention of the ambassador or the missing jet. It feels like a hell of a lot of smoke and mirrors, Boss."

The phone went dead. Kurt looked at the no signal icon flashing at the top. He knew that news of his foray into the city would travel among the gangs. He couldn't stays in the city, but he could lie low in the country if Connor needed him to. He still had contacts there he could call on.

He gulped down the Asahi he ordered and left the restaurant. As he walked across the road, he let the phone fall from his hand. It bounced once before a car shattered it into pieces. Just like his past, Kurt vanished into the crowd.

Chapter 15

Connor watched the drizzle spatter the hotel room windows. He clutched his phone, waiting for Kurt to call back. That call never came. Connor wasn't concerned as he knew Kurt would lay low, his short mission completed for now. Connor saw reports on the local news about gunfire in the downtown area of Tokyo City. It a made sense if Kurt was involved.

Connor looked away from the tv screen as Chapman entered their rented room.

"The building's fairly secure, Boss, as far as hotels go." He noticed the furrow on Connor's forehead. "Any more word from Kurt?"

"No," Connor said. "I got a call from Daniels before Kurt rang. I told him we were tracking down leads. He bit back, expecting results. I told him we would get them soon enough."

Chapman shifted to a nearby table, a duffle bag sitting on its surface. "Janus will be along soon enough. Kelly is scheduling a meeting with you and Hiroto Toyotami at short notice."

Connor expected no less from his second in charge, "Good, the quicker the better. Tori should be at the building shortly. Her update will be invaluable in our next phase."

Chapman pulled out a deck of cards. "Take a seat, Boss. I figured you had gone to sleep standing up."

Connor smiled, looking out at the view as the early morning dawn broke over the skyline of Tokyo. "It's a beautiful city, isn't it? It has an air of mystery and a shroud of darkness over it at the same time."

"You referring to the Yakuza?" Chapman asked, raising an eyebrow. Evans nodded.

"All big cities are like that," said Chapman. "New York with the gangs, Sicily with the Mafia. Hell, we came from North Korea a few days ago. No matter where we go, Boss, evil lies in wait. But if we don't do something, who will?"

Evans looked at him, a smile tugging at the corner of his mouth. "Smartest sentence you've strung together in a while, don't you think?"

Chapman laughed, the sound filling the room before it faded to a chuckle. "Next time we are up in the sky, remind me to accidentally roll the chopper with the door unlocked."

Chapman didn't let the silence linger. "There's something I want to ask you. Since the prison break, when you put your neck on the line for Tori, I've noticed something of a shift. Like you've seen something you wish you could unsee."

Evans knew that Chapman would let it lie if he chose not to respond, but he felt that he owed him the truth.

"After my father and I established the organisation, things were finally looking up for me. I had gone through a rollercoaster of hell from relationships, family issues, you know, the works. It was before you joined the organisation. There was a mission I undertook with Janus and Southgate. We were employed by the Nigerian government to work with a child trafficking ring taking African children away from their families and shipping them out to countries in Asia and the Middle East.

We arrived at a small village on the outskirts of Saudi Arabia, too small to have a name. Most of the villagers were inside their houses when the raid occurred. It was a joint operation. Approaching one of the houses on the hill; we moved in quickly. The authorities wanted the operation to be visible for media purposes. I just wanted the bastards who did this brought to justice. It felt like a circus to me. We busted the doors and moved in. What I saw that day will sit with me a lifetime. Cages upon cages, like an animal pound. Scared girls and boys of no more than ten years old kept in them. There must've been at least fifty or sixty of them crammed into a cage and stacked like dogs. Some of the girls shied away when unlocked their cages. Others had injuries too horrible to mention, and many more had a fear in their eyes that would most likely stay with them for the rest of their lives.

The Nigerian forces had a female army psychologist. The girls were attracted to her like bees to honey. I can still remember the faces of the men I had commanded, their faces drawn and grim."

Chapman looked at him, a deeper understanding now of what drove the man. "Sir, whatever you saw, it was not your fault, evil never sleeps. It's up to us to be the bastion of defence, the light that throws itself endlessly against that wall of darkness."

Connor nodded. "You're right, but since then I can no longer stand by and do nothing. Sometimes, someone just has to do the right goddamn thing."

"Never met your father, Connor, but I sure as hell feel like if he is anything like you, he must be a hell of a man." Connor didn't have the heart to reply.

"What about you, Chapman? I hired you all those years ago because you were one hell of a pilot and mechanic, but despite all we have been through, you're about as mysterious as they come."

Chapman laughed. He pulled two beers out of the minibar and tossed one at Evans. Chapman popped the top of his and took a long swig like it was water.

"My story is like yours, just a little different on the finer points. Child trafficking was one thing in Africa, but I saw other things, too. Flying medics into war torn Sudan and other parts of the continent made me realise evil doesn't sleep. I've seen children taken from mothers, and fathers killed over nothing. These people we fight stand behind an ideology that makes about as much sense as the idiot spouting the nonsense in the first place.

Connor's burner phone buzzed. He put the phone on speaker so they could both hear Kelly.

"Connor, I have good news and bad news. The good news is I've bypassed security at Toyotami Industries, and I've put you in Hiroto's calendar in the next two hours."

"Good work, Kell. What's the bad news?"

"I was getting to that," Kelly said, sounding annoyed. "The bad news is we haven't located the ambassador or the bombs yet."

"Did you manage to get anything from the video feed, or manage to trace it?" Connor asked.

"We traced the feed off a number of signal towers but couldn't pinpoint which of the three islands in the chain it came from."

"Get to work on cross-referencing them with the rest of the crew's run-down. One of those islands is our target."

Connor ended the call, looking at Chapman.

"Kelly will find something. Chapman, I need you to rent a helicopter. Use one of the company cards and an alias. Have it prepared for later tonight."

"What are you thinking, Boss?" Chapman replied, keen to be out of the hotel room.

Connor smiled, trying to let Chapman down easy.

"I'm thinking Janus and I need to see a good tailor."

Chapter 16

An hour later, Tori was sitting at a table in a Japanese restaurant opposite the main entrance of Toyotami Industries. The aroma of fresh fish, spice, and petrol made her want to gag. The hustle and bustle of people in the surrounding street blocked her view as she waited for Chapman to return from his permitter check. Tori wore casual clothing, a shirt and shorts purchased from a local clothing store. She nursed the small mocha coffee beside her.

The concrete and glass tower rose high into the sky, high enough she had to crane her neck to see all of it when she looked out from underneath the restaurant awning. She glanced at her phone. A shadow blocked the light. Chapman.

"Hello, little lady, is this seat taken?" he said.

Tori, not taking her eyes off the building to acknowledge his boyish grin, replied, "Sit down you idiot, you'll give us away. If you hadn't realised, we are the only foreigners here watching that building. Try to look like you belong."

Chapman obliged,

"Heard anything from Evans and Janus yet?"

Tori shook her head. Evans wanted to get a closer look at the company he suspected may have been involved with the ambassador's jet going missing. Evans had several theories. His first was that if it was willing to bankroll a private security force, there was more to the company than met the eye. He figured the only way to confirm this was to hack into their servers. Despite Kelly's best efforts, she had not been to achieve this externally. The second was that the ambassador's meeting may have posed a threat to the weapons manufacturer, meaning he needed to be removed from the equation. Connor's goal was simple: *access the servers, find out what they are hiding.*

Evans had tasked three additional company members to blend into the crowd on perimeter watch, observing while Tori kept tabs on the main entrance. The additional crew were keeping an eye on the underground parking garage, staff entrance, and emergency exit. Shifting uncomfortably on her chair, Tori felt the hard lump of the weapon in her shoulder holster. Although it provided comfort, she hoped she wouldn't have to use it, especially around this early morning throng of people. Onboard the *Serenity*, Kelly had tried to work her magic to get warrants for the guns, but Japan was one of the few Asian countries with very stringent laws regarding who could carry weapons, especially in public.

Chapman checked his watch. It's almost 8am. Where is Evans?" he said, his voice loud enough to be heard above the crowd.

"He is never late. He'll be here soon," Tori replied.

A jet-black limousine pulled up outside the entrance opposite. A woman got out and, as Tori watched, climbed the stairs elegantly. Reaching the top, she held up her phone, as if taking a selfie. Tori continued to observe this unusual behaviour, as the woman placed her phone in a small purse. She turned and looked directly at their supposedly covert position, before entering the lobby of the tower.

"Did you see that?" said Chapman. "She looked right at us."

Tori kept her eyes on the entrance as the limousine peeled away back into traffic.

"What has you on edge? We don't even know who she was. For all we know, it could be one the father's mistresses. Stay focused. We aren't here to gawk."

Tori had never been spotted so easily, and her frustration almost gave way to anger. She couldn't help thinking Chapman was right. The woman was clearly aware she and Chapman were watching. Connor would want to know about this. Tori punched a number on her burner phone and waited. Evans answered on the first ring.

"Boss, we may have a problem. Chapman and I *think* we were spotted by a visitor to the tower. A woman dressed in a dark blue knee-length dress. I couldn't make out any features, but this operation may be."

After a pause, Evans replied. "Alert the others, tell them to keep an eye on the entrances and exits for anything suspicious. Janus and I will be arriving shortly. We might be able to find out more about this mystery woman."

"Kelly can do a check if we manage to get a photo," Tori said, as another limousine pulled up outside the tower.

"Don't you worry about that, I'll see if I can get a fingerprint," said Evans.

The limousine driver got out and opened the rear door. Two men emerged. Both wore dark suits with matching ties, one carrying a briefcase. The two were almost in perfect sync as they climbed the stairs, then one paused, facing Tori, and curled his fingers into a symbol she knew all too well.

"You and Janus look good in those suits, Boss," she said. Is Janus wearing a fake moustache as well?"

"If need to know, Kelly suggested the moustache for me to hide my resting scowl, she reckons it makes me look more dashing or whatever the heck that means," Janus growled.

"Stay alert. I'll let you know what I pick up inside. Janus and I will leave our mics on," Connor interrupted

With that, Evans ended the phone call, and he and Janus strode purposefully into the lobby.

* * *

Evans and Janus stood shoulder to shoulder in the elevator. The stereotypical music playing was more soothing than its American counterpart. Evans placed a finger in his ear, feeling the earpiece designed expressly for this kind of mission. His team had been devising it for months for covert operations and it was still a prototype, so they had neckpieces tucked under their collars as a backup.

Evans checked the devices as they waited for the elevator to arrive at their stop. Tori's voice came through loud and clear. Janus indicated that his earpiece was also working.

"I hope you know what you're doing, Boss," said Janus. "The sudden procurement of a meeting may arouse suspicion." The man was as cool as ice and, unlike Chapman, Janus gave Connor chills. The notorious sniper worked well under pressure, and nothing could change that.

The elevator dinged as the stainless-steel doors opened into a plush atrium. Reflections from a hanging crystal chandelier painted the glass and tile in white light. They walked out onto a thick red carpet, Evans and Janus taken aback by the sheer luxury of it all. This was more opulent, and even more elegantly designed, than their luxury yacht. He knew Japanese culture was focused on Feng Shui, and he could feel the balanced energy in the room as they approached a reception desk.

"Glad we have the scrambler active. I've spotted almost ten cameras since we got out of the limousine," Janus said in a low voice.

The pretty receptionist had her dark hair up, kept there by what appeared to be a chopstick. She wore little in the way of makeup, but Connor felt she didn't need it. Her smile only enhanced her features.

"Mr Harding, here to meet with your CEO," said Janus, indicating Connor. "My name is Mr Ross." The receptionist clicked a few times, and the recognition on her face confirmed Kelly had done her job well. Connor decided a large bonus would be coming her way.

"Please take a seat, gentlemen," she said, gesturing toward a small seating area near two large oak doors. "Mr Toyotami is currently in another meeting. Would you like anything to drink?"

Both men declined. As they sat down, Connor knew Janus was already making an assessment on exit strategy should things turn sour. Connor, on the other hand, was wondering about the man they were due to meet. Hiroto Toyotami was the reclusive CEO of Toyotami Enterprises, according to Kelly's brief. The weapons builder had endured an illustrious era during the wars in the Pacific countries, until the past decade had seen a sudden decline in the value of their shares. Evans could understand why. Put simply, there were no more wars to be fought. However, Connor speculated this may not be for long, given the ongoing tension in eastern Europe, and the crisis occurring in Africa and the Middle East. Wherever dissent occurred, you could bet the weapons they came were from black market dealers that underhandedly sold weapons from companies like the one he was now visiting.

"What do you make of this, Boss?" Janus whispered, placing the briefcase on the table. The device inside was responsible for scrambling their faces on the cameras, and it was currently active. Evans knew the security guards would have tried to run facial checks on him and Janus. The scrambler within the briefcase was designed to distort their faces, but it also ensured any trace run on them would bring up the forged documents and identities of Mr Harding and Mr Ross. The reason they declined a drink was to avoid leaving fingerprints.

"Anything from Kelly yet?" Connor asked.

Janus didn't answer, as the receptionist stood up behind her desk. Evans tensed as she opened one of the doors and disappeared inside. He wondered if their cover was blown. Moments later, she reappeared, and both men got up made as she announced them.

With a sigh of relief, Connor straightened his tie and walked to the doors. The receptionist directed them inside. As they did so, the mysterious woman Tori had described glided out of the room. Connor was more focused on the mission at hand, but Janus, stepping aside to let her pass, raised his arm to check his watch, squeezing his gloved hand as he did so.

Evans was captivated by the excellent taste carried through from the reception to the room he now stood in, it combined both classical and modern Japan. Hiroto Toyotami's penthouse office was spacious, with a view from a property developer's dreams. Its central position in the business district meant it overlooked most of Tokyo. The white speck of a distant airliner was the single blemish in an uninterrupted view of Tokyo's skyline. On either side of the glorious view, stood racks of ancient Japanese armaments and weapons, some he recognised others he could only guess at. All looked deadly and sharp.

Enthralled in the view and weapons, Evans barely noticed the presence of Toyotami seated behind a voluminous desk. The CEO of Toyotami Industries made to stand, but his frailness betrayed his age as he could only rise from his chair, maintaining balance with his other hand on the desk before him. Connor and Janus bowed their heads before taking their seats in front of the desk. Though Evans felt the familiar desire to shake the elderly man's hand, it would go against custom. The man, dressed in traditional male garb called a Jinbei. The outfit was often worn in the summer months, consisting of a black short-sleeved jacket and short pants. This was crossed over at the front and tied by cord. It provided very casual look to the older man before them taking both men by surprise given the lavish environment surrounding them as he smiled at them.

"Welcome gentlemen. My name is Hiroto Toyotami, but you would already know that. Do what do I owe the pleasure of your company today?"

Evans saw right through the old man's façade as he gestured for both Janus and him to sit in two plush chairs before the desk. Despite the smile on his face and the warmth of his welcome, the man radiated a certain deathly chill when the smile faded, and his gaze settled on Evans. The receptionist left the room as Toyotami spoke, closing the door quietly behind them.

Connor didn't return Toyotami's smile.

"Thank you for seeing us on such short notice, Mr Toyotami. Seems we have something in common: our desire to make money and turn a healthy profit."

Kelly had done her research well. Connor breezed over the financials in the report she'd provided. He had to admit, he had never seen so many zeroes in a company's net worth. Morbidly, he wondered if that net worth was less than, or equal to, the numbers of those who had died because of Toyotami's weapons.

"That is true, Mr—" the old man said. Evans knew full well the man knew who he was meeting with, as Kelly's report said Toyotami had only one meeting that morning.

"Harding, Thomas Harding."

"Well, Mr Harding, what can I help you with?"

Evans crossed his legs and placed his hands in his lap, "Mr Toyotami, it has come to my attention that the war in Eastern Europe and the continuing escalation in the Middle East has highlighted a situation that cannot be ignored."

"What situation would that be?" Toyotami asked, his eyes twinkling with greed.

"It's clear, sir, that the world hasn't been on edge like this for nearly a hundred years. It was only a matter of time until the cauldron boiled over. What surprised us all is the direction it came from. Russia has been wanting to flex its military might ever since the Cold War, but the spread of communism was slowed to some extent by the Vietnam War. It seems their President has not only an ego, but a desire for expansionist policies. He wants to establish the original Russian empire created by Peter the Great. Advancing his ambitions under such a pretence is his prerogative, but what of our own backyard, Mr Toyotami? How long until China makes its move, and who will it be against?

Evans almost believed the drivel that was coming out of his mouth.

"We didn't see the war in the Middle East erupting as it did, the attacks in the Red Sea on neutral countries?"

Hiroto Toyotami had been sitting quietly, taking this in. "What do you propose, Mr Harding?"

Evans continued. "The fall of your own country was attributed to the success of the Americans in the Pacific. Liken this to China. Once more, if the bear is poked and a war comes with it, who falls first? Japan, Taiwan or even Australia, and the other southeast countries? If anything, we were wrong in presuming the Russian military was strong and united. Evidently, it was nothing more than a front. The real power comes from its nuclear weapons arsenal. An arsenal that China also carries. Your nearest ally is America, and we sure as hell don't have any. So, what I am proposing, Mr Toyotami, is that my Australian company works with your company in building or acquiring nuclear weapons to prevent such an act of war occurring.

Hiroto nodded thoughtfully. He had been listening intently to Evans, making him feel that potentially he may have overstepped the mark in what he had to offer, but Connor knew the man was racked with greed.

"Gentlemen, this is quite an unusual proposition. I agree with you that the Pacific may become the next battleground and very soon. I also understand your concern for both our frontiers, Japan particularly. We have three communist countries around us in possession of weapons that could send us back to the Stone Age. I see your offer as one of goodwill, fostering the alliance between Japan and Australia. I will have to get back to you on the matter, as I must discuss this with the board. This is a great undertaking that will directly put us in a position where China may wish to flex its muscle against us—"

Connor jumped in, not wanting to lose the old man. "If Japan has nuclear weapons, they will act as a deterrent."

Toyotami shook his head, "Your proposal is sound, Mr Harding, but as history serves, the USSR placed missiles in Cuba to deter America from flexing its own muscle. A situation, if you remember, that almost brought about World War three. If we were to construct and place such weapons on the doorsteps of two sleeping giants, it may only serve to bring about our own doom. If not for the logic and reasoning of Kennedy, the world would be very different."

When the door opened, Toyotami cut his response short. His eyes narrowed.

Janus and Connor turned at the disturbance.

The new arrival was every bit the striking image of a younger Toyotami, making Evans conclude that this was the missing link in the chain: his son.

"Excuse me, gentlemen, please accept my apologies. My son, Kenji, has rudely interrupted our meeting." Hiroto went to rise as Kenji marched toward the desk and, in hushed whispers, bent low to talk into his father's ear. Evans only caught a few Japanese words, but nothing that he could piece together. To Evans's surprise, rather than leaving, Kenji Toyotami sat in a chair near the desk, staring coolly at his father's guests. Evans had little information about the son that wasn't already public, but Kenji's sudden appearance and Hiroto's glare were enough to confirm the growing contempt between the two men. There was no love there, and Evans saw an opportunity he could exploit. He addressed Hiroto again.

"Information has recently come to my attention of weaponry that Russia possesses: a Poseidon torpedo that can cause radioactive tsunamis. Whether such a weapon exists is hard to confirm, but reports suggest it may have been invented during World War Two and hidden from the eyes of the Axis. Such documentation that is now unclassified states that tests were performed but were unsuccessful. Between you and I, Mr Toyotami, I believe these weapons do exist, but their whereabouts are unknown. It would be in our interests to invest in this technology, given the propensity for our neighbours to do the same. We are playing with millions of lives, gentlemen. We would be wise to be prepared."

Evans notes of Kenji's demeanour, the old man's knuckles whitening on the armrest as his son fell for Evans's ploy. Evans felt he had everything he needed to know now. Not from the old man, but from his heir.

"What exactly are you after from me and my company?" Hiroto Toyotami asked.

"I have an interest in anything experimental you may have for instance. If you offer me exclusive rights on such weapons, then I will make you an offer of a lump sum payment of a hundred million upwards. Provided of course, the goods are satisfactory."

Toyotami nodded, clearly in thought. Evans made sure to keep Kenji's reactions within his vision, casually averting his gaze between them.

"Please think on my offer, Mr Toyotami. The world may soon be at war. Power is shifting once more. Countries like ours must stand together to deter the imperialist expansionism that once existed. There's an old English expression, one his father had used often when talking about his military days, 'All it takes for evil to triumph is for good men to stand by and do nothing.' Which side will you be on, My Toyotami?

Evans had played his hand. He only hoped Hiroto, or his son, called his bluff. He glanced at Kenji. The offer had the expected effect. The younger man looked as if he wanted to leap out of the chair and shake his father until he saw reason and accepted the offer. The company's shares continued to tank, but an investment like this might see their fortunes turn around. An offer, Evans could see, that, unlike his father Kenji wouldn't refuse.

"Very well, Mr Harding. Leave your details with my secretary and I will get back to you in due course. I must ask, given your significant wealth, why this is the first time I have heard of you and your company?"

Evans remained unmoved by the question. He knew Toyotami would have doubts, as the man had been in the game for decades. He would know all the players and, just like at a roulette table, experienced players were often wary of newcomers.

"Forgive me Mr Toyotami. My company is directly endorsed by the Australian government. You would likely recognise my name elsewhere, but with the way the world is shaping up over the next few years, I think my investments would be better placed in the field of weapons."

Evans knew he was dancing on a fault line, but unmoved by the substantial cash offer and Evans's reply, Toyotami only smiled. *A smile of death,* Evans thought. Rising, Connor bid both men goodbye, Janus following closely behind. Hiroto buzzed the secretary as one of the doors swung open, indicating their departure.

Evans had got a lot more than he had bargained for. He instructed Janus to confirm with Hiroto's secretary, that they booked accommodation at a five-star hotel a block from the company's headquarters.

The rented limo was waiting outside the building. Once inside, Evans and Janus peeled off their outfits. Underneath, they wore t-shirts and shorts. They also replaced their shoes, and Janus peeled off his fake moustache.

"God, that hurts," he said as the glue holding it in place tore away his stubble. "Damn thing feels like pulling off a band aid," he said.

"You've taken bullets to almost every part of your body, and you are moaning about a little bit of glue," Evans said, as he knocked on the screen behind the driver. The limousine pulled into the traffic.

Evans texted the team waiting on the perimeter, telling them he and Janus were out.

Now we play the waiting game, Evans thought.

Chapter 17

Onboard the *Serenity*, Kelly saw the email notification. Twirling a pen in one hand, she clicked on it, and the pictures from Janus began to download. Accompanying the email was a message: *Run a facial scan. Find out what she was doing at Toyotami Industries. Has Australian accent.*

The indication of an Australian accent would narrow the parameters of their facial recognition software. She uploaded the photos and waited.

The search results didn't take long. *Connor's going to like this,* Kelly thought.

* * *

In their hotel room, Connor reached for the laptop in Chapman's duffel bag. He opened the email from Kelly, his jaw tightening as he scanned it. It seemed that Daniels had kept tight lipped about the ambassador's entourage containing not one, but two ASIO agents. Government spies. While Connor had been focused on the mission objective, Janus had kept his eye on the woman. Connor cursed himself for being so blind. The facial scan had come up with a report. Laura Goddard. Personal assistant to Ambassador Joshua Davidson. Kelly had dug deeper, signing off the email with *Looked into ASIO files, thought you might like this.* It told him everything he needed to know.

Janus came out of the bathroom, noticing the laptop screen.

"Say what you will Boss, it was plain to see she was no employee of Toyotami's."

Connor gave him a look. "If she is at Toyotami's then where is the ambassador? Was she in on it?"

Janus grimaced. "We won't know till we find her. Fortunately, I had Kelly's team on that as well."

Connor smiled, clicking speed dial on his phone. Kelly answered.

"I take it you got my email," she said.

"Seems Daniels has his secrets as much as we do," replied Connor. "Janus said you were keeping tabs on Laura Goddard.,

"She's staying where you are, Connor. Same hotel, floor above you. The information was in Toyotami's calendar. Patching through the details now."

Connor didn't believe in coincidence. He knew none of his team did either. "I'll investigate it further. Keep at it, Kelly. You find anything, you let me know."

Connor ended the call and looked at Janus, "I need you rested and ready to go later tonight. We need to see what's on those servers."

"Don't you worry about me Boss. Being a ghost is my specialty."

Minutes later, Connor walked out of the elevator, looking both ways before heading to the room number Kelly had sent. He wasn't sure what surprised him more, their run-in at Toyotami Industries, or that fact that Goddard was in the same hotel.

Reaching the door, he pulled out a skeleton key card, a device that resembled a bank card. He slid it through the card scanner on the door, and the door unlocked. Checking his surroundings, Connor entered the room and closed the door behind him with his foot. He fished a pair of gloves out of his pocket. He was careful to limit how much he touched, wanting to ensure everything was left as it was before he entered. Though he'd trained for break and entry, he had worked with Kurt to hone his spy craft. It had paid off more often than he'd expected.

At first glance, the room was identical to his own. Given Laura's background, Connor had brought a few devices to ensure his break-in remained undetected. The room's layout was simple - desk, lounge chairs, a queen bed, and a small dining table. The room's walls were adorned with photographs of local landmarks, nothing out of the ordinary. He moved a small electronic device slowly over the frames on the walls, then the desk lamps beside the bed, searching for listening bugs. *Nothing.*

There was no luggage in the room. It was almost too clean. He walked to the ensuite bathroom and turned the handle. As he did so a man fell toward him. Connor raised his arm to deflect any blow.

What happened next was something Connor had never experienced. The man didn't put up a fight. He didn't even raise his arm to break his fall, as he dropped to the floor and lay unmoving.

"Who are you? are you with him?"

Connor looked at the stiletto in the man's back, then at the woman in front of him, holding a supressed pistol.

Although she still wore some makeup from her previous meeting, Laura Goddard was naturally pretty. Her features were petite, her hair an auburn brown, and her eyes were a jade green, searching his own for any trace of a lie.

"My name is Commander Connor Evans. I work for the Australian government. I was sent to search for you and Ambassador Davidson."

Laura kept the pistol steady, evidently trying to decide if he was telling the truth.

"When your jet went missing, we were hired by George Daniels to find you," he said. "You must believe me."

"Why should I? You were at Toyotami Industries earlier." Her voice remained steady. "Are you one of them?"

"No, I am not one of them. In fact, I'm all you've got at this point." Connor wasn't sure if his answer would be enough.

Laura lowered the gun but kept the safety off. "What were you doing there?"

Connor lowered his hands., "I could ask you the same thing. Where is the ambassador?"

"Sit on the bed. Now." Connor did as she asked.

Laura stood over him.

"Don't make me repeat the question."

Connor nodded. "I was at Toyotami industries for the same reason as you were. To find out whether they were responsible for the ambassador's disappearance, and to find out the location of a doomsday device."

"What doomsday device?" Laura probed.

"We received a video from the kidnappers, who are yet to be identified, holding a katana to Davidson's neck. They threatened to bring about a new dawn in forty-eight hours and create a new ring of fire. The video featured a digital timer on a device of some sort. We have no idea what weapons they possess and what the device is at this point. But we are running a dangerous race. We have been hired to find Davidson, but now we also need to find these weapons."

Laura's voice held no trace of panic.

"What did you find out from Hiroto? Anything related to these bombs?" she asked. Connor noticed her Australian accent was barely discernible. He was lucky to have Janus there, someone foreign-born who could pick up subtleties he couldn't.

"The man is a traditionalist and an idealist. A relic of the past. But he knows what nuclear weapons can bring about the son, on the other hand, wanted to jump at the offer I made to develop such weapons."

Laura nodded, "I wasn't there for Kenji's appearance, but on Hiroto, we both see eye to eye."

She settled into one of the lounge chairs near the bed.

"What if I told you that the ambassador's recent visit to Japan was meant to prevent what you just told me actually happening?" she asked.

"Then you would've caught me off guard. We haven't figured out that angle yet. But that would be part of the missing link we are searching for," he replied.

"The ambassador was supposed to meet his counterpart in Tokyo, collaborating to ensure Japan's nuclear weapon policy remained unchanged. The Australian government was also seeking counsel on limiting the manufacture of weapons and tackling black market dealings."

"Why Japan, though? I can't imagine Japan is as much a problem as the Russian AKs every terrorist or extremist possesses?"

"Not Japan, but Toyotami. The old general's power extends beyond weapons into political circles. We believe he could influence policy once more."

"But he won't," Connor concluded, "because his son is a bigger concern."

Laura nodded. "Hiroto is getting on. Kenji holds a stake in the company that allows him to take control if his father dies."

Connor could see the problem if someone like Kenji, who was drawn to his lie like a bee to honey possessed such power.

Connor switched topics. "What happened to the jet? You've been missing for days now."

Laura looked out at the city before she replied.

"I don't remember much. We were taken captive by the 'security force' that was on the manifest. From there, a military jet diverted us. Everything went black after that, and I woke up in some prison cell. A tiled floor and white walls. I saw Davidson once, and he was being beaten for information. Once they left, I wanted to save him… he was too weak and…" Laura's throat caught.

Connor wanted to console her but was still unsure if Laura trusted him. The pistol still rested in her hand.

"My team is trying to work out where the ambassador is," he said. "Where did you escape from? I can help you get him back. You're not alone in this fight."

Laura looked at him, making the decision he'd hoped for. She clicked the safety on her pistol and put it on a small table.

"I may be angry, but I'm not stupid. I will accept your help. I need to contact my superior first, back in Canberra. I need to let him know that Steven, my partner, didn't make it."

"You can use a satellite phone in my room to make the call," he said. A glimmer of a smile touched her lips. As she left the room, he looked at the body lying face down on the floor. "I think I might make a quick call to room service first," he called after her.

An hour later, Connor stood in the hotel room with his most senior team members. Kurt was still lying low on the outskirts of Tokyo after his messy run-in with the Yakuza hit squad. Connor couldn't ask for more than that. He wasn't in the game of asking questions of his team, unless it jeopardized their desired level of secrecy.

The rest of the team were either in the hotel room with Connor, or back onboard the *Serenity*. Laura had joined them, despite the team's objections. She was privy to their plans now. Connor had informed them of her credentials, and Kelly had verified them with Daniels, who had been relieved to hear one of the consulate staff had survived.

"With Laura onboard, we can get down to business once more. I asked Kelly to put a digital timer back at the Hub to monitor how much time we have left. We must move on this now. Laura has some information to share with us, so the floor is hers."

Laura explained where she was kept, the ordeal she went through with the ambassador, and described the location of the facility she'd escaped from. Kelly took the new intelligence provided, and, with a quick scan, highlighted an island of interest within the Izu Island chain. Tori-shima Island. An island they might never have picked as the location of the ambassador.

"Alright, team. William and Janus, scout ahead on Tori-shima Island. William, I want your gun dogs to be ready at a moment's notice onboard. Tori will work on the logistics with Kelly."

Connor ended the meeting. His part in the plan meant breaking into the servers later that night with Laura. Janus and William, he hoped, would find the ambassador alive and still in one piece.

Chapter 18

"It's not every day you visit a volcanic island to find a missing ambassador," William said.

William waited for Janus to retort, but the man said nothing.

William shrugged. "Thought you might want to offer your two cents, big man. You ready?"

"I was born ready," Janus said, making William chuckle.

The chopper blades whirled up to speed as William performed the preflight checks onboard the Robinson helicopter. William was not usually pilot, a role normally reserved for Chapman. He had little in the way of flight experience, but since he doubted this mission would involve aerial acrobatics or evading Surface to Air Missile turrets, he wouldn't let Connor and the team down.

To ensure they covered the ground evenly, Connor had ordered the *Serenity* to move closer to the island chain and maintain a position between it and Tokyo. That way, if his mission in Tokyo was successful, he could return to the *Serenity* rather than the hotel room they now occupied.

For William and Janus, this meant their flight would take no more than four hours. The flight time also allowed Kelly to create their credentials and email them the necessary paperwork for the island, seeking the permissions they needed. The only way to get to Tori-shima Island was by air. This worked in their favour as they had their own chopper fuelled and ready to go. Not only that, but further research showed the island was a protected national bird sanctuary, meaning it was only visited by research scientists with special permission on government registered flights. Tori-shima was so protected that even tourists to the island were only taken around by boat, and not permitted to land on any beaches, due to a combination of rough seas and unsuitable landing spots. It gave Connor even more reason to investigate, given the Toyotami's great influence in the government due to their military connections. It wouldn't be too difficult to hide anything extra onboard those flights or switch out personnel at the last minute. If he was in their position, he would do the same.

Janus's phoned chime, as William piloted the helicopter toward the sloped circular shaped island of Tori-shima.

"We have our documents now, though I can't imagine there will be many people here to show them to," Janus shouted, apparently forgetting he was wearing a headset.

"We won't know until we know. Janus, keep an eye out for a landing zone. They'll have locations for us to put down somewhere," William replied, wincing at Janus's voice coming through his headset and from behind him at the same time.

Janus didn't reply, instead looking out the window for a clearing. They found what they were looking for as they moved toward the south side of the island. Among Japanese black pine trees inland, they saw the small asphalt landing zones reserved for helicopters, a large letter H in the middle of each. William took the helicopter down and gently kissed the tarmac, letting the rotors come to a standstill.

William climbed out as Janus pulled open the rear door to grab their belongings. To both men's surprise, the area was deserted.

"I expected a red-carpet greeting, if I'm being honest," William said, cracking another joke that didn't land with Janus.

"Let's find out what we are dealing with," said Janus. "The quiet is both an ally and an enemy. It would help if I had somewhere suitable to set up so I could recon the island better. It's much too flat and confined here."

William looked up at the towering expanse of the volcano.

"Plenty of space up there for a good view, if you need it. Come on, we will find you a nest later. Kelly's briefing mentioned a facility not far from here for us to investigate. It's listed on official records as being reserved for visiting researchers and scientists. Let hope we find the ambassador there."

Climbing down from the helipads that floated off the ground on metal supports, they found a parking garage with two jeeps parked inside. They were in an empty office off to the side of it. It looked like it had been used at one point. Scratching their heads, they climbed into a jeep and shot off onto a dirt road leading to the coast. The road brought them out to a wide expanse of volcanic ash and dust. The jeep bounced along the road in grooves well-worn and recent. That thought alone gave both men hope that there were people on this island. Another hour had passed before they saw a concrete facility built on the southern side, nestled among rocks and trees. The sun had dipped lower in the sky and beat down hot and dry, giving William the feeling he was in a Mad Max scene, the barren terrain a perfect apocalyptic backdrop to their mission.

As they got closer, William left the road, parking the jeep behind a pile of volcanic rocks. He didn't want to draw any more attention to themselves, knowing that the dust kicked up by the jeep's tyres visible for miles, had already announced their arrivals. William was a former SAS commando for the British army, experienced in break and enter and hostage rescue. Janus was skilled in recon, surveillance, and becoming a ghost in any terrain. William deferred to the big man's expertise on this mission.

Janus scouted the area ahead with well-trained eyes, and a pair of binoculars held ready. William watched him scan back and forth. Neither man knew who was posted at the facility, and they weren't going to take any unnecessary risks to find out.

After some time had passed, Janus hadn't seen any life outside of the local fauna. Both men had brought the necessary equipment for the operation but had no way of covering the ruts caused by the jeep's tyres or hiding the vehicle effectively. They decided to leave the jeep behind the rocks, uncovered. Shouldering their packs, they set off toward the facility. William felt a sense of unease but trusted in Janus's judgement. They approached the forlorn building from the west.

Both men appreciated precarious situation they were in on the island, and that their mission essential to the survival of the ambassador. It was left to Connor and the others to defuse the bombs, when and if they found them.

William followed Janus, impressed by the man's ability to remain so stealthy despite his size, his feet barely touching a stray twig or making a sound. It gave William the impression Janus was hovering over the ground. His own footstep placement was not so precise, with the occasional twig snapping under his boot.

They reached the western side of the structure, both men crouching, allowing Janus to recon the facility once more. The lack of life put William on edge more than the alternative. William paused, as Janus indicated through hand movements for them to drop to the ground.

Less than fifty metres from the building, William could see the facility more clearly. The building was constructed of concrete and glass. It was as large as any warehouse, with an angular roof designed to disperse any rainfall. The bare concrete reminded William of an institutional prison complex, rather than a research facility. From their position, there was no entry point that wouldn't require breaking the exterior glass. Something William doubted they could manage, as it would likely be toughened safety glass, and that kind of noise would surely raise an alarm all over the island.

"What are you thinking?" William asked.

Using the ashy terrain underfoot, Janus drew their best points of entry. The area was naturally cordoned off by black pine trees on two sides, giving them only two options. William saw a concrete wall tapering off at the far side, but from their angle he couldn't be sure what it was.

"Should we just try the front door first? Kelly gave us all the paperwork we need on our phones," William said.

Janus nodded in understanding. Scrubbing out the plan on the ground, he wrote 'Plan B'. "We can't be so sure, William. It's possible, Toyotami has spies among the scientists here. We cannot risk being caught."

William agreed. "Let's not delay. I say we move now."

Janus shook his head in response,

"Better to wait, see if anyone surfaces in the next few hours."

William didn't like the idea of sitting still and getting caught doing so.

"The sooner we get inside, the sooner we can find the ambassador. What if he's there right now, spilling the beans on Australian secrets?"

"He would've done that long ago, if the Honourable Ones are behind this,' Janus replied.

William was about to ask who the 'Honourable Ones' were when Janus placed his hand up. William remained mute, waiting. After a few minutes, Janus dropped his hand to his side.

"I'll keep an eye out ahead, check our equipment and make sure we are ready to go at a moment's notice."

With that Janus melted into the trees, and William was alone, except for the distant cry of sea birds.

Hours later, Janus returned, William asking the obvious on where he disappeared too. The big man knelt and drew in the dirt what he had seen. Janus explained he was gauging who was in the area and other than the building, movement was minimal except for the odd bird in the trees. William once more conceded to the big man's ability to remain invisible, noting the dimensions in the dirt before letting Janus take point. They approached the structure carefully. As they got closer, it occurred to William that the concrete was older than he'd first thought, the building showing signs of visible age, and even the occasional bullet hole.

The building likely originated during WWII, but William couldn't imagine what purpose it had been built for. He tapped the big man on the shoulder, indicating he would take point as they moved in.

The front of the building was solid concrete except for two metal doors at the top of a set of steps. It was apparent to both men that the doors were a newer addition to the building. William knew Janus' head was on a swivel for any form of surveillance, and a tap on William's shoulder indicated they were clear to go.

Pistols drawn, they approached the entrance and climbed the steps to the double doors. William set his backpack on the ground to fish out his lockpicks. The door clicked.

William looked up. Janus was standing to the side of the open doorway.

"What the hell," William hissed.

"It's not even locked. Makes you wonder if we really are alone," Janus replied.

"You'd think for a government facility, it would be up to the nines in cameras, scanners and security, but we get an open door?" William said.

Both men stood at the doorway, looking down a long corridor, bright white light coming from buzzing LEDs. The corridor was empty. The silence was eerie. No alarms, no cries for help. The white corridor and tiles made reminded William of a hospital wing, rather than a research facility.

"I expected seven levels of resistance, hell, even one, but not this," William said, as they stepped inside. Though he walked slowly, the sound of boots on tile echoed along the corridor. "I think we're alone." Even William's whisper echoed hoarsely down the hallway, so he switched to hand movements, Janus nodding in understanding.

William had hoped they would find the ambassador, but he hadn't expected this. He remained silent, scanning ahead for any sign of an ambush. They found each door open, each room within void of anything but lint and specks of dust dancing in the air.

Satisfied they were alone, they moved into one of the rooms, the echo there non-existent, allowing them to talk.

"Nothing but an empty building. Looks like the government abandoned this facility ages ago. We are only wasting time now," William said in disgust.

"I don't think so," said Janus. "You didn't see what I saw. The building is old, but the interior is new. That's nothing out of the ordinary. What is out of the ordinary is how clean it is. If it was abandoned, it happened recently. It warrants a closer inspection before we report in."

"Maybe so. Let's check the exterior as well. Being alone is starting to creep me out."

Outside, on the far side of the building was another vehicle bay, complete with two more jeeps. A quick inspection showed the interior of the jeeps was missing, probably stripped for spare parts. While Janus continued looking, William looked across the open expanse, seeing new plant growth over old, rusted fence posts. Vines slithered around the metal and in between the barbed wire tips on top.

Janus came up alongside him. "Something wrong?"

William pointed at the metal posts and wire,

"I figure this was a WWII bunker at one point. This fencing helps confirm that. This must have housed POWs at some point, too."

"Are you thinking what I'm thinking?" Janus replied.

"Depends. I am thinking Toyotami chose this island for a particular reason. You think he used the old bunker to hide the ambassador? Hide him in plain sight?"

"We won't know until we have a closer look." said Janus. The men went back to work, scouring the building further. They examined every inch of the building as quickly as they could. The only thing that stirred was the dust.

"I'm calling it," William said, pulling the sat phone from his.

"I wouldn't do that. Come check this out." Janus pointed to something they hadn't noticed before. To William, it was nothing more than a white wall.

"What are you seeing?" William said.

Janus walked up to the wall and tapped a particular spot. The sound came back hollow.

"So what? They put cladding all over this building. The temperature in here is cooler than outside by about ten degrees. The insulation in the walls would normally moderate it."

"You would think so. Unfortunately, the building's heating units are all gone. The air-conditioning units, too. When I was scanning the roof, I noticed the fans weren't on. A further clue that the building has been abandoned. While you searched the front rooms, I searched the upper and lower levels."

"So? What are you saying?"

"I'm saying that this wall doesn't contain insultation, but something else. Look at the carpet. Are you seeing that as well?"

William looked at the scuffing on the floor, then at the wear on the carpet near the wall.

"That doesn't happen from furniture. That's movement William, a lot of it, too. I think we stumbled on how Toyotami keeps his business on the down low, away from prying eyes.

"Are you sure?"

"I take it when you walked in here, you smelled it too?"

William raised an eyebrow, "There was a lot to smell. Bleach and paint mostly."

Janus nodded, "Exactly. You smelt the paint too. Doesn't it strike you as odd the smell is strongest in this room? I'd place money something in this room doesn't belong."

"You think the walls have been replaced…?" William asked.

"Or covered up…Let's find out," Janus said. He kicked the wall, and his foot went straight through it. There was, a dull clang.

Both men looked at one another. Janus reached for the knife belted to his hip and plunged it into the wall, sending white particles into the air and onto the floor.

William helped Janus saw through the chalky material, and - to William's surprise - Janus was right. An elevator door lay in front of them.

"How in the world did you know that was there?" William asked, respect in his tone.

Janus shrugged. "My mother always said I had a nose for detail."

"I think you mean 'eye for detail, Janus. Still challenged in the nuances of the English language?"

Janus scowled, which was as close as he ever came to smiling.

"Next question: how do we get it open?" Janus said, returning to the task at hand.

"We could pry it open?" William said, pulling his own combat knife out.

"No. The electricity still works," Janus replied, shaking his head. "It runs off solar panels. Why would you pack up everything internally and leave the panels on the roof. Why leave the vehicles, too?"

William didn't have an answer for that.

Janus approached the open doorway. "I have another hunch," he said, inspecting the door frame, and pointing to three buttons on the light switch.

He clicked the first one, and it turned off half of the lights in the room. The second button turned off the other half.

Standing in the semi-darkness, Janus clicked the third. A low sound came from the walls.

William stepped closer to the door, hearing the whirring noise of machinery. "Well, I'll be damned," he murmured.

The two men drew their pistols as they waited for the elevator to arrive. While they focused on the door, another sound carried through the empty corridors. They barely heard it due to the thick walls of the concrete bunker. The thumping sound of helicopter blades.

Chapter 19

The first thing Janus or William knew about the missile fired from the helicopter was when the explosion shook the whole building. The bunker was built to survive, but repeated artillery strikes would surely level it.

Another explosion rocked the outside of the building. Glass shattered on the upper levels.

"How did they know we were here?" Janus yelled, as another booming strike hit.

William looked out the doorway at the dust kicked up by the chopper, but he couldn't make out the make or model. It didn't matter. They would both die if they didn't couldn't get out of that room.

"I don't remember seeing demolition signs outside when we arrived. Unplanned maintenance, I guess," William said.

"Not the time for jokes, Will," Janus said scowling, as he climbed into the elevator.

William joined him as a section of the roof caved in, filling the main hallway with rubble. She pushed the first button he found. The doors closed. The explosions carried on as they descended into the unknown. William didn't want to tell Janus he felt like he was in a metal coffin being lowered into the earth.

* * *

Jiro Ikeda's orders had been clear to the men on the island and keep an eye out for anything unusual. The men had been stationed on the island for a week, keeping watch on the abandoned research station. For the first few days, the scientists removed much of their equipment, and by the third day, it had all gone. An official notice claimed there was a gas leak in the building. The men knew otherwise. Hired to protect Kenji Toyotami as part of his private security force, their remit included protecting any of his interests as well. The facility was one of Kenji's closest interests. The ten men assigned considered it an honour to serve the Toyotami lineage. When Janus and William arrived, the guards had been alerted immediately. When the two foreigners set off the motion sensor embedded in the wall, their orders were clear.

* * *

The elevator plunged into the earth. Janus and William were both pressing their bodies against the sides of the elevator when it signalled its arrival at the bottom.

Once the doors opened, both men pointed their pistols out, expecting a hail of bullets. Their surprise at being met with another empty corridor made their situation more concerning. Janus didn't know how far below they were, but the explosions had stopped. He couldn't say that was a bad thing, but it wasn't good either. He hoped whoever was responsible wouldn't come after them.

As Janus stepped out with William, a section of roof came down. Janus only just managed to pull William out of the way. The debris caught William a glancing blow, sending him stumbling into the wall, despite Janus's efforts.

"Jesus, I thought it was over," William said. "Thanks Janus, I owe you one."

Both men were covered in a fine white layer of dust from the particle board they had pulled apart. It gave Janus's beard a salt and pepper look. William's boyish face looked like he possessed a smattering of white freckles.

Chunks of debris hammered down the elevator shaft behind them. The combination of tons of cement, timber, and glass caused an almighty crash as the elevator was buried under the rubble. The lights above flickered like something out of a horror movie as, one by one, they shut off. The buzzing increased in volume, then stopped.

"Great, just great. Stuck in an abandoned facility with a colleague in the darkness. Tick that one off the bucket list," William said.

Ignoring William's complaints, Janus clicked on a flashlight pulled from his backpack, shining it around the room.

"So, the solar panels were powering this place. There must be a backup generator in case of emergency down here," Janus said.

William coughed as he inhaled concrete dust, "Good thing neither of us smoke." He coughed again, clearing his lungs, before adding, "What do you think was down here that caused them to bury us?"

"Could be anything. The ambassador, some kind of research, or maybe weapons that make the nuke of '45 look tame and ineffective."

William shivered, not so much because of the comment, but the way Janus said it.

"You know, Janus, it's dark down here, but you're darker."

Janus ran the beam over the rubble. There was nowhere to go apart from the way they'd come. "You'll realise one day, William, that despite fighting in the light, it's the wars we fight in the darkness that define who we truly are."

Janus moved away from the choked elevator shaft, leaving William to think on what he'd said.

"We can't go up, so might as well see what secrets the darkness holds for us," Janus continued, as William jogged after him.

"They will still be waiting for us. I mean that's what I would do if the situation were reversed," William said.

Both men still clutched their pistols, safeties off, and pointed at the floor.

"We can't wait them out. We won't last a siege like that," Janus said. "Do your comms still work?"

William tried his in-ear microphone and got nothing but static. Janus got the same.

"What about the satellite phone you had?" Janus asked.

William fumbled inside his bag, Janus shining the torch for him.

"Shit. I must've dropped it topside.'

"Well, I'm all out of suggestions. Let's find something down here and see if we can get out a signal."

The two men walked the hallway shoulder to shoulder. At points, it narrowed before widening once more. They checked each room, only to find each of them empty.

"Do you think they will come after us?" Janus asked.

"Depends on how badly they want us dead. It's a slim possibility that they know we escaped into the shaft. It's more likely they think the building buried us when they brought it down."

"If it were me, I would check for bodies, confirm the kill," Janus remarked.

"You're a trained sniper. You kill from afar. You don't usually need to confirm anything."

"You're right. I don't miss, but I have seen amateur snipers miss their mark. You should never assume a spray of blood means your target is dead. Sloppy work, if you ask me."

"What are you getting at?" William asked, confused at the point Janus was making.

"Never assume," Janus said. He stopped William commenting further by pointing his beam at a closed doorway in front of them.

"Seems we have struck a dead end," William said.

"You speak Japanese at all?" Janus asked, playing the beam over the doorway.

Written in red letters both men translated the warning as *don't enter*. This only served to arouse their curiosity further.

"This far down, it could be an emergency exit to the top," William suggested, reaching for the handle.

"Or something worse," Janus remarked.

William preferred his option. He pushed down on the handle and opened the door. The metal groaned in protest as rusted hinges bit back. He stepped away as Janus directed the beam inside.

"Looks like a passageway," said Janus, trying to fit through the door.

William added his weight to it, and the door gave way, sending Janus forward into the dirt floor.

He grabbed the torch and rose to his feet, dancing the beam around the room.

"Hold up, this might help," William said, cracking a glow stick and tossing it down the passageway they stood in, before pulling out his own flashlight.

The stick skittered along the floor, illuminating the passageway in a bright green glow.

"It's a passageway alright, carved out of the stone. Where do you reckon this leads?" Janus said.

William ran his hand over the wall, feeling grooves made from pickaxes, not modern machinery.

"This explains the POW camp we encountered up top. Wonder why they needed so much manpower?"

"I think we will find out soon enough," Janus replied. The air temperature remained cool as they delved deeper, following spiralling passageways. They soon discovered an antechamber. They could only assume it was an extension of the Japanese occupation above. The room measured fifteen metres wide by five metres.

"We might be in luck on that generator down here," William said, shining his yellow beam on a bunch of cables that ran along the wall, leading to multiple bulbs above their heads. The next antechamber they found, just a few metres from the first, gave them their first real clue about what the real Japanese purpose on the island was.

The second chamber housed steel framed beds, most with stained mattresses. A quick inspection of the copper-coloured stain confirmed it was blood. They traced the stains along the floor, where some led further into the passageway.

"You don't think they experimented on people here?" William said.

"Difficult to say. The Japanese weren't so different to the Nazis in that regard, looking for the next scientific breakthrough thing to make their conquests."

"Jesus. I feel like our world grows darker every time we stumble across something that happened during that era."

They found three more chambers in similar states as they progressed further. Without knowing what the other was thinking, they shared a common feeling of hopelessness wondering whether they were marching toward a dead end.

"You can see why Toyotami is the way he is, can't you?" Janus said as they walked. "Ruthless and efficient was the Japanese way. If they were experimenting down here, something tells me that they would have made horrific discoveries and God knows what else. I wonder if he knew this was here."

"Let's ask him next time we see him, shall we?" William replied. "It's amazing how the scientists that came to this island to study its flora and fauna had no clue this was under them the whole time."

A deafening explosion came from behind, making them both react.

"Debris falling, or an entry point?" Janus said, his pistol pointed behind them, searching for a non-existent target.

"Neither sounds good to me. Come on, surely there is an end to these blasted tunnels. I've inhaled enough dirty air for one lifetime," William responded.

They quickened their pace and rounded a corner, emerging in a cavernous chamber that raised more questions than answers. A huge wall of darkness greeted them.

"What the hell is this place?" William said.

Janus's beam was swallowed by the vast darkness. As he moved it either side of them it illuminated a small, brick-like machine near the entrance. He kneeled and scanned the piece of equipment, as it dawned on him what it was. He looked for the cord. Finding it, he holstered his pistol, placed one foot on the generator and pulled it three times in quick succession, with no luck.

"This stupid piece of shi—" With one final pull, the generator kicked over and spluttered to life.

The buzzing sound of electricity filled the air as it snaked along the cables to multiple lights that hung overhead, illuminating the huge cavern they stood in.

The circular chamber was well over a hundred and twenty-five feet high, and about same in width. The hanging lights flickered but didn't go out. They examined the horrors before them.

Their gaze swept over neatly stacked wooden crates on one side, a sparkling blue-green lagoon on the other. Their primary focus on the crates nearest them. a quick inspection had both inhaling sharply. Instead of being full of weapons or shells, they were full of human bones. Thousands of them. The first row of crates had spilled and burst open. A skull rested in front of William, who felt sick looking at so much death.

"The sooner we leave this place the better," William said, gritting his teeth in revulsion.

Janus did not reply, moving past the bone piles and finding another antechamber. Around the room were a collection of antique radios, communications equipment, and - in the middle surrounded by chairs - a large rectangle table, pinned with maps and minifigures. Along the walls were posters emblazoned with the red and white sun of the Imperial Japanese army. William pointed this out to Janus, silently agreeing with the point he made earlier.

* * *

Janus left William in the cave to explore what the Japanese had left behind, as he walked across to calm lagoon located on the other side. The Japanese had constructed a concrete pier, perhaps to receive goods. A scan around the chamber confirmed Janus' fear. There wasn't an exit. The room was a curved dome, a dead end. With the lights buzzing above them, he traced iron railroad tracks embedded in the rock, leading from the piles of crates to the pier. A quick inspection of the pier told him that at one point a crane would've been situated on it.

William entered the chamber, noting the pier and the tracks they had somehow missed in their excitement at finding the cavern.

"How in the world did they get ships in here?" he said.

"They didn't. Look for yourself, this is a subterranean cavern. Not ships, submarines," Janus replied. "Did you find anything in the other room?"

William nodded, raising a bound folder. "I think this place is a former a weapons facility converted into the modern research station after the war. I think Kelly struck out on this one."

Janus took the binder and flicked through it, pausing halfway through. "They were working on some serious hardware here."

"Guess someone forgot to shred it. Either way, we need to find a way out before they find us sitting here. I'll find something to wrap it in. We can bring it back up for the team to go over. Connor might be interested. He is into that history stuff."

The two men looked at the lagoon, the same grim thought in both of their minds.

"Looks like we are swimming out. This is a volcanic island after all; the exit might've been buried some time ago by a landslide," said Janus.

"Maybe one of us should go first, check that it's a clear run?" William suggested.

William was set to flip for it, but Janus had other ideas. He had already stripped off and was lowering himself gingerly into the lagoon. He took a moment to acclimatize to the cool water. The plasterboard particles floated aimlessly around him as they washed off his olive skin and beard.

"Give me the rebreather in my backpack. It should be inside my glasses case."

"You wear glasses?" William replied incredulously.

"No, it's something Connor acquired from the Americans after seeing it in action. Never had to use it till now," Janus replied, ignoring William's comment.

William unzipped the backpack, pulling out the case and opening it. Inside lay a small rebreather, two miniature air tanks on either side cased in aluminium. A clear rubber snorkel piece covered the nose and was brought together by a central 'o' mouthpiece. *An ingenious design*, William thought, trying to remember where he had seen it before. He passed it to Janus, who placed it on his mouth.

"Good luck mate, make it count and don't be too long about it," William said, keeping cheerful, despite their circumstances.

* * *

Janus chose not to reply to Williams comment and plunged into the icy cold water, diving under the once-calm blue surface. At first, all he saw was darkness and the blotchy outlines of rock, then the view cleared. Jagged stone outcroppings gave way to a tunnel spanning almost fifty feet in diameter; more than enough to accommodate Japanese World War Two submarines. A distinct blue glow in the distance gave Janus a mix of hope and dread. Unless it was a trick of the eye, the distance looked too far to swim, and he wasn't sure how much room there was to escape.

The miniature rebreather gave him freedom to navigate the tunnel. William didn't carry one of them, so the two of them would have to share it on the journey. Janus kept his mind clear, and his body relaxed as he swam. A weakness he didn't share with the team was any discomfort in tight spaces. The more pressing problem he faced now was being stuck in a tunnel underwater that was beginning to taper. The rebreather had enough air for fifteen minutes, at a guess. So far, he had almost expended five minutes just swimming toward the ray of sunlight, which didn't seem to be getting any closer. He was about to turn around when he noticed a change of light above. Curiosity getting the better of him, he changed direction, swimming upwards. He rose out of the water in a small culvert of no more than three feet in length and width. It would be an ideal place for both men to rest as their made their way out. He returned the rebreather to his mouth and dove under the cool water once more.

Moments later, Janus resurfaced as William dangled his feet over the edge of the pier. He pulled the rebreather from his mouth and took grateful swigs of the humid air.

"Isn't the whole purpose of a rebreather to scrub carbon dioxide and provide fresh air?" William asked.

"It's stale air, Will. You'll see once we go under. There is a tunnel that stretches for a distance. I didn't go the whole way as the rebreather has a fifteen-minute limit on the air."

Janus coughed loudly in the chamber, clearing his lungs after the swim.

"We will have to share it as best we can. We leave as soon as you're ready"

A minute later, once both men were in the water, they headed for the tunnel opening and dove. At Janus's suggestion, they'd left backpacks behind, only bringing what they needed, strapped to their person. If the backpacks were discovered, there was nothing that could lead their enemies to the Company. The men still clutched their flashlights but relied more on the light ahead of them. Janus counted the minutes as they shared the rebreather. They quickly used most of what little air remained. They took turns using it, then holding their breath.

Turning his flashlight on at intervals, Janus pointed it toward the top of the cavern, searching for the air pocket he had encountered on the initial swim. He was met with nothing but blank stone. There wasn't a clear pool to be found. The situation was even more desperate for him, as William was using the rebreather.

Despair seeped into his normally relaxed mind. He had a choice to make. A mad dash for the unending tunnel exit, if it existed, or a search for the air pocket, praying for a miracle until William appeared. The desperation began to rob him of his ability to navigate. Trying to register when he was, he turned to look for William but was met with darkness. *Where the hell had he gone?* Janus was not one to panic in any situation, but he felt its first stirrings. He knew William had the last of the air in the rebreather. Once that was out, they were both going to die. The bitter taste of defeat set in, and he felt oxygen deprivation begin to hamper his movements. He opted for one last ditch attempt for the exit. As he went to commit, he felt something grab his ankle. He swung around and pointed the flashlight into William's face.

William frantically gestured that his oxygen was also depleted. Janus realised William was trying to signal something else. He was pointing upward toward something. With great effort, he forced himself to follow William, who clutched at his arm swimming toward the roof of the cavern. Both men exploded into the air pocket like dolphins at a display, gasping for.

"Jesus Christ, remind me to never let you lead the way again, Jan," William said in between bouts of hyperventilation, his chest heaving below the waterline.

"I didn't get further than this. The rebreather was lucky to get us here at all, considering how much air was left," Janus replied in exasperation.

William clutched the rebreather, "This thing's out, now anyway. I don't think I can hold my breath for that long again."

Janus scowled. "Suck it up, princess, we'd better leave before we use up all the air in this pocket."

Janus took a large breath and dove under once more with a renewed sense of purpose, heading for what he hoped was sunlight. William tapped his ankle to signal he was close as they continued through the darkness toward the crystal water at the end. The water switched from navy blue to azure as they approached the exit, at least that's what Janus hoped.

His lungs were burning, chest aching to draw in breath. Janus realised he wasn't going to make it. He felt the flutter in the base of his throat signalling his brain that he was out of oxygen. He kept swimming, the physical movement burning up his final oxygen reserves as the carbon dioxide built in his lungs. He didn't notice they had exited the tunnel and were in open ocean, he saw only the final swim of twenty metres to reach the surface. He had never been so close to drowning before. The feeling in his limbs was fading, the darkness draining the light from the edge of his vision as his starved brain did everything to preserve itself. He had come so close, but not close enough....

Unaware of William coming to his aid once more, he felt a sudden acceleration as his colleague grabbed his limp arm and pulled him onto dry land. William would have struggled to carry the bigger man; underwater, he was nearly weightless. Janus kicked with all the strength he had left, certain William was drowning too, but had chosen to ignore it. Unceremoniously, the two men burst through the surface, spluttering and coughing. Their chests were heaving and burning as they floated on top of the water. Janus let himself be manoeuvred again by William, who dragged him toward rocks at the base of a cliff. With his last remaining strength in him, William pulled Janus out of the water and collapsed. Both men savoured the sun's rays on them, their bodies on solid ground once more. Neither man wanted to talk about the experience they had just gone through.

William smiled. They had survived to see another day. An hour later, both men climbed their way out of the lagoon, s battered and bruised from their foray underwater. They looked a sorry pair, two hardened soldiers looking like castaway survivors as their feet finally sunk into the ashen sand of one of the island's beaches. Janus had regained little strength, but his determination to return what William had found to Connor drove him on. He wasn't sure if it would blow their operation wide open, but they had risked their lives for it, and it had to be good for something.

Chapter 20

Connor had no doubts about the two men he sent to Tor-shima Island to investigate the weapons facility. His own operation was about to begin as day turned to night. The shrinking glow on the horizon gave him pause. In the Hub, the timer continued to count down. He wanted to witness this sunset. It might be his last if they didn't accomplish their mission.

Hours had passed since Janus and William had arrived on the island, and since then there had been no contact. His men knew the risks of each mission they undertook, but he prayed today wasn't the day they paid the ultimate price.

"Kelly told me you would be up here. She said you like to clear your mind before any operation," said Laura.

Connor closed his eyes, inhaling, before turning away from his tranquil thoughts. He wasn't usually disturbed on the wing bridges. Laura's glossy auburn hair danced in the trailing breeze as her green eyes focused on him.

"How are you feeling?" she asked.

"I've been better. Unlike other missions, this hits closer to home," Connor replied. "What about you?"

"Well, it's not often that I'm part of an international mission, onboard a mysterious yacht filled with even more mysterious people. My missions were always simple. Protect ambassador Davidson at all costs and maintain secrecy about who I really worked for."

"Plausible deniability, right?" Connor said, smiling.

"Exactly," she said, returning his smile. "I'm curious. How long have you been doing this? At the hotel, I didn't get to ask much about you. Nothing intimate, anyway." She moved toward him, arms folded.

She was so close, Connor could smell her perfume.

"You had a gun pointed at me. I don't think 'intimate' was on the cards. To answer your question, I've been doing this long enough to have seen what people will do for any cause, no matter the cost to them or others."

Laura reached out and touched him gently on the arm. Connor reacted at the touch, hoping she didn't notice.

"If not you, then who else would do this?"

Connor chose not to reply, instead changing the topic to their shared interest.

"Have you remembered anything else about your escape from the island?'

She looked away. He caught her reaction immediately.

"I remember parts of it. There was a guy who ran the show on the island, called himself Shinigami. I didn't see much of the facility at first, just the four walls of my cell. I think the men who took us captive on the plane were part of the Honourable Ones."

"I know of them," Connor said. "Kenji's private security force. He must have some deep pockets, or access to his father's money, to have that kind of army at his disposal."

"Exactly," Laura said. "If they were involved, that ties at least one of them into the kidnapping. I am sure we will find everything we need when we leave tonight."

Connor hesitated, before adding, "I don't think you should come. your mission has always been to protect the ambassador. Mine is to find him, I don't think—"

"That I can handle myself?" Laura replied. "My mission hasn't ended yet. I can't protect him from afar. You need my help, Connor. Don't think for a second I can't handle myself."

Connor saw the fire in her eyes, burning more brightly than the setting sun. He could see she had already made up her mind. He sighed.

"I already have a plan for how I intend to approach this. I can't have you jeopardising it. This is not a personal vendetta. You stay behind, understand?"

Connor had sensed the change, the warmth no longer apparent between them. He watched as she went to argue once more, before throwing her hands up in disgust and striding away. He had a job to do. He couldn't afford to let his guard down now. Not even for a feeling he hadn't felt in a long time when she stood close to him.

* * *

Connor answered on the third ring, his personal phone vibrating in his pocket.

"Kelly, what do you have for me?" he asked, one hand over his ear, having to yell to be heard over the noise inside the helicopter cockpit.

"I had to jump through some programs, but I pulled the blueprints for the tower. According to the plans, there is a server room down the hallway from Hiroto's office. It's situated between his office and Kenji's. No guarantees on whether either will be there. That's your problem Boss. Clearest entry point is from the roof. Security is pretty much what you'd expect. I can hack the cameras from here, but it may take me time."

"Good work, Kell. Upload the documents to my personal drive. I will check them out from here."

His phone buzzed again, and Connor checked the screen. He had been expecting this call for hours. He only hoped the two men had pulled off a miracle for them. He merged the call with Kelly's.

"What do you have for me, Will?"

"The facility was bust. No one was there. We weren't alone for long, though. Seems someone wanted the facility guarded closely. Some nutcases in a helicopter tried to bury us alive five minutes after we got in there."

"You fellas come through alright?" Connor asked.

"Yeah, we pulled through alright. We needed to improvise at points, but we managed to evade whoever they were. No guesses as to who they were hired by. We stumbled across some horrific shit, Boss, but we came through with something."

"What do you have?" he asked.

"We found an old folder. Seems, during the war, Toyotami was developing some doomsday weapons of his own. Far as I remember from

122

history lessons, the Nazis and the Allies were the only ones doing that kind of thing."

"I didn't get that from Hiroto when I met him. Seems the man is a wolf in sheep's clothing. Does the folder contain anything of value to us?" he asked.

"My Japanese is rusty, Boss. Kelly could translate it quicker through our system. But it appears they were unsuccessful on all fronts. And that's not all."

Connor paused, waiting to hear what William had found.

"The Japanese must've had spies planted within the allied chain as they had some documents here in English. One of the weapons of particular interest belonged to Uncle Sam and our closest ally, New Zealand.

"What was it?"

"A missile or torpedo. Capable of levelling fortifications by using mother nature. Basically, Boss, something capable of harnessing the sea and destroying everything in its path, washing away all trace, allowing the Japanese to stroll in. The document calls it a 'tsunami bomb.'"

"According to Allied reports, the weapons only ever reached prototype stage. You think that's what Toyotami has up his sleeve? Don't you remember what the video we received said?"

"Capable of *washing* away the western world's sins. A new Pacific dawn," Kelly said joining the conversation.

Connor swallowed heavily, "Get on it, Kelly. Find out everything you can. If Hiroto Toyotami developed these weapons, we need to know now. Fill Daniels in as well and tell him to prepare for the worst. We cannot keep him in the dark any longer on this." His mind cut to Laura onboard the *Serenity,* part of him wishing she could have accompanied him on this mission. "Good work, fellas, beers are on me when we get back to the mainland after all of this. I need you back onboard *Serenity* as soon as possible. Kelly, I need you to find out where Kenji lives and pass that information onto Kurt. As far as I'm concerned, both men are equally dangerous, but Kenji seems unhinged enough to be the brains behind all of this."

Connor ended the call, gazing out the window at the endless nightscape sweeping past the small window of the helicopter as they passed the city blocks. He knew the risk he was taking going in solo. With the break in at the facility, and Laura on the run, the Toyotamis' surely knew someone was onto them now.

Chapman hit the button that silenced the blades as much as possible for their descent to Toyotami Tower's helipad. The unique technology muted the thundering blades with no overall loss to the powerful blades' motion.

Once they were above the pad, Connor pulled open the door and threw down the rope. He slid down it with practiced ease, throwing a thumbs up to Chapman who repeated the gesture, before pulling away from the pad and disappearing into the night sky Alone on the pad, peeled back a glove to check his watch. He had two hours to get what he needed before Chapman was returned. *That should be more than enough time*, he figured.

He moved toward the stairs leading to the rooftop access door and elevator. The weapons manufacturer's security would be top-notch, so he was wary in his approach. Connor likened it to breaking into Fort Knox. He didn't need to know all the dirty secrets contained within the building; just two. The helipad hadn't been lit, so Evans moved in total darkness; the tower rising high above the city, so its lights couldn't reach him. The only betrayal would be if the stars disappeared behind the clouds.

Pulling the lock picks from a pocket on his Kevlar vest, he kneeled and slid them into the lock. Without the aid of a torch and in semi-darkness it proved difficult at first, but the better of two options. The second option meant mounting C4 on the door, a louder entrance than he wanted. It took forty seconds to hear the click he was hoping for. He pocketed the keys. A random thought came to mind as he did. When he was very young, his mother had told he had the fingers of a musician, and that he should play piano or one of the string instruments. She would be sorely disappointed if she knew how he was putting his hands to use these days. Ignoring family sentiment, he edged the door open. He didn't hear anything indicating an alarm and could find no electronic device attached to the door, but that didn't mean there wasn't a silent alarm going off somewhere inside.

Pulling out an aerosol canister, he sprayed the area in front of the. To his relief, there were no signs of a laser tripwire or motion sensor. He hoped his only real challenge was to contend with the cameras hidden all over the interior of the. Moving inside, he clicked a small device concealed in a pocket. No bigger than a cell phone, it distorted his image on any camera that picked him up. Descending the metal stairs, he arrived at another door and performed the same process, surprised once again at the lack of alarm. Leaving the access doorway, he moved through the brightly lit upper-level passageway he had visited only hours earlier. Every other light was on, meaning every step he took cast a shadow. Swallowing heavily, mouth dry, he knew tonight was a risk, but a necessary one. Connor pulled up the building schematics on the small screen strapped to his right wrist. He noted the server room was on the same level as Hiroto's and Kenji's offices. Like most entrepreneurs, they liked to keep things close, *even their dirty little secrets,* he thought. Sliding along the wall with the grace of a cat burglar, he reached the doorway that led to the server room. Under the harsh hallway lighting, he felt terribly exposed, and a voice within almost led him to abandon the mission there and then.

There was no turning back. He had committed to the mission. He didn't owe it to the past, but he felt the owed the scared faces of those girls that he had seen all those years ago. Although he didn't commit the crime, whatever sin lay in the room he stepped inside had never truly washed off him. At the key card panel, he slipped an electronic master card into the reader and frowned as the red light came on beside it. Trying again, Evans sighed, knowing that accessing the server room wasn't going to be easy. With the red light flashing again, he figured the third try might trip an alarm, and he pulled a small packet from a vest pocket, unrolling it. Alongside the lock picks and other smaller utensils, he pulled a miniature tool consisting of eight smaller ones. Using the screwdriver, he pried away the key card panel and stared at the wire's underneath.

A bead of sweat ran down his neck. He stared at the mess of wires, summoning up the level of concentration he would need to apply. If he messed up now, Chapman would be too far away to get to him in time. Their schedule was set, and - so far - everything had gone off without a hitch, this was the final hurdle to get inside. Connor had defused bombs in his military days but hadn't practised that skill for some time. He figured cutting the wires was one option but bypassing them might be the lesser of two evils.

Not wanting to leave a trace, a motto he lived by, he switched to a smaller knife tool. He took a quick breath, held it, and cut one of the wires, The red light stopped blinking. Not wanting to waste time, he reached for a small clip within the rolled-up packet and clamped it between the two wires. The red light chirped and glowed green, the door popping open a fraction. He coiled the cables and placed the key card reader back into position. Rolling the tools back up, he slipped into the server room.

Chapter 21

The heat of room hit Connor first, the air stale and dry. Dozens of blinking lights surrounded him. He estimated the room to be ten metres by ten metres, reminding him of a convenience store layout, with three lanes of server towers before him.

He located the main terminal on the far side of the room. The sweat gathered at under his arms as he sat at the terminal. A small whooshing noise above anticipated the fans which now started up throughout the room. The room changed temperatures immediately from a dry heat to a more bearable temperature as the air in the room was cleaned, no doubt to prevent humidity short-circuiting the delicate hardware within.

Opening the last of the three pouches on the vest, Connor removed a small USB stick and slid it into the first USB slot on the tower. Though he waited patiently, his fingers drummed a beat on the table beside him. The USB was uploaded with a trojan virus of Kelly's own design to bypass the security firewalls of even the largest corporations. The next phase of the program was effectively a malware that wormed its way through the securely encrypted viruses. The program took two minutes to run. Connor watched as the program did its thing. He couldn't help but feel a nagging doubt he had overlooked something.

He moved to the door, placing his ear against it. Nothing. Pushing the handle, he peeked through the thin crack and scanned the room once more. Down the hallway, double doors led to the office where he had meet Hiroto Toyotami and Kenji. Something moved at the receptionist desk at the end, He thought it was a trick of the eye, but needed to be sure.

The sound of the elevator arriving drew his attention.

Kenji's appearance surprised him. Connor watched from his hidden position as Kenji moved purposefully across the room, covering the distance from elevator to desk in a few strides and initiating a conversation with someone behind it.

Evans tried to make out the conversation barely louder than a hushed whisper, but his limited Japanese let him down.

The conversation gradually increased in volume to the point where Kenji loomed over the desk and brought his hand palm-down on the polished wooden surface with a slap. Kenji's body blocked Connor's view of the next slap, but he thought it was skin on skin contact.

Connor's impulsive to leap out and confront Kenji over the matter almost gave him away. He slipped back into the shadows as Kenji turned from the desk, praying the younger Toyotami would be too heated to notice the light from the server room. Evans kept an eye on the scene as the female receptionist came from behind the desk, wearing similar attire to the previous day. Kenji hissed something at her again.

Who was this guy... Connor thought, as the woman walked stiffly toward the office door. Kenji grabbed her hand and ran a single finger through her black hair, whispering something in her ear. He then pushed her away from him and toward the door. She pulled out a key card and, though Evans was a few metres away, he saw her handshake as she fumbled and dropped it. She retrieved it quickly, Kenji leering at her with a mixture of derision and lust. It was evident to Connor Kenji had no respect for the woman, and even less so for his father. Evans knew then that he was dealing with a sociopath. The man possessed no morality, nor regard for others. A person like that was dangerous and would stop at nothing. Connor was certain he was their man. The office door opened as Kenji slapped the female's behind. Evans tightened his gloved fist as Kenji and the secretary walked inside, the door closing after them.

Connor's mind began to work overtime.

All it takes is for good men to stand by and do nothing... his father's voice echoing in his mind.

The download would soon be complete, but he couldn't leave Kenji to assault the young woman. He made up his mind in a flash. Moving to the computer, he input a command to download anything that related to prototype or experimental weapons, adding the Ogasawara Island chain to be certain the search didn't miss anything. Redirecting the download back to *Serenity*, he knew Kelly would process the files as they arrived back onboard. The USB had a built-in kill switch rendering it useless once the download was complete. He activated it now and moved back to the door.

After checking the corridor was clear, Evans made his move. At the closed office of Hiroto's office, he slid the skeleton master card through the reader. The door handle disengaged and pushed it open, only to be met with darkness broken only by the lights of the city below. His eyes adjusted as he caught sight of what he had hoped not to see. Kenji was in the act of assaulting the receptionist. Kenji was so enthralled in the act, he didn't sense the movement behind him as Evans appeared and pulled him away, throwing him to the floor in a controlled rage.

The young woman screamed as she staggered away. Her shirt was open, and her panties were caught around her ankles. He urged her to run as he switched his attention back to Kenji. He heard the receptionist's sobs behind him as she left the room, pulling the door closed behind her. *Muscle reflex,* he figured.

Kenji reacted like a lion while Connor was temporarily distracted, facing the intruder who had let his prey get away.

"Just who the hell are you?" Kenji yelled.

"Your worst nightmare, Kenji. That girl did nothing to you, you just wanted to exert what little power you have. The way I see it, you're pathetic."

Evans knew he was poking the bear, but that was deliberate. The angrier Kenji got, the more volatile and predictable his movement would be, in contrast to Evan's own controlled state.

Kenji rose from the floor, adjusting his pants. The two men sized each other up, a gap of only two or three metres between them. A sudden bolt of lightning arced through the night sky, illuminating the combatants. Evans's expression remained unchanged. Kenji's expression rippled between anger and realisation.

"I have seen you before. Mr Harding, isn't it?"

Connor didn't reply, staring Kenji down, willing him to make a move.

"I did my research on you, Mr Harding. Seems our cameras started playing up when you entered our premises. I was alerted to this by my security staff. We have never encountered such a glitch before today. Foolish move to try to hide your face. If you truly are a manufacturer of weapons, you have quite advanced technology. Dare I say prototypes?"

The statement was posed as more of a question, though Evans didn't wish to discuss anything with a man who assaults young women. The look on her face still burned in his mind, fuelling his own rage. Connor was wise to Kenji's attempt to throw him off-guard with the line of questioning.

"You are right, my technology is advanced. Too advanced for your father's company. To put Toyotami Industries back on the map, you are willing to create a terrible weapon just to drive up your share price," Connor said, betting on a hunch. He thought Kenji's ego would win out.

Kenji smirked. Whether it was because Connor had worked out his plan, or because Kenji considered Evans as someone too far beneath him to pose a challenge, it was clear neither man would get the answers they needed.

While trapped in this small room, Evans had nowhere to run. His only escape route lay past Kenji, who was unarmed.

Without warning, Kenji leapt for him. Connor shifted to the side to follow up, but Kenji slid over the desk, reaching for something on the nearest wall.

He pulled a long blade from a rack of ancient weaponry, deliberate and slow.

Connor sensed the power shift in Kenji's favour, his opponent standing taller as he felt it too.

"The choice is yours, Mr Harding. Either you join me or die here in this room. When the police come looking, they won't find whatever is left of you. My dogs at home are hungry, and fresh meat is their favourite."

Kenji adopted a fighting stance with the ancient samurai sword situated above his eyeline position. Connor had seen it in textbooks. The pose was known as *Koncho-no-Kamae*. The defensive stance was supposed to intimidate the samurai's opponent. It allowed the attacker to move in any direction without warning. Connor had only the combat knife strapped to one leg, and the silenced pistol strapped to the other. Kenji had yet to strike. Connor wasn't going to delay any further.

Evans knew he only had one chance to even the odds. In a single movement like that of a gunslinger out of the Wild West, he drew his pistol and fired. At the same time Kenji leapt at him. Connor's split-second shot missed, but Kenji's swing didn't. The hardened steel blade drove sliced through his pistol down to the grip, Connor barely pulling his hand away in time. Kenji swung again as Connor leapt to the side, throwing himself over the desk like Kenji before him.

He landed heavily, tipping the desk over as the samurai blade came at him, driving through the wood, missing his head by inches. As Kenji pried the embedded blade out of the desk, Connor reached for whatever weapon he could reach in the rack.

He pulled the blade from its scabbard, noting to his dismay he'd selected a *wazikashi*, a short Japanese sword used by samurai in close quarter fighting. could deflect Kenji's longer blade but it lacked the reach to do any harm to his opponent.

Kenji freed the blade as Connor used the distraction to move into the centre of the office, where the two men circled one another like predators.

Connor needed a game plan, something to gain him the upper hand. Kenji swung the samurai blade again, slicing the rug as he brought the sword up and over in a wild slash. Evans rolled toward him, lashing out at Kenji's legs. One of them buckled, making him grunt in pain. Kenji slashed again, but Evans followed through, maintaining momentum, leaping to his feet and slashing at Kenji's hand.

Kenji roared in pain as the blade sliced through his skin like paper, severing muscles to his thumb as the blade clattered onto the exposed floorboards. Evans charged at Kenji, who absorbed the blow, knocking the blade out of Connor's grasp. Evans placed two well-aimed punches into the man's chest in reply, knocking the air out his opponent. Kenji responded by throwing a punch of his own, sending Connor reeling back, tasting blood as it ran from his nose and busted lip.

"You won't win. This war is Japan's to win. You will see, the world will see. The land of the rising sun will finally bask in the light of an empire my family has longed to create."

Evans disregarded the maniacal speech, keeping the upturned desk between them. Kenji grabbed his blade with his good hand, the other pouring blood.

"My father is a weak old fool. He only believes in the past. Unlike him, I see a better tomorrow, Mr Harding. You were right when you said the world is changing. No longer can countries stand idly by when what was once ours belongs to someone else. China gets it, Russia gets it. Soon our time will come."

Evans couldn't believe what he was hearing. Where the father dreamed of a commercial empire, Kenji evidently wanted the real thing.

"You're mad. Killing innocent people for what? To relive history? a past that paints Japan in a bad light. You inflicted untold misery on thousands for your Empire of the Sun," Evans said, goading Kenji.

In a move that tested the laws of physics, Evans righted the desk and swung under it in a move that threatened to pull both his shoulders out of their sockets, landing on his back and sending pain up his spine. He brought one leg up and pulled out his knife, racing to plunge it into Kenji's exposed thigh while he had the momentum. Kenji, still in shock at the move, barely kicked it away in time, leaving Connor unarmed once more.

A blinding beam of light blasted through the windowpanes. Both men were blinded by a spotlight attached to a dark object hovering outside. The silhouette revealed itself to be a helicopter, the blades suddenly beating loudly, rattling the windows and the floor beneath them.

"Looks like you're in a bit of a bind there, Boss. Let me even the field for you." Chapman opened up with two short bursts of gunfire from the sides of the MH/AH-6M helicopter, affectionately known as 'Little Bird' by American special forces. The lightweight helicopter was kitted out with two smaller mini guns on its flanks that could send more than a thousand rounds per minute at multiple targets. The bursts shattered the towering glass panes, sending razor shards of glass down around Connor and Kenji.

"Climb on," Chapman called into Connor's earpiece. Connor tried desperately to get his bearings through the chaos unfolding around them. He spotted Kenji lying a metre from him, hands over his head to protect himself from the glass, as well as the buffeting wind and rain that assailed them both. There was no sign of the long blade as he climbed to his feet, careful not to slip on the wet floorboards. The little chopper rocked wildly in the wind as Chapman held her steady. Connor had no more than a five-metre run up, but he had to take the risk to escape.

* * *

Chapman pushed the autopilot button and threw open the rear passenger door, bundling the rope out with it. He returned to his seat in time to see Connor use every ounce of his strength throw himself at the chopper. A freak gust of wind pushed the chopper away from the building, Chapman fighting it back into position, but too late. Connor plunged out of sight, down into the heaving streets of Tokyo.

"Connor!" Chapman called, trying to control the Little Bird.

"Damn you, you stupid bloody thing, if I could turn you into scrap, you bet I would. Turn, you bastard!" Chapman grunted as the bird slowly regained altitude and levelled out. The blinking lights that had been beeping loudly at him fell suddenly quiet.

"Remind me never to go on a rollercoaster with you, crazy man," said someone behind him. Chapman jumped with considerable fright. He thought he was seeing a ghost, when he saw Connor's grinning features.

"How did you—" Chapman started.

"Story for another time. Best get us out of here. I don't like the look of the backup," Evans said, as gunfire began to fly around them. Members of Kenji's private security force and three security guards stood in the open window, firing at the chopper. A few shots ricocheted off the sides as Chapman, still perplexed by Connor's survival skills, pulled away from Toyotami Tower and out across the city, leaving behind the chaos Connor had created.

Chapter 22

Kenji climbed to his feet, shoving off the help of the security guard who came to his aid. He watched the chopper disappear across the city, eventually fading into the distance. It was the last thing he'd expected to see when he came into the office tonight. He felt the inner rage boil inside him, threatening to erupt. The men nearby shuffled nervously, knowing his outbursts all too well. He wanted the men to both respect and fear him, a delicate balance. His rage wasn't targeting the perceived failures of his men but was focused on one man in particular. Mr Harding was no ordinary businessman from Australia; that much was now clear.

He tasked two of the security guards with finding the security footage of how Connor had broken in, and what he had been able to achieve in that time. The two security guards left to do his bidding. leaving three of his private security force standing to attention.

"Sir, we just received news from one of the men stationed at Tor-shima. The facility has been levelled with the intruders inside. The men report no survivors."

Kenji looked at the man.

"Did they check, or just call it in?"

"They searched the ruins for hours but couldn't find any bodies," the man replied.

"Tell them to search again. The last men to let me down became fish food. Do not let make the same mistake. Send for my helicopter. This place is no longer safe. We leave for the Sanctuary immediately."

The soldier saluted, the two others following him. Kenji was alone in the windowless office.

He stood on the glass, peering over the precipice to the streets far below.

His homeland had been attacked once more, and he felt compelled to defend it. His orders had been clear. If he was ever attacked, his force would go underground until the bombs were detonated.

Moving away from the edge, he found the telephone on the floor and made a call.

Jiro answered straight away,

"Sir, I just received the news from—" Jiro started.

"Shut it, Jiro, I am tired of your excuses. Tokyo isn't safe now. I have already moved what was necessary in preparation for the final countdown. I want the Sanctuary operational immediately. I will be there shortly."

"Yes, sir," Jiro replied.

Kenji hung up the phone, before suddenly hurling it across the room and out of the window, his rage finally erupting like a volcano. He was compelled to defend his homeland. He would not lose, like those so long ago who lacked the ability to defend their own. He would be victorious.

As for Mr Harding, he would deal with him as he dealt with anyone who crossed him. He would make his death a slow and painful one. With one last glance out into the night sky at the coming storm, he made his way to his office. The police would arrive at the building soon, followed by the paparazzi no doubt. He wanted the cameras to see his good side, after all.

* * *

Janus crawled carefully through the dense bush, a branch whipping his face as he arrived at his destination. The villa was large and spacious, its geometric design and abstract lines making it look as though it clutched the cliff edge to prevent it falling off. Janus peered through his night vision binoculars.

So far, there had been no word from Evans on the success of his mission, but Janus preferred it that way. He believed any distraction, however small, might become a fatal chink in his armour when out in the field. He didn't let anything get in the way of his sole focus. That was the plan, anyway. Much had changed since arriving in Tokyo, and he sensed a shift in his commander's unshakeable persona. Normally reserved, Connor had developed an emotion that was drawing him into dangerous territory.

Almost twenty-four hours had passed, and their straightforward mission of finding the Australian ambassador felt like it had turned into a manhunt for the son of a weapons manufacturer. It wasn't for Janus to comprehend the finer points, but the bigger picture was clear. The ambassador was their first and only matter. He vowed to talk to Evans when he returned to *Serenity* about the constraints of time and prioritisation.

Janus scanned along the jutting balconies, corners, and entry and exit points with the expertise of a trained sniper. He spotted six guards in total with, no doubt, more inside. Each carried a lightweight, compact submachine gun. He didn't care for the design, but its lethality in tight quarters was the real challenge. Janus had no idea what he would find in there, but when Kelly handed him the brief, he suited up and took one of their zodiacs to the mainland.

That was almost nine hours ago. He had brought his suppressed rifle and a small backpack. He figured removing a few of the patrolling men would be the better option than sneaking into the villa into unknown territory. Those he couldn't remove from this range; he would deal with up close and personal. He relished the thought. Opening the backpack, he pulled out rope and a harness. He spotted a rock that would hold his weight. Janus was positioned fifteen metres higher than the roof of the villa below, and - as he threw the surrounding rope - he clamped it together with a clip and settled it beside him. Methodically, he pulled out the rifle from its shoulder bag, removing a small case of bullets from an outer pocket. Janus had a sweet spot for his weapon, considering it an extension of his body. Though his only talent only caused death, he had embraced it willingly, hardening himself against feeling anything for the enemy, no matter who it affected in the end. He popped the magazine, examining the bullets in their neat row, before shoving it back into the weapon, racking the chamber, and dropping the bipod at the front, resting the butt of the gun on his shoulder.

He had darkened his face with paint and had rubbed dirt on his skin to ensure that the moonlight didn't expose him. Wiping around his eye, he pulled out a digital barometer and held it up. After a second, it showed both wind direction and speed. He could hear the incoming storm. As though on cue, a lightning bolt cracked in the sky, followed by booming thunder. *Just great,* he thought. With the first of the raindrops pattering against his back, he nestled the barometer beside him. He looked down at the sight and picked the first target. The man lighting a cigarette, leaning over the balcony, as Janus lined him up in his crosshairs. Wrapping his finger lightly around the trigger, he exhaled, then lightly tapped it. The gun jolted, and he watched the man jerked back like he had been zapped, before falling over the railing. Janus shifted his sight to the next target, watching for any sign of them hearing their comrade fall onto the rocks below. Removing two more from the equation after that, he was in the process of lining up another when he heard distant gunfire.

Normally not so easily distracted, he dropped his sights and stared toward the sound of what sounded like a mini gun being fired. He saw a small chopper hovering around the tower. Pulling out the night vision binoculars, he zoomed in fully, the city lights making it hard to make out the small bird in the air near one of the tallest towers. *Bloody hell, Evans and Chapman know how to throw one hell of a party, or even better, one hell of a distraction.* He looked back down the sights of his sniper, watching as three more men poured out of the villa, hearing the shots as well. Janus knew it was now or never. Moving his sights he aimed at the nearest group of men, fingering the trigger as they stood almost in line he fired, the bullet not only passing through the first, but the other two as well. He smiled. *I just keep getting better.*

With them removed from the equation, there were three men left by his count. One of them appeared from around the balcony corner in time to see his comrades fall like bowling pins. He shouted to others inside, ducking down behind a concrete pillar. The man searched for the hidden shooter as Janus sent another shot his way, the bullet sinking into the brickwork, but not felling the man. Janus couldn't see the other two inside, until one made the mistake of moving close to one of the lights surrounding the house, his shadow giving away his position behind a pillar.

Popping the magazine out quickly, he tossed it into the bushes, reached into a small pocket in the bag, pulled a single bullet from it, and slid it into the empty chamber. The full metal jacket round would cleanly pass through most surfaces, and with the serial numbers scratched off, bore Janus's own signature of writing something corny on it. He sighted the man behind the pillar, letting the bullet do the rest. The armoured round passed straight through the concrete and the man tumbled forward. Though no one could see it, he knew the bullet had *To whom it may concern* engraved on its side; a fitting message.

He shifted his sights to the other pillar, felling the last of the two men in a similar fashion. Not wasting any more time, and with Evans now providing the perfect distraction, he threw his rifle over his shoulder, pulled his harness on, and clipped himself to the rope. He abseiled down the side of the cliff face, drawing his pistol at the bottom. He pulled himself over the surrounding fence and ran across the open yard through the open front door. Stepping over the prone form of one of the guards, he paused.

Janus had spent his career in hostile nations. Most eastern European soldiers did not possess army tattoos of note, but it didn't stop Janus observing the tattoo located on the dead guard's neck. It was not one he had seen before. He could only assume it was the mark of the Honourable Ones, the elite security force loyal to Kenji. He snapped a photo, sending it via secure encryption to their database to find a match. Ghost-like, he searched each room. After five minutes, he had covered the ground floor, which followed the standard layout of most houses. He hoped the bedrooms might have something worth looking for. As he moved upstairs, he heard a steady thudding sound, followed by several more. It didn't sound like explosions, rather someone stamping their feet behind the closed door.

He leaned closer, hearing a low moan. He recoiled in shock. Grabbing the handle, he slid inside, weapon held ready,

Tied to a chair in the middle of the room, the floor covered by a white sheet with dark burgundy stains, Janus didn't need to confirm what he saw. Seated near the covered sheet was another man, this one breathing, his head tilted forward and resting on his chest. At the sound of Janus entering the room, the man lifted his head slightly.

The man had one black eye and a series of small cuts across his left cheek. His once crisp white shirt was saturated with dried blood. Janus pulled out a pocketknife and sliced through the ropes, catching the man as he fell forward.

"Hey, you're going to be alright, mate. What's your name?" Janus asked.

The man struggled at first, Janus wondering if there was more to the story as he saw the caked blood around his mouth. Then he spoke

"'Harry, Harry Yates. Who are you?"

Janus knew this was a distraction he did not need, but - like his name suggested - he was not only a taker of life in Roman mythology, but a giver. Evans would decide the man's fate later. For now, Janus did not reply, instead asking if the man could walk, before hefting him to his feet. Yates walked unsteadily at first, with one arm wrapped around Janus's broad shoulders for balance.

"It seems, Mr Yates, that fate had something different in store for you tonight. I need you to do me a favour and follow me. Do as I say. I need you to be my eyes and ears if you can."

Harry stared at Janus through his one open eye and nodded. Moving outside the door, Janus made to go downstairs. Another guard Janus had missed in his startled him, but his training kicked in, and he dropped him with a double tap to the head and chest.

The action awakened something in Harry, the man's jaw dropping open.

"What the hell was that?" he asked.

"Military training and years of experience. Now take his gun and watch for anyone else. I will be right back."

Janus went to return upstairs when Yates called after him.

"I think we can help each other; I believe I know what you're searching for," he said. Though his voice was timid, he tried to stand proud, as though he had control of the situation.

Janus paused, turning.

"I don't have time for games Yates—"

"You're looking for the bomb, aren't you? The one that causes an underwater explosion, effectively leveling fortifications, buildings, you name it. Am I right?"

Janus remained stony faced, though he couldn't help but wonder how the hell the man knew that. There was time for that later, however. He had never put his faith in someone he had just met, but his plan of remaining silent had changed given he had picked up another he doubted was versed in stealth like he was so he might as well try his luck.

"How do you know about that weapon?" Janus asked, his expression impassive.

"My father spent his life looking for it, and it cost him dearly. I was hoping to find it myself, because it meant so much to him. I figured it would only be right to acquire it."

"How did you know of its existence? I can't imagine your father talked to you about something that could cause so much death."

Harry shook his head. "No, he didn't. My grandfather left letters, diaries, and journals from his time in the Pacific Fleet. When my grandfather went missing in the Pacific, my father assumed his ship had been sunk. He packed all the papers away and forbade me to ask him about it again. So, I didn't, until I recently found his notes. I wanted it for myself. My father wasn't someone who obsessed over such things. But whatever this thing was, it almost cost our family legacy."

* * *

"If you know of their existence, tell me where the bombs are now." he quizzed.

Harry stood quiet for a moment. "They are here as we speak."

Janus eyes boggled. The idea that the doomsday weapons were in this house changed everything. Not normally one to break radio silence, he tapped his earpiece twice.

"Janus to *Serenity*, do you copy?" He watched Harry looking out at the flashing lights hovering around the distant tower.

"What the—" he said. Janus cut him off as a response came through his earpiece.

"Go ahead, Janus, *Serenity* reading you loud and clear. Connor wants an update. What's your status?" one of the crew onboard said. *Kelly must be preoccupied*, Janus thought.

"The residence has been recently 'vacated' by its occupants, so far there is no sign of the primary package."

"*Serenity* copies. Commander Evans wants to speak to you, standby." The voices of the crew faded away, replaced by Connor's.

"Janus, there have been complications on my end. Expect trouble in the next thirty minutes if they catch on. Get what you can and get out of there fast."

Janus looked at Harry, "Copy. In addition, secondary package has been secured. Will need exfil as quickly as we can."

"Fifteen minutes, Janus, be ready when we get there," Connor said.

Harry looked at Janus. "Who do you work for? are you a government agent? A spy maybe?"

Janus ignored the questions, gesturing with his pistol. "Show me the weapon. We are expecting trouble soon. Best we get to it."

Harry understood. They moved into a room Janus had already inspected. Harry approached a panel and punched in numbers, surprising Janus.

"You know the code?"

Harry tapped his forehead. "Photographic memory. Works like a camera."

To Janus's further surprise, a floor panel in the corner of the room hissed open to reveal a set of polished metal stairs.

"You first," he gestured.

Their footsteps clanged on the metal stairs as they descended metres underground, arriving at a room that looked like the testing site for a nuclear bomb. Desks, stationary, charts, and whiteboards were scattered everywhere. They were arranged in an organised manner, each station displaying something in Japanese. The central table had designs and plans on it.

Janus passed a mini camera to Yates, "Take photos of as much as you can," he said, as he checked the room. After a few minutes, he looked into the smaller rooms off the sides of the larger lab. He only had one question for Yates.

"Where the bloody hell are they?"

Yates didn't have an answer. His lack of awareness for the kind of risk the bombs presented angered Janus. His normally stony-faced expression cracked, his eyes narrowing as he did.

Marching up to Yates, who was still taking photos, he grabbed the bloody collar and threw him against the table, scattering papers all over the floor.

"Tell me what you know, because if the bomb isn't here then we have a problem, a very *big* problem. It's my job to stop the lunatic who has them from unleashing them on the world, or - selling them to the highest bidder. Now where has he taken them?" He shook Yates, ignoring the man's current condition.

"I don't know, I swear I don't know," he said, stammering as Janus shook him violently.

"Connor to Janus, exfil in five minutes. We are closing in on the location. Are you out of there yet?".

Janu rage at the casual attitude of the man who sold death to the highest bidder only heightened his frustration, but he let the man go, leaving him lying on the table

"Janus to Connor, we have a problem. The weapons aren't here. They were, according to my source, but no longer. Heading to exfil now."

"I copy. See you at the rendezvous location," Evans replied.

Janus dragged Yates off the table. He pushed him in the centre of the back toward the stairs. "You're about to have a lot of explaining to do. You think you went through hell. You haven't faced the heat yet, boy."

Chapter 23

Joshua Davidson remembered the stories his grandfather had told in the letters his father had kept from decades ago. He remembered his father constantly admonishing him for not having the backbone to defend his country. He was barely seven years old at the time. But he also remembered his grandfather writing in his first letter, *'the first casualty when war comes is the truth'*. He didn't understand that then, but he began to wonder now, what truth would come out about his kidnapping, was this a prelude to something much worse?

Davidson remembered Laura approaching with two men by her side. The rest was a blur. At the time, he was more focused on the turbulence of the plane as it vibrated during its slow descent. He remembered the screaming and pleading of his defence attaché, Laura Goddard, as she was subjected to some form of torture. All he could do was yell loudly into the bag over his head, which stifled his voice, making him feel like he was only begging himself for another chance.

Plenty of time had passed since the vibration and the shuddering, and since Laura's screams, for him to admonish himself. Joshua didn't know what he had done to deserve this. He had been strapped tightly to the chair by cable ties, given the cutting feeling in his wrists when he struggled. He remembered the plane banking right, taking them off the planned course to Tokyo, instead taking them north toward the east coast of Russia or Korea. He had felt no other human presence near him for some time, and a sense of abandonment passed over him like a wave.

The sound of a door opening and closing interrupted these thoughts, leading to a flood of fear as he sensed movement in the room.

"One more time, ambassador, tell us what we ask, and the world will soon know of your miraculous survival. The other option is well, a small spread in a newspaper somewhere," the man hissed, close to his ear.

The distinguishable Asian accent had permeated much of Joshua's thoughts as he wondered who was responsible for this heinous act. Any act against him was a direct attack on Australia itself, and it wouldn't go unpunished.

"I don't know anything about any weapons. I am an ambassador, an envoy between two countries. I don't know war or weapons. I am a man of peace."

With that reply, the bag was whipped off, and the sudden onset of light make dots appear in his vision. He closed his eyes, opening them slowly, taking in his surroundings. He had been brutally beaten in a whitewashed and tiled room. Evidently this had changed. Davidson was in the last place he could imagine *onboard the government jet*. Bewildered, he took a moment to register the two men standing in front of him.

"Where is Stephen? Where is my aide?" he demanded. The quiver in his voice betrayed his fear.

The man closest to him was dressed in black. He wore a mask that increased the shock running through Joshua's nervous system.

"Your aide sleeps with the sharks. Your lack of information meant my master had to make the easy decision to remove one of you from the picture," the man replied coldly, a dead look in his eye.

"What about Laura? Where is she?" he said, trying to sound tough, his voice barely a whisper.

"We ask the questions, *ambassador*," the masked man replied. "You will find out soon enough."

The man turned to the other and signalled in a slicing motion. His colleague, a bald Asian man moved toward Joshua as he shrank back into his seat. A knife sliced through both cable ties easily and he was jerked to his feet.

Joshua was dragged by the collar, not having the fight in him, his bruised and battered body's sagging as he was brought to the plane's exit. The man in the mask stepped outside before pulling him out. Davidson's eyes took a few seconds to adjust as he took in his surroundings, unused to natural light after being left in a windowless room and cell.

The temperature outside was cool, almost temperate. He couldn't place where he was, but he figured by the trees surrounding him that he was still somewhere in the Pacific. A dark mountain loomed over them in the distance, its jagged peaks flattening out in a way that Joshua thought suggested the crater of dormant volcano.

Someone shoved him down the steps parked against the plane's hull. His legs felt like jelly as he descended, only getting some strength back when he reached the bottom. There were no horrors there, and nothing to explain why he had been taken. He looked around at the large clearing in the forest before him, where simple log cabins were built in a semi-circle. There were three of them in total.

The second man pushed the butt of his rifle into Davidson's back and shoved him unceremoniously toward the door of one of the cabins. Joshua stumbled on a rock and fell. His weakened condition meant nothing to the second man, who hoisted him to his feet like a ragdoll and pushed him on. Joshua limped awkwardly due to his now sprained ankle, but his senses sharpened due to the pain, and he noticed smaller details. The cabins had a series of antennae on their roofs. The men guarding them looked more like hardened veterans of war than civilians, each wearing a similar mask to the one who had dragged him out of the plane. He noticed the fencing around him, chicken wire with barbed wire on top. He felt like a prisoner of war, but which war? The door of the third cabin opened and two civilians were pushed outside, landing face first in the dirt. Both wore Japanese clothes common among the poor farm folk who worked the rice fields of the mainland. *Am I in Japan?* Joshua thought as a bullish looking man marched from the cabin, stalking the two civilians before kicking both the man and the woman hard in their backsides. Joshua tried to help but was forced back by the bald man. The other man noticed Joshua's reaction.

"What difference could you make?" he said. "We are armed, you are not. You wouldn't understand that these people deserve it. You should not steal from people who protect you, especially when you did not protect your country when it mattered most."

"You call that protection, attacking unarmed civilians?"

"Yes. The civilians are protected by the fear we place in others. If we set an example to a few, it doesn't just resonate with them, but also sends a message to our enemies," the masked man replied, as they reached the cabin door.

"It tells me that you are weak. No good leader would attack civilians to send a message. Your lack of power is on show right now, whoever you are," he said.

With no further comment, Joshua was pushed inside the cabin.

"Now, we can do this the easy way or the hard way, it's your choice. I will let you be your own judge, jury, and executioner."

A scan of the room revealed a table filled with nasty implements on silver trays. White sheets underneath them were stained red. He was directed toward the table, and pushed into a seat hard, feeling his spine complain under the pressure.

"I will ask you again," the masked man said, as he moved deliberately and slowly toward the table of torture. He took the time to admire each implement in turn, as beads of sweat appeared on Joshua's forehead.

"I don't understand what you want from me. I came to sign a deal banning the construction of nuclear weapons and preventing a third Cold War in the Pacific as part of the Quadrilateral Security Dialogue Summit," he stammered.

The leader settled on a nasty hooked instrument that reminded Joshua of his last dental visit, then moved swiftly to stand over him.

"That's not the answer I want," he said, his dark eyes menacing from behind the mask making Joshua sink lower into the chair. The other man held him down as ropes were tied around his hands once more, binding him to the chair.

Joshua's pain-addled brain remembered who the man in the mask was. *Shinigami.* At least that's what the guards had called him when the man tortured him the first time, using the standard terrorist technique of waterboarding and vicious beatings.

"I am the ambassador for Japan. We can come to some arrangement. Please. My country will pay for my return. Ransom me, don't kill me in this place, please, I beg you." Joshua continued to plead as the man moved the instrument closer to his face.

"It's too late for dialogue, it's time for action. I expected more from a representative of Australia. I guess your country is not as great when the Americans aren't standing alongside it," the man answered, as what was about to happen dawned on Joshua.

The door banged open, and Stephen was pushed into the room, beaten and bloody. His tie was pulled low around his neck and his shirt was bloody. His jacket had been ripped in several places, and his glasses had a crack on the inside, making the left lens impossible to see out of.

"Stephen, thank God you are alright. I was told you were fish food," Joshua said, the relief in his voice apparent, as the bald man pushed Stephen into a chair facing Joshua.

"What is going on?" Stephen asked. His usual confidence was gone, much the same as Joshua's.

"They want me to support nuclearization of Japan, Stephen. That's what they want. I will never support a decision like that." Davidson glared Shinigami in defiance.

"We have yet to find your briefcase," said the torturer. "Your assistant didn't have it, and neither does Stephen. Tell me where it is, or your aide will suffer the consequences."

Joshua inhaled as deeply as he could, thinking about the choice he faced. His father's words echoed in his head, telling him he wasn't man enough. "It's in a safe at the back of the plane, hidden behind a panel in the wall. The code is 6-4-2-2-3."

Shinigami ordered the bald man to check it out as the three men waited in silence. The only sounds were the shallow breathing of the two men who feared for their lives.

The door reopened a few minutes later, both men exhaling in relief at the briefcase in the bald man's hands. He placed it on the table between them. Shinigami input the code, and the locks on the briefcase unclipped.

The contents consisted of papers for the meeting that had never gone ahead, stationary, and other government documents. What he was looking for was located in the upper lining, Shinigami plucked the red leather-bound book from the briefcase and opened it carefully, scanning the pages. His otherwise lifeless eyes glimmered behind his mask

"Take this to him, he will be expecting it" he said to the bald man, then turned to Davidson.

"We aren't finished with you yet," Shinigami said.

Joshua's ropes were cut, and he was hauled to his feet, protesting. He screamed at Shinigami as he was dragged outside, watching the door shut with Stephen still inside. The look of horror etched on Stephen's face was seared in Joshua's mind as he fought against his captor.

Joshua was dragged to the third cabin and hurled inside. The door was slammed shut and darkness consumed him. There were no windows, and not even a single crack of light came from under the door. When Joshua tried to move from the cold floor, he felt his hand sink into something soft.

"Watch where you are going," a young voice whispered in Japanese, startling Joshua. He retreated. He hadn't seen the interior of the room before the door closed and was shocked to find someone else in the darkness with him.

"Stop moving, idiot," a man said, as Joshua landed on another human in the darkness.

"I want my parents," a young girl's voice sounded in the room, she sounded on the verge of tears.

"They are more than likely dead; they spoke out against them and were overheard plotting to escape," another spoke harshly in the darkness.

"My parents are not bad people," came the little girls reply.

"I'm sorry to hear that. I'm sure your parents are going to be alright," Joshua said, though in he knew that was, at best, a half-truth. He didn't see where they were taken, but it was unlikely the two children would ever see their parents again.

"You lie, don't put the child through any more hell," the harsh voice rasped again.

Joshua tried to move slower this time focusing on the young girl's sobs in the darkness.

"Hey, hey, you will be alright. I will protect you if they come for you," he said reassuringly, wishing he could envelop the young girl in his arms and tell her it would be okay.

Though he didn't believe it himself, he didn't want them to try to avenge their parents.

"How long have you all been in here for?" he asked. This time, a chorus of voices replied, with the loudest suggesting almost a month and a half.

"How often do they feed you?" he asked.

"Not often enough I think they are starving us for information, but I don't know what for. My parents were simple farmers. We lived on this island."

"*Island?* Where are we right now?" he asked quickly, his tone sharp, realising he was probably scaring the poor child who was still sobbing.

"We are on Aogishima Island, off the coast of Japan. How do you not know where you are?" an older female voice asked.

"Because I was kidnapped. I am an Australian citizen. I work for the Australian government. They want me because they believe I know things," he replied, unsure whether telling them was in their best interests or not.

"What kinds of things do you know?" added another voice in the dark. It was a good question. *What else should I know?*

"Has anyone tried to escape?" he asked. The chorus of voices sounded a resounding no.

"They keep us hidden from the world. The mountain looms over us, but a large camouflage net is draped over us day and night, hiding us from the world. I have never seen anything like it. the guards are confident they will not be found. They say it shields us from above, from what I have no idea. No one can find us, and no one has come. The authorities must've been bought off by them," one voice said.

"Or live in fear of them," another added.

Joshua couldn't work out how many children were in the room with him, or how old they were. He couldn't see, no matter how hard he tried. There wasn't a single glimmer of light in the room. His breathing wasn't shallow, and his lungs weren't desperate for air. Somewhere in these cramped confines, air was getting in. The prisoners told him there were no beds, so everyone huddled together on the floor. The air wasn't stale, but the heat from multiple bodies in a confined space produced a feeling of claustrophobia he had never experienced before.

"I didn't see a net when I arrived," he said, trying to take his mind off how close the walls felt to him.

"Then you are lucky. Sometimes they remove it for deliveries, of what we cannot say."

"Who are *they* exactly?"

"They call themselves the Honourable Ones. Though there is nothing honourable about them. They deprive us of food and steal our lands.

"That's horrible. Are you the only ones left after they did this?" Joshua asked.

"No, there is a small village on the south side of the island. We spoke out when they arrived a few months ago. My family worked for a company in Tokyo, but they complained about the harsh working conditions and were placed here," a voice in the darkness replied.

"We lived on the land we are imprisoned on. My family farmed the rich soils around the volcano for what we could," another added.

Then one of the girls asked the million-dollar question.

"Will your government come for you? Will they come for us?"

Joshua fell silent. So far, there had been no word from any authorities concerning his release, though he doubted he had been forgotten. Australia protected its own, but he feared he was being kept for some express purpose by his captors. What that was, only time would only tell. And time, unfortunately, was not on the ambassador's side.

Part 3
Into the Fire

Chapter 24

The high-definition monitors displayed every angle of the *Serenity* as Kelly sat in her customary spot in front of Connor. The lenses on her frames mirrored the news feed on the Hub's larger wall monitor. They watched the local news channel, which was broadcasting the damage to Toyotami Tower.

"Seems Connor has bitten off more than he can chew. Blowing up areas of Tokyo wasn't on the cards," Kelly muttered.

"I don't think it's just Connor. I'd say Kenji has finally joined the party. The commander has only drawn him out and exposed him. Now the real fight begins," Tori replied.

"Maybe so. We don't yet know whether they are responsible for the ambassador's kidnapping," Kelly said, eyes still on the screen.

Kelly's console beeped, and she pulled up a secondary screen. "We may have a problem."

"No, they are all maintaining radio silence. Standard protocol, Kelly, you know the rules." Tori punched her sister lightly on the shoulder.

"External scanners show two Japanese coastguard boats moving toward us. Radar pinpoints them at no more than one hundred metres off the bow," Kelly said.

"We have nothing to hide," said Tori. She looked around the room at the extravagant and advanced setup, adding, "Well, nothing they need to see, anyway."

"Should we prepare for boarding, or do you have another idea in mind?" Kelly asked, looking at Tori.

"Keep trying to get Evans on the line and fill him in on the situation" Tori said. "I'll need two of Will's boys from down below to pull off what I have in mind."

* * *

A faint orange glow on the horizon told Evans what time it was, as he returned his gaze to the man sitting in the cockpit across from him. The small chopper thundered across the brightening sky toward the *Serenity.*

"I don't normally deal with prisoners, but my man Janus here thinks you're important," Evans said, looking at the state of the man before him.

"I don't know what Janus thinks of me, but I know some things you may be interested in," Yates replied, yelling over the chopper's engines.

Evans had yet to be filled in on the finer points by Janus, so asked for the brief version of events. After Yates finished filling in the gaps in his story that Evans required, he appealed to both of them.

"I am on your side," Yates said, looking at Janus's stony-faced expression. He swallowed. "I can help you, fund your ventures through my company, or even provide you with weapons if you need them. Hell, I am American, guns are our specialty. Well, that and stirring the pot around the world. If that's what you need, I can do that too."

Evans sighed, "We aren't the stereotypical type of mercenaries, Harry, let me make that perfectly clear. Secondly, we have a backer already. Thirdly, when you looked at the weapons, did Kenji tell you they were ready to go, or were they still in the design phase?"

"He told me they were still in the design phase, but testing was underway. According to his reports, they were in the stages of perfecting the design."

"Testing is already underway. Did he expand on that at all?" Evans asked, as he rubbed his chin in thought.

"Nope, not one bit. Kenji said that by the time the deal I had offered came through, they would be ready to ship to parts of the world that needed them."

Janus sat forward, concerned. "I'm confused on one detail. How many did you order?"

"Seven, with more on the way. Before you ask, I didn't want to use them. I wanted to give them back to the government that designed them to begin with."

"So, you're telling me you didn't want to purchase them for yourself. But you wanted to honour your grandfather's dying wish and sell them - for a fee – back to the American government. Let me guess, this would help you rebuild your brand and image in the process?"

Harry looked at him, long and hard. "You know, if you weren't such a hard arse, I would hire you in heartbeat to work for me. You've got a big ol' brain in there."

Harry's comment drew a thin smile from Evans.

"Don't jump the gun there, Yates. We need you to debrief us in full when we get back to base," Evans said.

The internal intercom squawked from Chapman in the front.

"Sorry to interrupt your private conversation there, commander, but we are on final approach to the *Serenity*. Best buckle in now." The three men took his advice.

"What the hell are those?" Janus said, pointing out the window at the approaching Japanese craft.

"They don't know I am here, do they?" Yates quizzed, worry marring his features.

Evans shook his head.

"Not possible. Unless they've been keeping tabs on us, they couldn't have found you this quick."

Evans believed what he'd told Yates, but stranger things had happened. "Get Tori on the line. Tell her to expect company. She will know what to do."

"Never mind that, sir, they are buzzing us now. Should I put it through?" Chapman asked. Evans nodded.

"This is Evans," he said, when Chapman transferred the comms.

"Are you seeing our new friends incoming, Commander?" Kelly asked. Evans looked out the window. The approaching craft were less than forty metres away now.

"I see them. Is Tori prepared to accept our guests for dinner?" he asked.

"Sure is, Connor. The tables all set," Kelly replied.

"Ensure the crew maintains complete silence. No doubt they are creating a drag net around the city and its surrounds. We are flying the Australian flag. You know the drill."

Chapman brought the helicopter in low on the bow of the yacht. It lightly kissed the helipad as Evans threw back the door, not waiting for the blades to slow. Janus and Yates jumped out behind him.

Tori met them on the pad, her shirt being whipped by the still-spinning rotors as Chapman wound down the helicopter.

Evans approached her, smiling, "We made a hell of a mess, but we got what we came for. Have Kelly run the data as quickly as she can. I need to know everything that's on it within the next few hours. Time is critical now."

Tori noted the look of concern on Evan's face.

"What is it?" she asked, knowing such a grave look meant trouble was near.

"It may be nothing, but Janus picked up a stray, Mr Yates there—" he began.

Harry interrupted, giving Tori a once over before sticking out his hand.

"I'm Harry, but you can call me—" Tori put up a hand.

"I've heard it all before, cut the crap. You're lucky my colleague here didn't put a bullet in you. What use are you to us?"

Harry looked like he had been physically slapped. Janus whispered, "She's like that, pal, might as well get comfortable with it."

Evans suppressed a smile at Yates's confused.

"Seems our man here knows about the bombs were searching for. He will need to provide us with a full debrief of everything he knows. I figured you would be perfect for the job," Evans said.

The look Tori gave Yates would have made flowers wilt. He tried to grin at her but she flicked her hair and turned away.

"This way, college boy, we have much to discuss," she said, not looking back.

"She is going to tear strips off him," Janus said to Connor,

"He wasn't that bad. He just talked the whole trip is all," Evans said as Janus shook his head.

"We can't have two Chapmans on this yacht, Connor. I would have to resign."

Chapman chose this moment to come up behind them, his helmet tucked into the crook of his arm.

"What did I miss?" he said as he ran a gloved hand through his oily hair, not having taken the helmet off for almost six hours.

"Our guest is about to go toe to toe with Tori; want to wager how long he lasts?" Evans asked. Janus was in before he had even finished the sentence. Chapman looked at Yates still trying to make small talk with Tori,

"You're on, he won't make the night," Chapman replied, laughing, as he shook Evan's hand.

"Let's hope we do, too," Janus murmured, his expression once more as hard as stone.

Leaving his men to their own devices, Evans grabbed a pair of binoculars and walked back out to the helipad.

* * *

Jiro Ikeda stood silently on the deck of the coastguard vessel, his jet-black hair pulled back into a bun, a few strands lightly lashing has face. The grey vessel bounced over the waves, leaving a foamy streak behind it. He undid the Velcro fastening on his glove, pulling it tight again as he gazed at the large black yacht in front of him. He had to admit it was a beautiful vessel, elegant and streamlined, an object of such beauty that he believed only German manufacturers could pull off. A man wearing black fatigues came up alongside and him and bowed, handing him a pair of binoculars. He zoomed in on the vessel, scanning its black length from stern to aft until he rested on the lone man on the rear helipad looking look right at him through binoculars. Pulling out a walkie, he spoke into it.

"Pull alongside the vessel as though performing a general inspection of the ship for general purpose. I will pull along the other side," he said.

The helmsman of the other coastguard vessel acknowledged his message and sped past, flecks of sea foam spattering Jiro's face in its wake.

Wiping it off with one hand, he returned the binoculars to their owner and walked back to the rear of the vessel. He climbed downstairs and entered his cabin. He opened a cupboard, revealing a small radio inside. He tuned it to a different frequency than the one the vessels used.

"Kenji, we are almost alongside the yacht now. It is flying the Australian flag. It could be him."

"That means nothing, you fool, see that you search everything. I have men at the airport terminals seeking him out. He will have nowhere to run."

"We are more than prepared to board the yacht. If Mr Harding is on board, we will find him."

"Ensure you do, Jiro, I am losing my patience with your incompetence, and that of your team," Kenji replied in frustration.

"I brought almost a dozen men, all our most experienced. Nothing will get by us. We will turn the vessel upside down until we find what we are after," Jiro replied.

"Do not underestimate him. He could unravel everything I have worked so hard for. Find him and bring him to me," said Kenji.

"My men are ready for anything. We will not let you down."

Jiro's walkie talkie crackled at his belt.

"Sir, we will be pulling alongside the vessel in two minutes," the helmsman said.

"I will report back once we are finished, Kenji," Jiro said, putting down the microphone. He opened a weapon locker, taking an assault rifle.

He returned to the deck as the helmsman manoeuvred the vessel to rest lightly against the yacht.

"This won't take long. Stay alongside the yacht while we will search it bow to stern. If they try anything, tell the men onboard to open fire."

The two coastguard vessels rested just short of *Serenity*. Two crewmen threw rope ladders down in response to their arrival.

Evans had watched the men aboard the vessel's bow as it pulled up. Their outfits were those of the Japanese coastguard. Satisfied, he shifted his attention to the other vessel. Unlike the men on board the first, they wore black fatigues and carried military style weapons, moving with a level of military discipline. Evans had prepared for this eventuality on previous missions. For his plan to succeed, his crew would have to play their roles perfectly. Janus appeared at his side, making the hairs on Connors neck stand up.

"My God, man, you move like a ghost, make some noise for once, will you?" Evans said as his heart skipped a beat.

"They don't look like coastguard," Janus said, ignoring the comment, "What do you think they want?"

Evans didn't look away as he replied. "We are about to find out. Wouldn't have anything to do with our little foray on the mainland, do you think? We may have rustled some feathers."

The first of their visitors climbed aboard.

Chapter 25

It seemed to Evans that their visitors had only come aboard to spend thirty minutes gawking at his yacht. They admired the craftsmanship, the wood panelling, and the plush carpet. He watched them tread dirt into the carpets and internalised his frustration at the footprints they left in their wake. He had a mind to send a bill to the man in charge.

One of the black-clad soldiers approached, an insignia on his shirt identifying him as the captain.

"Are you the captain of this vessel?" the man asked, his eyes burrowing into Evans's skull, probing for something other what he'd just asked.

"I am. My name is Captain Andrew Waller, and this is the *Chimera*. She is a private yacht owned by me and my company. Can I ask why heavily armed men, and the Japanese coastguard, are searching my yacht and scaring my crew?"

"Forgive me. My name is Captain Jiro Ikeda. There have been a series of events on the mainland, and I have been instructed by the port authority to accompany the coastguard vessels as they investigate all ships within our territorial waters. We believe those responsible have fled the city and may be stowing away on ships that have recently left our harbour."

"Events?" Evans asked innocently.

Jiro nodded, unmoved by the question, "That's right. We believe a person, or a group has conducted terrorist activities in Tokyo. So far, no one has claimed responsibility. Due to this, we suspect those responsible may be operating separately from traditional terrorist groups."

Evans nodded. It was understandable to think that way. Jiro wasn't far off, but they weren't a terrorist group. The man before him was about as much of a captain as Evans was a chef and - in his opinion - a poor one at that, or so his team told him.

"Well, Captain Ikeda, if your men are done snooping around my yacht can I request that they get their dirty boots off my clean floorboards, stop treading dirt into my carpet, and desist from running their oily hands along the wood panelling?" Evans played his part well. "This is not an art exhibition to be admired. My crew and I are quite uncomfortable with your presence."

Jiro tilted his head, staring curiously at Evans.

"I am not familiar with the accent, where are you from?"

Evans hadn't considered their accents, and a quick gaze confirmed the *Serenity* still bore the Australian flag, flapping in the early morning breeze. The Hub was well hidden on the lower levels, but he hadn't considered his own accent might give him and his team away. A massive oversight on his part. The cogs began to turn quickly in his mind. He knew the longer he delayed answering, the more suspicious he would appear.

"I'm Australian. I normally come this way as the weather suits me and my crew, along with our clientele. You may not know this, but the air is cleaner here than down south. Also, there is more excitement in the air up here, if you catch my drift," he added

"I don't understand—" Jiro began.

"I mean, the power of these waters makes you feel alive, don't you think?"

Jiro looked at Evans as though he had lost his marbles.

"I can assure you the tension is very real between our neighbours and us. I do not take these jokes lightly. You would be wise not to make light of such matters," Jiro replied, hissing the last few words like a threat.

Evans smiled, nodding at the man, "Maybe you're right. Either way, can your men say their goodbyes, please? We normally rest at this time of the day, and I don't want a grumpy crew to contend with later."

The excuse was a poor one, but Jiro appeared to accept it. Another soldier approached them, offering his apologies for interrupting their conversation. He leaned in and whispered to Jiro in Japanese that the yacht was all clear.

Jiro returned his attention to Evans. "Thank you for your time, Captain. I apologise for the inconvenience we may have caused you and your crew. If you have any concerns, or wish to report anything, please contact the port authority. You have a good day now and may fortune smile upon you."

Not on your life, pal, Evans thought as he smiled and shook Jiro's hand, continuing to watch as the man and his team climbed down. A few minutes later, their vessels pulled away, moving back toward the mainland.

The foam from the retreating boats hadn't yet settled as Evans went to the lower decks, pausing at a wall which displayed a bird's eye view portrait of Sydney Harbour. The iconic 'coat hanger' bridge spanned the harbour in all its glory. Nestled behind, were the outlandish sails of the Opera House. The casual observer saw only a painting, but it hid a secret purpose. Connor pressed a small yacht in the harbour: *Serenity* was painted within the artwork. Pressing it opened a panel behind the artwork's descriptive panel. When he entered the code, a section of wall to his left slid away, leading to the hidden section of the yacht.

* * *

Connor marched into the Hub, where Tori hadn't yet taken her eyes off the retreating coastguard vessels.

"Where is Chapman? Get him up here now. I have a hunch I want to follow."

Moments later, Chapman sat at a console on Kelly's right, controlling an aerial drone that zipped over the brightening azure waters of the northern Pacific. Chapman deftly manoeuvred the drone to conceal it within the rising sun's rays, and maintained a safe distance from the coastguard vessels, ensuring it would not be seen. Connor looked at the digital timer. They were running out of time. The clocked ticked away the seconds. *Twelve hours remaining…*

He looked back at the console screen as his hunch came through. The vessel with the black outfitted crew turned and headed in east.

"Chapman, show the rest of the crew our new toy," said Connor his expression blank despite his small victory figuring out their visitors had not been part of the coastguard's watch.

Chapman switched from the fisheye lens to a newly installed lens that allowed them to zoom in to almost five hundred times their usual capacity. It looked so close, Connor could spot individual men onboard the targeted boat.

"Acquired it from an old friend of mine in Germany. I couldn't miss the opportunity," Connor said.

"Bit like you and German cars, hey Boss?" Kelly said.

Connor winked at Kelly before William came over to tell him Tori had finished working over Yates in the hold.

The idea that the American might have kept information back didn't surprise him. He had felt the same way about Laura, at first. His heart beginning to race as an image of her crossed his mind for a moment. He excused himself, leaving Kelly to watch over the operation, making his way to the interrogation room. He knocked once before entering. Tori sat in front of a metal table, Yates on the other side. To Evans's surprise, he had his legs up on the edge of the table, looking more relaxed than he should've been. Evans raised an eyebrow, as Tori shrugged.

"What have you got for me?" Evans asked. He grabbed a chair from the side of the room, spinning it around and straddling it, his arms on the back of the chair, his expression remaining neutral.

"Well, like I told Tori here," he said with a wink that drew a withering gaze from her, "it's not Hiroto that runs the show, but Kenji. The man is unhinged as they come, and he strikes me as the kind of psycho that wants to prove something to someone because his ego is so fragile. Truthfully, I think that's what he is going to do." Yates's posture was relaxed, but his tone was serious.

"We already know this," Connor replied. "Tell us something we don't know."

"Alright then, how's this for you? Back in '99, the Americans and the New Zealanders were working on this kind of weapon that could cause untold devastation. The weapon was designed and tested in two separate locations in the Pacific. Problem was, the war ended, so like most things it turned to dust at some black site. But recently, say in the last ten years, earthquakes have become more frequent around the area. An Egyptian newspaper report suggested the Indian Ocean quake of '04 may have been caused by a nuclear bomb going off underwater. Let me be the first to say it. That wasn't us."

Connor sat up straight, listening intently. "If it wasn't you, who was it?"

"That's the million-dollar question," Yates replied. "I did a little digging and contacted some of my father's old sources from his military days. The ship my grandfather was on carried unique missiles capable of causing such quakes. They were codenamed T-Bombs. These suckers were supposed to reduce coastal fortifications to dust. My father's notes suggested that, just as key German scientists defected to the Western Allies, some eastern scientists did the same."

Evans held up his hand. "So, you're telling me the Allies worked with Japanese scientists to create a bomb and, where the Americans might've failed, the work is now complete, and those exact bombs might be in the hands of Kenji?"

Yates looked sheepish. "I don't have all the details, but according to my father's notes, the Office of Strategic Services were involved in the whole sordid affair."

"Well, that checks out," said Tori. "The blueprint folder we found at the weapons facility had the seal of the OSS on it, and that was a World War Two era bunker not far from here. We thought it was a bit far-fetched, but you're confirming what we found."

Connor looked at Tori. "Just when we were you going to tell me this?"

"You were on a mission Boss, that's what I was coming to tell you when those coastguard vessels showed up," Tori replied.

Connor turned back to Yates. "What ship was your grandfather on when it went down?"

"My father was tight-lipped, but I found out through his naval friends. The *USS Redmaine* was a destroyer class ship, part of the Okinawa Campaign, and my grandfather's final posting. According to my grandfather's letter, they were gearing up to attack the Japanese mainland before the bomb was dropped. They were enroute to test the T-bombs for the first." A call over the internal intercom interrupted them.

"We will finish this conversation later. For now, I need to know you are completely on our side in all of this," Connor said, in a serious tone.

Yates hesitated before nodding. He had nothing to fear from Evans or his crew, and evidently Tori had managed to keep the American in his place.

"Tori, find Yates somewhere to clean himself up, then come find me in the comms room," Evans said.

Before leaving, he faced Yates. "Did I forget to mention there's room service?" he added. Connor remained impassive despite the look on Yates's face, as the door closed behind him.

"What the hell is this place?" Yates asked Tori

"You don't want to know," Tori said, as she too left the room, leaving Yates scratching his head, a perplexed look on his face.

Chapter 26

"What do you have for me?" Evans asked, re-entering the communications room of the *Serenity*, and sighting the land mass on Chapman's console. This time Laura joined them. Connor felt she hadn't yet forgiven him for leaving her behind. She gave him a half-hearted smile.

"I tracked our boat's trajectory to an island in the Izu Island chain."

Kelly typed at her computer, a picture of a volcanic island appearing on screen. It was shaped like a sombrero hat, its centre a large volcanic crater. It was ringed with cliffs and inhospitable looking beaches. It was lush with vegetation and dense jungle, due to the fertile volcanic soils at its core.

"This is Aogishima Island. The entire island is a volcanic crater, part of the Pacific Ring of Fire at some point. The island is sparsely populated. It has a small airfield and working dockyard. It's roughly three hundred and fifty-eight kilometres south of Tokyo, and inconspicuous enough not to draw attention. Perfect for someone who, for instance, is trying to hide an Australian ambassador."

Evans examined the land mass, noting the large rise in its centre, and the small inner crater surrounded by its outer rim.

"The island has a thirty-hundred-and-sixty-degree view, so impossible to approach by air. The only option may be the zodiacs, but even then, Kenji may have defences prepared. William and his boys are going to be hard pressed to find an easy solution. Even with sixteen of the best men money can buy at his disposal, the most advanced weaponry, and gadgets to play with, this island might be a challenge."

"I heard that, sir," William said entering the room behind Connor. "I'm glad you think that, because I reckon, I've got a strategy they will never see coming,".

"In daylight, stealth is going to be a right mess. The cliffs are sheer, so scaling the sides of the island would be a rough go, even during the day. There is a road that snakes along the coast; maybe we can use vehicles."

Connor shook his head, telling Chapman to move closer. He used the drone's advanced magnification to full effect, focusing on the dockyards.

"I've got a better plan for you and your boys, Will." He told William and Kelly what he needed from them. William could only shake his head after Evans had explained it.

"The plan checks out, but we need to be careful," said William. "We can't have someone tipping them off, otherwise we'll end up paying the bill for the ambassador's funeral."

Such a morbid idea quietened everyone in the room. Connor ordered one of the crew in the Hub to keep an eye on the coastguard's vessel as it pulled into the docks. He was taking a chance on the drone battery holding out long enough.

When William left to prepare his team, Connor and Kelly remained behind, watching the drone footage. "I'm going with William to the island," he said, "but not because he needs me. It's self-evident now that the men we encountered on the coastguard vessel are all part of Kenji's security force. The weapons they carried are as good as ours. It will be a tough slog, when push comes to shove."

"It will be like history repeating itself, then," Kelly chimed in, as she typed away on her computer.

"Australians never made it the full stretch in World War Two," Connor replied. Kelly spun around to face him, pouting and crossing her arms.

"Well, we didn't think that the New Zealanders were building weapons co-jointly with the Americans, now did we?"

Evans laughed, "You have a point, but according to history, the Americans fought the rest of the way through the Solomon Islands and as far as the Okinawa Island chains."

Kelly agreed to disagree on Evans's point, as he shook his head,

"Keep an eye on things while I'm gone."

His final of the statement left Kelly at a loss. The mission was starting to chip away at their commander. Janus had made the comment to her when he returned about the efficacy of their mission and priorities.

Evans left the communications room and marched to the rear of *Serenity*. He had a single thought in his mind. It was crazy, but he figured it just might work.

William was briefing his men as Evans entered the room, the big man turning to look at him. "I didn't think I'd see you down here until later," he said.

Evans wore a serious expression on his face, making William clam up in an instant.

"I need to adjust my plan," Evans said. The rest of the men sat studiously in plastic chairs in front of the whiteboard William had been using to explain the upcoming operation.

Evans and Southgate shifted to the side, away from prying ears.

"I am going to go this one alone, for now." He saw the expression on William's face, holding up a hand to allow him to finish. "Before you say anything, hear me out, Will. Your boys will be great when I need them to cover for me, but for now, it needs to be me alone. One person can be better than three heavyweights. especially when they have Australian accents and appear on the island out of nowhere.

William nodded slowly. Connor could see his mind ticking over,

"Are you sure, Connor?" Will asked.

"No point in sending in all of us, it would be a suicide mission. Not until we know what we are up against on this island. For now, it's better just one person goes. This is the new plan. Kelly already knows about the change. See it's followed to the letter."

Connor slapped a hand on William's shoulder. "We have less than twelve hours to perform a Hail Mary on two objectives. It's all or nothing now. Take no unnecessary risks yourself unless you have no choice."

Connor knew William wouldn't argue with him once he had set his mind to a task. Kelly was the only one who could sway him, but then again, she had that effect on William too.

"As you wish, sir. Watch your back. My men will be ready when you make the call. Speaking of, how are you going to make the call exactly?" William asked, one eyebrow raised,

Evans grinned at him. "Just keep your eyes peeled, mate. I am sure you will know what to do when you see it." He left William wondering what he meant by that, and anxiously awaiting the night to come.

* * *

Later that night, Kelly stood on the raised ramp, arms closely folded, looking at the lapping water as it gently kissed the tops of her flip flops. She surveyed the darkness as though he could see something Evans could not, watching, waiting, an anxiousness passing through her at what might come during the next few hours. The normally white led lights had been dimmed to a dark battle red, one of their zodiacs bouncing on the water. Evans arrived wearing a dry suit, the neoprene material hugging his form as he dipped his exposed feet in the water.

"Good thing I don't feel the cold," he said, as calmly as possible. Kelly nodded, worry etched on her face.

"Is this really the best we can come up with, Connor? Why are you going in alone - you know we are a team, right?"

Evans moved up the ramp toward his second in command. "It's better I go because I don't want anyone risking themselves needlessly. This has gotten dangerous enough without me putting the rest of my team on the line."

"Then you'll be surprised to know Laura left earlier. I meant to tell you before but—" Kelly said.

Evans moved toward her. "When we picked her up, she struck me as someone that couldn't be tied down, even on our beautiful yacht. I'll find her, but I am sure she can take care of herself. We share a common interest. We love our country, and we would do anything to protect it.

Connor paused as Kelly, her skin shining under the red lighting, looked into his eyes. She smiled at him, as he embraced her. The moment didn't last. Connor, he moved toward a small piece of equipment near the ramp, prepared earlier. It was something William insisted he wear when performing solo dives, especially when hoping to float along the water without drawing attention to himself.

The device in question was a Draeger unit. It was essentially a portable dive device that provided regular fresh air to its user, filtering out carbon dioxide in a looped system, allowing the diver to remain invisible, eliminating any stream of bubbles. With a depth limit of no more than thirty feet, it was ideal for the conditions he was using it for. The only other equipment he took was a knife strapped to his thigh, his flexi minicomputer on his wrist, and his suppressed Glock pistol. He was almost positive that the men he encountered before were wearing state-of-the-art Kevlar body armour, so he'd swapped out the regular ammunition for armour piercing rounds.

Kelly looked across at a small computer near the exit ramp.

"The monitor shows the water is no more than 21.6 degrees Celsius. You're lucky. If we were in the waters back home, we would have to wrap you in several layers of towels at this time of the year."

Evans ignored Kelly's nervous humour. He could see it on her face and wanted to say what was on his mind, opting against it. He climbed into the zodiac as one of Will's men did the same, another following him to sit in front of the engine. He looked back at Kelly.

"Make sure William is ready on my go. He will know the signal when he sees it."

The pilot of the zodiac started up its motor, which buzzed loudly as it reversed into the water. The propellor churned the waves as the driver twisted a button. In a heartbeat, the engines turned near silent, with only a small froth underneath as they pulled away.

Evans looked back after a time, but just as he'd envisioned when he had the yacht designed, it was enveloped by the surrounding darkness.

"Get me as close as you can to the island. I'll do the rest," he said to the pilot of the boat, as he looked at his wrist computer. Kelly had already synced it up his computer to Chapman's drone that idled over the island, its battery freshly replaced. He looked up at the twinkling night.

"I know you can see me," he said, throwing a finger to the team above.

Back in the Hub, Kelly grinned. "At least he has a sense of humour," she told Tori. "I'd be losing it right now."

"It's better he's like this. Because if he wasn't, you can bet we wouldn't do half of what we do sometimes," Tori replied.

Ten long minutes later, Evans and the two men with him in the zodiac, bobbed quietly on the tide. Evans rechecked his Draeger unit as Chapman's voice came through his earpiece.

"Port checks out, nothing moving down there. If there is any activity, it would likely come by the small shed near the end of the furthest pier. Happy hunting." Chapman signed off.

Evans doubted the man would leave him be. He knew Kelly would be breathing down his neck to use the thermal imaging to scout ahead, making sure the coast was clear.

Attaching the rebreathing unit, he closed his eyes and took a few deep breaths, clearing his mind of any anxiety, and reminding himself why he was doing this. Slipping his dive shoes on and pulling down his dive mask, he fell back into the surf, sinking four feet before opening his eyes. It took two heartbeats for the bubbles to clear, leaving nothing but a deep blue and black darkness. He couldn't gauge depth, as it was too dark to even see his feet. He looked down at his wrist computer, which was working perfectly.

Rising to the surface, he focused on the sporadic distant of the dockyard and moved under the surf once more. Seconds passed before sudden movement nearby made his pulse race. Connor figured it was the zodiac moving away to ready itself for later, then realised it was nothing more than an undercurrent. He breathed a sigh of relief.

It was amazing to him how calming an effect of the ocean could have at night. Despite being all alone and surrounded by darkness that would put most into a state of panic and disorientation, his heartrate was steady and his breathing normal, as though he were out for a leisurely stroll. Kelly had been right about the temperature of the water. It was lukewarm, almost like bath water, and he moved through it effortlessly.

Time seemed to stand still as he swam until, eventually, the outlines of the concrete pilings came into focus. Moving toward one, he ran a hand over its surface, a mixture of barnacles and smooth concrete providing a perfect route to the surface. The deep blue gave way to the night sky as his head broke through. He stayed still underneath the pier, his dripping hair casting ripples around him. After waiting a full minute for any sounds of movement, he swam between each pillar until he reached the one nearest to the shore. Listening closely, he heard faint voices, but nothing close by. He slung the re-breather over his head and tucked it into the rocks that formed the break wall, before moving slowly into the open. Unlike when he was diving, he felt very exposed now, and wanted to leave the water as soon as possible. He spotted a rusted ladder nearby. Clinging to it, he pulled himself out of the water, waiting as the bulk of the water dripped off his body. He climbed the last few rungs quickly, reaching the top. He hid behind a pair of barrels, holding his breath, praying no one would come.

"Connor to *Serenity*, can you hear me?" he whispered.

"*Serenity* copies, how was the swim?" Kelly replied.

"Like taking a bath," he whispered back. He weaved his way through the nearest buildings, stopping at what looked to be a warehouse. A rancid stench hit him from barrels crammed with fish offal, almost making him dry retch. Hunkering down behind them and holding his breath again, he surveyed the dockyards. His first obstacle was the sliding chain-link fence. Cutting a hole might mean losing the element of surprise. Instead, he ran, scaled the fence, rolled over the top in one streamlined movement. The wire rattled as he climbed down the other side. Laughter echoed from a nearby building as he ducked into the shadows.

So far, so good, he thought, as the faint sound of music came from a side street. He was in a small coastal village. The buildings around him were no more than ten storeys tall, most of them only two storeys. Among these build-ings, he felt like an ant, and almost certainly looked like one to the drone high above him that watched his every move.

"Chapman, do thermal scans show any signatures nearby?" he whispered.

There was a slight delay before Chapman answered. "I am seeing multiple heat signatures around you. Most appear to be civilians."

Always a good sign, Evans thought, as he continued weaving his way among the buildings. He wasn't sure exactly what he was looking for, but he was sure he would know it when he saw it. A sudden chill passed through his body, so he ducked into an alleyway to slip out of his dry suit. He wore dark clothes underneath to remain invisible in the shadows.

The plan had gone off without a hitch so far.

He peered out of the shadows as the sound of a roller door opening drew his attention. A group of men wearing masks walked out of a rundown old storage facility. They sported the advanced weaponry he had seen onboard the coastguard vessels. Putting two and two together, he watched them climb into a nearby jeep and drive away, the roller door closing behind them.

"Connor to *Serenity*, Kenji's security is already here. I think I have found another facility. I'm going to take a closer look."

Making a split-second decision that might cost him, Connor sprinted across the badly paved road, diving to the ground with a smothered grunt, using his momentum to roll under the closing door as it shut behind him.

Chapter 27

Thin beams of light filtered through the warehouse windows high above him, as his eyes adjusted to the interior of the dilapidated building he stood in. He pulled out his pistol and clicked on the flashlight attachment attached to the muzzle.

Vehicular parts of metal and aluminium surrounded him, stacked in rusted metal crates. Moving deeper inside, he shifted the yellow torch beam higher for a moment to get a feeling for the interior, noticing halogen lights typical of warehouses, floating high above. Out of the corner of his eye, he noticed something unusual about a pillar in front of him. A closer inspection concluded it wasn't a pillar at all, but something else. Hoses and electric wires were wrapped around its landing gear, and at its base were two large bulbous tyres, worn but still inflated. This wasn't a pillar, but landing gear for something big. *A jet?* Evans thought.

There was a loud noise nearby like metal piping falling on concrete. Unsure if he was alone, Connor edged around the landing gear to hide behind some stacked crates. He noticed a, rocking slightly on its hinges. It had fallen open and was caught on an overhanging piece of metal, which had made the noise he'd heard. He walked slowly toward the doorway holding the torchlight steady, pointing it at an angle that wouldn't betray his position. At the doorway, he turned off the beam and leaned inside.

So far, he figured this place was likely a scrapyard, a metal graveyard. Leaning against the frame, he looked around at yet more stacked boxes stacked on top of one another, a seemingly endless from what he could tell at ground level. Stepping into the next section, his eyes made out more details due to the moonlight filtering through small, thin windows above. A curtain of dust hung in the air, making him stifle a sneeze. It was then he noticed it, between two towers of boxes, almost like a trick of the light.

He had to shimmy his way between the two boxes, not finding a way around them. His shirt caught on the edge of the metal, tearing the fabric as he fought to free himself. Whether from the subtle breeze, or some sense of foreboding, a chill ran up and down his spine. Stepping out from the gap he had shuffled along, he looked at the large, looming object above.

An old Boeing 747, its once-white hull caked with dust and grime, sat forlornly buried among the rusting graveyard. It could only fit in the warehouse because it was missing its wings.

Ducking under a series of overarching cables to get close to the 'spirit of the sky', as they were known in Australia, Connor encountered the remains of flight chairs chucked in a pile. The fabric chairs were, amazingly, in near-mint condition. Evans continued to search the jet's undercarriage, coming to an open hatchway.

Curiosity got the better of him, and he pulled himself inside the underbelly of the forgotten plane. He shone his flashlight down the length of the cavernous baggage compartment area. Remnants of stripped-out wires and cables hung in various areas, as he crawled along. Reaching the end of the compartment, another hatch opened into the passengers' compartment. Again, he shone his torch down the long tunnel. He spotted the holes in the floor where the chairs were once bolted. Connor wondered why such a plane was hidden in the warehouse. The Boeing 747 was the peak of the world's fleet for decades. Now one of its hallowed models was here, hidden away on an island far from any major airfield.

The haunting atmosphere moved him as he reached the flight deck. Opening the door and shining the torch inside, he saw that all the navigation aids and electronics had been stripped back to bare metal. The only thing that remained in the gloomy interior were the chairs that two dedicated and skilled pilots would've occupied. Evans could see that the work was done by professionals rather than scavengers. Shining his torch up high, he looked for any kind of serial number, anything that might identify this aircraft, but and found nothing. That was strange, but not surprising, given the 747's current home. He thought about what Janus had said about serial numbers being misaligned. He wondered if they came from a plane like this.

Turning around, his shoulder caught on something that shifted downwards. He'd moved a lever, with a faded *on and off* marked on the metal.

Just as Connor was wondering what the lever did, someone out of the darkness.

Evans jumped backward and dropped to a shooting position, but nothing moved. He shone his torch at the intruder, the light picking out a cardboard cut-out, similar to those used by the military in training drills. *What in the hell,* he thought, as he rose from his kneeling stance and pushed against it, feeling it flex under his fingers.

He heard it before he saw it: a clicking sound, like a chain rattling. Bright neon orange lights flickered around him as more of the cut outs slid out from the floor. Evans knew stealth was now out of the question, as the sound from the klaxon alarm would bring Kenji's soldiers in droves to his position. He ran down the length of the plane, its interior lit up like a main street Climbing down, he crawled quickly until he reached the plane's exit hatch. His rubber-soled shoes barely made a sound as he landed on the cement floor. Stepping away from the plane, the warehouse now lit by the flickering orange lights within, Connor realised the klaxon couldn't be heard outside the 747, making the aircraft's interior look like a silent disco.

Retreating into the shadow of the metal crates, he watched and waited for anyone to appear, straining his ears for shouts, or engine rumbles. None came. Connor directed the torch beam back toward the open doorway where he had seen the landing gear.

He wasn't sure what he had just escaped from, but as he stepped into the next room and flicked his light toward a corner he had yet to explore, it dawned on him. He was looking at a specially built armoury, with racks of weapons and ammunition.

On a small desk, papers were neatly stacked in a document tray. Evans flicked through the papers, looking for anything incriminating, certain he was onto something. Taken together, these papers provided the evidence he needed to prove Kenji was behind the kidnapping of Joshua Davidson. When he reached the last of the papers, he noticed an envelope at the bottom of the tray. It had already been torn open. The paper inside bore the Toyotami Industries letterhead. The document detailed an order of weapons, ammunition, and special equipment. Connor took a photo before replacing it in its envelope and tucking the papers away.

"Connor to *Serenity*, do you copy?"

"*Serenity* copies, Commander. Have you contacted William yet?"

"Negative. I'm sending through a set of documents. I need confirmation of its contents."

He sent through the document via secure email and waited while Kelly did what she did best. While he waited, he examined the weapons, pulling one from the rack. A Howa Type 20. Introduced in 2020, it replaced the previous model Type 89. Japan's defence ministry ensured domestic weaponry were used instead of international rifles such as the Heckler and Koch G36 or American-made SCAR assault rifle. The rifle had not been fired. Picking up another, he noticed the same thing. The third had been fired, and—from the smell of the gunpowder residue, it had been fired recently. He wondered if the group he had seen leave were responsible. *What were they training for?* he thought.

"*Serenity* to Connor, come in." Kelly's voice came through loud and clear. "The document lists equipment which is standard in Japanese land infantry forces. I cannot say the same for the specialised equipment listed."

"Any guesses on what it was used for?" Evans whispered. He caught movement in his peripheral vision, a shadow shifting behind him. The hairs on the back of his neck rose.

"Glad you figured it out the same time as I did." stepped out of the darkness.

Their reunion was short lived as the sound of the roller door clattering behind her drawing both their attention. They had company.

Chapter 28

Connor pulled Laura behind the desk, both shocked and glad to see her again.

"It seems this time you brought guests," Connor whispered.

She shrugged. "This isn't on me. I figured I had learnt enough from you and your team to go it alone."

There would be time enough later for disagreement. For now, they had to contend with whoever had returned to the facility.

"Kelly, its Connor. Switch to thermal imaging over my coordinates. We have company."

"Negative, Connor. Chapman had to pull the drone back. He won't be in your airspace for another few minutes at least."

Great. With no eyes in the sky, he was blind to what was coming. Keeping low, Connor and Laura hid behind the desk near the small armoury as five hostiles entered the warehouse floor, judging by his count of their torch beams. Leaning around the desk, he watched one figure break away from the group, the flashlight - which was attached to his gun —bouncing as he approached them.

Looking down at his watch, its luminescent green face told him that almost thirty minutes had passed since he'd entered the building.

Laura was so close. Connor could hear her breathing and feel her warmth. He reached for her hand, cupping it in his. "There's one coming toward us. Follow me and keep low. We might be able to slip past him."

She squeezed his hand in understanding as they crept around the corner. Fortunately for them, the torch beam had moved on as they slid along the sides of the metal boxes, pausing each time they heard a sound. Most of the light beams had disappeared into the other room where the orange neon continued to flash. To Connor, it was odd that only one man was stationed behind to guard the only exit, an oversight on the enemy's part. It was an opportunity they weren't going to pass up.

Guiding Laura back to the door where he'd entered, Evans hesitated when one of the soldiers called out in Japanese that he'd found something in the other room. The call drew the attention of the lone guard, giving Connor his cue to emerge from the darkness, startling the guard as his hand connected with the man's windpipe. Behind his face mask, a gurgle came from the guard's throat as he tried to breathe. Connor dragged him into the darkness behind them, continuing to cut off the man's air supply until he went limp.

Piece of cake, Evans concluded as they left the building. Checking to make sure no one was guarding the still-idling vehicles the men had arrived in, he and Laura ran across the street and hunkered down behind a large steel bin in the alley. The stench of fish and what might have been soy sauce drifted deep within their nostrils, making Evans never want to touch either again.

With the moonlight directly overhead, Connor saw Laura had pulled her brown hair into a ponytail, her green eyes looking at him in a way that made his heart race. The feeling troubled him greatly. Shaking his head to clear his thoughts, he looked back at her.

Evans couldn't help but feel her arrival meant he wasn't just looking out for himself, but also for her. Laura had proved she could take care of herself, but he doubted she had dealt with anything like this.

Two men emerging from the warehouse drew their attention, along with the sound of an engine, then headlights appearing on the street. The engines revealed themselves to be two all-terrain vehicles.

"The island is criss-crossed with mountainous bike tracks; they're the only way to get to the island's centre. That where Kenji and his force are hiding. I am positive," Laura said in his ear.

Four more men arrived, suited up in body armour and resembling a SWAT team.

"I was kept a short distance from here," said Laura. "It looks like just another building, but it's a lot more than that. That's where they are keeping Joshua. I won't be happy until I've killed every one of the murderous bastards for what they did to him."

Her word sent a chill down his spine, and suddenly Laura didn't look so inviting to him.

He looked back as one of the men shouted orders to the others.

"Did you see what was inside the warehouse?" he asked her, to which she nodded.

"I saw the flashing orange lights you set off," she replied. "I figured I'd ambush whoever came out. I didn't expect to see you. What do you suppose the plane is doing in there?"

"I wasn't to know that Kenji had set up a training facility in a 747. I would've had more time to explore if you hadn't brought half of the land force here with you," he said, nodding toward the men fifteen metres away.

She pouted, which only frustrated him further.

"Look," he said. "I don't know how you got here tonight, and frankly, it's better I don't ask. It looks like we are stuck in this together. According to those documents, the jet wasn't there for show. The jet inside was where Kenji practised kidnapping the ambassador."

"Except it didn't go down like that," Laura murmured, staring past him, as though her mind was far away.

A man emerged from the warehouse, communicating via walkie talkie. Neither of them could make out what he was saying. Evans watched them climb back into their vehicles and head in the same direction they'd come from.

"You need to smile more," Laura said.

Connor raised an eyebrow. "You just say whatever comes to your mind, don't you?"

"Pretty much. Got a problem with that?" Laura replied, grinning.

Though her appearance had increased the danger, he was glad she was there. More so because two heads were better than one. He knew Kenji would be onto them now, especially as they had triggered an alarm in the facility.

Connor began to backtrack to William's position when Laura tapped him on the shoulder.

"Are you thinking what I'm thinking?" she asked.

"Men," she said. She gestured for him to follow her.

Connor followed her to a corner convenience store. He peeked around her, spotting the truck parked up on the kerb, silhouettes in the store moving as the faint sound of music filled the air.

"We aren't going to take that. Surely you can't be serious?" he said.

Evans thought Laura had lost the plot. The sound of the engine starting up would bring whoever was inside out to confront them.

"Do you have a better idea?" she asked

Moving from behind her, he walked to the rear of the truck. He left Laura to wonder what he was up to. When he reappeared, the look on her face was priceless.

"So, instead of stealing a vehicle and driving it away, you propose these?" she asked, as he stood holding the handlebars of two bicycles.

"Stealth is the best option. Let's not mess that up. Not yet, anyway," he said as she shook her head in the dark. He climbed on and started pedalling.

Thirty minutes later, they had left the twinkling streetlights of the small village behind and begun to weave their way through thick jungle, unable to see more than a few feet before them even with the faint light from the stars. Evans moved to the side of the road, steering the bike into a dense thicket as Laura followed.

"If I had known tonight would've involved riding a bicycle of all things, I would've brought my bike pants with me," she joked. Evans laughed.

"Being Australian means being preparedly unprepared," Evans replied. Laura's laugh was infectious, and it brought a smile to his face.

Parking their bikes away from a bike trail, they sat under the stars on a flat rock. She sat next to him, placing her head on his shoulder, a move that caught him off guard,

"Preparedly unprepared, Mr Evans," she said, as he felt warmth grow inside him.

He looked up at the night sky, a faint light trace catching his eye. A shooting star crossed his vision as he looked at what the northern hemisphere had to offer above. Laura's breathing became deep and steady, making him wonder if she had fallen asleep on him. He couldn't imagine what she had been through, or what it must be like to return to where she had been held captive. He felt lucky in more ways than one.

Their momentary respite was interrupted by the sound of voices. Connor gently shifted Laura off his shoulder. The movement made her eyes flutter open as Evans placed a single finger to her lips. She understood immediately, as she registered the faint voices. Moving back toward the bushes, they saw a group of people walking along the road, their voices rising and falling in a mixture of excitement and passion.

"Teenagers. They must've come from the camping ground up in the crater," Laura whispered.

Connor looked at her. "There's a campground in that crater?'

Laura nodded. "It's likely the group is enjoying the scenery and thought about taking a merry stroll into town, probably going to the same place where that *truck* was parked."

Evans, not bothering to argue, retrieved their bikes and pointed up the mountain. "Come on, we have a fair way to go."

They rode back out into the open. The only sound was the steady rhythm of the bike chains as they made their way along the weaving roads leading to the crater above.

A low rumbling sound grew louder as they neared the summit. Evans didn't get a chance to react as four ATVs pulled out of the jungle, moving in circles around them, then stopping. The low rumbling of their engines made Evans wonder what they did to get them achieve such minimal engine noise.

One man climbed off his bike. He spoke rapidly into his internal headset, listening to the reply. Without a gesture, weapons were pulled from the side holsters of the bikes - military shotguns.

Evans knew once more that he was at the mercy of Kenji. His luck had run out. One of the guards toward smacked Laura with the butt of the gun, knocking her out cold. She hit the ground hard. Evans tried to throw a haymaker at the soldier when the leader stepped in, gun raised, butt first. Connor's world went dark as the ground raced toward him.

Chapter 29

When Evans regained consciousness, he was cable-tied and made to sit on the back of one of the bikes. Laura had been placed the same way, hands bound in front of her.

They drove through jungle tracks, deeper into the forest that covered most of the island. Unlike the riders, Laura and Connor had no helmets and were mercilessly whipped by low branches and anything that came their way, dirt and dust included. Evans copped a low-hanging branch to the face, tasting blood. If he hadn't been tied on, the impact would've sent him reeling back and off the bike.

When he felt like his bruised and battered face and body could take no more, the bikes surged out of the forest into a large clearing, lit by lights plugged into generators. The area was the size of a football stadium and was clear except for a collection of small buildings and containers. To the side of three cabins, stood an older brick building, looking out of place in the dark jungle. It may have looked old, but Connor he assumed that was all part of the ruse. The sound Lauren made convinced him this was where she had escaped from.

Connor and Laura were hauled off the bikes and thrown onto the ground roughly, winded in the process.

"You, Mr Harding, have become quite the pain to Kenji," came the heavily accented voice of Jiro Ikeda. "It's time you learned the consequences of your troublesome antics."

He ordered two guards to frisk them. Evans endured it while he kept his attention on Jiro. A deep scar along the man's face made it look like his head had been split like a watermelon by a samurai sword, then pulled together and sewn shut. Jiro's mouth curled at the edges making his face look like something that should only come out at Halloween.

"Who are you, and what do you want with us?" Evans demanded.

"It doesn't matter who I am. I want to know what brought you onto my island, and why you broke into my warehouse. So, tell me, what were you looking for?"

Connor looked around him and a thought came to mind.

"I'll answer your questions once you take off your mask," he said, a cruel smile at his lips. He knew Jiro wasn't wearing a mask like his men. The dozens of grotesque Oni masks resembled demons.

Jiro seethed with immediate rage as his men hoisted Laura and Connor to their feet by their tied hands. He barked an order, and his men shoved them roughly toward one of the cabins. It was then Evans noticed something parked behind a stack of shipping containers.

The government Gulfstream, revealed by the lights around the clearing, was parked among the trees as if it belonged there. A large, camouflaged netting, often used to confuse radar scans, covered the jet and part of the brick building.

Evans fought to make out more details as they were dragged roughly past, his view obscured by one of the men clutching him. Tired of Evans's writhing, one of the masked men punched him hard in his gut. doubling him over before he was painfully held up straight again, lungs gasping for air. Still, he studied the jet. Connor could see nothing to suggest how it had arrived here. Under the projecting lights he could see a large majority of the jet, almost pristine as though it had just rolled out of the factory. It carried no sign of outward damage. Thinking back on what his team had discovered with the Taiwanese authorities, he began to wonder what wreckage his team did discover, was it a hoax or another kidnapping Kenji had orchestrated?

He had to admit it had almost worked. If not for Janus and his superior attention to detail, he was certain he would have concluded the ambassador, and his plane had gone down for good. That was until he met Laura. She stood beside him now, hair dishevelled, full of leaves and pieces of twigs. He felt a pang in his heart that he hadn't just let his team down, but her as well.

"You have proved to be quite a resourceful man, Mr Harding. Kenji was most impressed that you managed to find our island sanctuary. But this is where is where your adventure ends."

Two masked men pulled down a large, camouflaged netting, revealing more airplane parts. But it wasn't the parts that caught Connor's eye. It was the large jet engine turbine. Evans looked at the engine, guessing it must have come off the Boeing housed in the warehouse. He traced wires and cables snaking across the grass toward one of the far cabins.

One of the masked men walked over to a makeshift panel. The box was half-covered by bunches of wires and cable tied together and stuffed into it. It looked very much like a makeshift bomb. A few clicks on the panel triggered a whirring sound, low and slow, from inside the huge turbine.

Jiro smiled, baring his teeth like a shark looking at its prey. The turbine nestled inside large the large white outer casing started to move in a mesmerising pattern, slowly rotating, the low whirring building up power, and pulling air from where they stood behind it.

The noise was getting louder all the time as three of the masked men moved away to a safe distance. Evans checked Laura, who looked horrified at their hopeless situation. Jiro stood directly in front of Connor. If Evans thought he was ugly from afar, he almost gagged up close.

A beeping sound made everyone turn toward a John Deere Tractor crashing out of the trees. Its normal shovel head had been removed, and all that remained were the two end pieces, like jagged toothpicks. Evans estimated there was at least twenty feet of wrapped rusty chain hanging from the arms. The tractor stopped five metres behind him, and Jiro smirked, slapping Evans gently on the face before moving behind him.

Connor's hands were tugged behind his back as the turbine thrummed and a further sound joined the chorus. Behind him, the arms of the tractor were raised, and he realised he'd been attached to the chain He rose almost four feet off the ground, feeling the tractor shudder once when the height was exact. Another judder followed, as the tractor was thrown into gear and pushed forward.

Evans could feel moisture gathering under his armpits, his black, torn t-shirt soaked through as it dawned on him on what was about to happen. He had to admit, Kenji employed some real psychopaths. The setup suggested they likely did this often. The tractor ensured the only person sucked into the voluminous fans was the individual attached to the chain.

His body ended up pointing forward like an arrow. From out of his peripheral vision, he saw Laura fighting the guards that held her. He heard her cussing and hurling insults at the men around her, her voice a familiar sound in the hostile environment. Jiro watched, the scar on his face rippling. It made Connor think of feeding time at the aquarium.

"Comfortable, Mr Harding? It's not too often you face first class like this?" The men nearby were resting on their haunches as events unfolded, as casually as they might watch a football match.

"I wouldn't say comfortable Just hanging in in there if I'm being honest," Connor quipped, before his expression and tone changed to one more serious. "For a group that calls themselves the Honourable Ones, there is no honour among you. You take what you want, you lie and steal. You are only thieves and murderers. You aren't descended from the samurai. Through your actions, you only dishonour them."

Jiro flushed with rage, Connor betting the man would make a mistake. He was working on an escape plan, but he needed more time. So far, Laura had made it easier for him with her own performance.

"That maybe so, Mr Harding—" Jiro started.

"You aren't too smart, are you? My name is not Harding. My name is Commander Connor Evans. You would do well to remember that. Not too many that hear that name live to tell the tale."

Jiro burst into laughter, the sound hollow and empty,

"I don't care who you are *Commander Evans,* you are already dead to me. Enjoy your quick death. Your lady friend, on the other hand, won't be as lucky as you."

With that Jiro moved away, telling Connor everything he needed to know. He had little chance to communicate with his team, shouting to be heard over the spinning turbine, as it came close to maximum speed. The fan spun at a rate where its blades all came together in a whirling pattern, like a blender.

"Whatever you think you'll accomplish by removing me from the equation, you're dead wrong. What follows me will only be worse for you and your men," Connor shouted as loudly as he could manage, struggling against the chains that bound him.

Jiro gave him a deadpan look followed by further laughter.

"I'm sure we will be able to handle whatever *team* you have. I am most certain there is nothing you can throw at us that we can't handle."

Evans felt his weight shift slightly as the tractor approached the fan blades. The loud whirring made it impossible for any further talk, Evans knew that if he didn't make it out, the world would suffer a fate far worse than his own. He closed his eyes, willing himself to figure a way out of this. His hands were tied tightly behind his back, his weight not making much of a difference to the strong metal arms of the tractor. Evans found himself thinking of his father then. His father didn't know, wouldn't know, that his son had faced adversity, almost overcome the odds, only just coming up short. He was certain his father would have had a few choice words and expletives for his actions, urging him to never give in, never resign himself to such a fate. He opened his eyes again, seeing Jiro standing just behind him, the man's carved pumpkin face full of glee at what was about to happen to Connor.

Connor had no plan; the last of his fight died with the thought of his father's disappointment. The tractor steadily moved close to the point where it would only need to extend the arms, the forced suction doing the rest.

During the high-pitched whirring, Laura had been pleading, fighting, and screaming at the men who held her. She had heard Jiro's words, but Connor hoped hers would be a clean death, unlike his own.

* * *

When the whirring reached its peak, Jiro rubbed his hands together, knowing that removing the thorn out of Kenji's side would earn him the praise he had always desired. He would take his place beside Kenji in the new Japanese empire. The thought brought a tear to his eye. His dream would become a reality. Jiro's passion fuelled his hate. Connor had not just caused Kenji much pain, but him as well. He had been subjugated by Kenji for his mistakes and failures, all caused by Connor. His blood boiling, he climbed onto the side of the tractor, throwing open the door and pulling the masked man out, leaving him to fall into the dirt. Jiro watched his adversary hang less than ten metres from the blades. Evans closed his eyes.

Resigned to their individual fates, neither saw the man near the turbine's head explode, or fall forward onto the panel.

Chapter 30

William knew something had gone wrong the moment Connor checked in with him. He and his men were laying low while waiting for Connor's signal. He had hailed a local fishing boat and paid the owner handsomely to take them in as part of his crew. The captain of the boat helped further by providing outfits that they changed into, aiding their covert operation. They had dirtied their hair, rubbed dirt on their faces, and smeared grime and engine grease on their clothes to look like poor farmers and fisherman.

An hour after Connor's last check-in, and with no further signal, William – as field commander after Evans – was ready to make the call. He crouched with his team in the hold of the boat. The smell of fish and algae drifted into his nostrils. Though he had an iron stomach, one of his men had gone topside, green around the gills and white faced. He told him to not bother coming back but to replace the man already on watch.

"Kelly, it's Will. Any word yet?' he said, his pommy accent muffled by the wooden hull.

"Not yet. It's not like Connor to miss checking in. We have no choice now. We go to Plan B."

"Alright, I'll get my boys topside. Do you think you can activate his tracker, find out where he is?" William ordered his men to move, so they shrugged out of their outfits and checked their weapons.

"I'm on it," Kelly replied. Moments later, her voice came through. "According to his tracker, he is inland, toward the far side of the island."

"Got it, far side of the island. Send it to my nav pad. The boys and I will take care of the rest. Connor didn't say anything about not going loud. It's time we had some fun of our own. Think you can get Chapman and Janus to provide air support?"

"I'll see what I can do. Be careful, Will, and good luck."

Will signed off, climbing the wooden stairs away from the safety of the trawler's wooden hold.

* * *

That was twenty minutes ago. Since then, they had moved into an elevated position overlooking a large clearing that had Janus wanting to take a closer look, despite Will's protests.

He had scanned it with his night vision. Nothing had appeared. Switching to thermal vision, he was surprised to have caught a large expansion of heat coming from the centre of the clearing. It highlighted several people positioned around it, the heat turning them into candles near a flame.

William waited for Janus to take the first shot, then watched as the man nearest the control panel collapsed into a heap, falling forward, and sliding off the panel.

"Goddamn, that was an impressive shot, now let's see about saving our boy," Southgate remarked through Janus's earpiece, watching the action through binoculars, seeing Connor positioned in front of the turbine. He had heard the unfamiliar sound as they powered through the bush in the truck that Connor and Laura had disregarded earlier. The road had ended thirty metres from their current position, so they had to hike the rest of the way.

"Keep them pinned down for now, Jan. We will do the rest."

Janus didn't need telling twice, as he racked the chamber once more. He exhaled as he sighted his next target and squeezed the trigger. On his third heartbeat he fired, the suppressed rifle kicking violently back into his shoulder

* * *

Evans didn't see the kill, but Laura caught it as the masked men beside her continued to watch, unaware of what had happened due to the noise of the turbine. The body on the panel initially caused the turbine to speed up before his weight pulled the lever back. It began to power down, the loud whirring gradually subsiding to a more comfortable level.

In one smooth movement, Laura reached right, yanked the small dagger from nearest guard, and plunged it into his side, kicking the other's leg, producing a satisfying crack as it bent inwards. She pulled the knife from the guard, slicing the rope with its sharpened edge. The teeth bit into the woven thread. Within seconds, she was free.

Despite the pain of the man's twisted leg, he raised his submachine gun and pointed it at Laura.

The man didn't get a chance to let off a shot, as his body kicked violently, before he fell forward. Laura - not wasting time on who her guardian angel was – grabbed the dropped gun.

Another shot cracked the tractor's glass near Jiro's head, piercing it and thudding into the centre of the wheel. Laura watched Jiro dive out of the far door as another bullet tore into the glass. She aimed at him, locking eyes with as bullets thudded around her, making her run and dive behind a stack of logs that had likely stood before the clearing was here.

She hazarded a peek around the wood as bullets sunk into their thick trunks, seeing Evans swinging wildly after the tractor stopped. The gunfire toward her position stopped, but the firefight still raged around her. She gauged the distance to Connor as she broke cover. Out in the open, she instantly drew gunfire. Laura sprinted across the field and, in a single leap, reached the tractor's flailing door and climbed inside. She hit the control arm that lowered Evans to the ground as a stray bullet from one of Ikeda's men caught her in her hip, making her fall to the ground, grimacing in pain. She tumbled off the ladder onto her back, crying out.

Chapter 31

Evans's feet had barely touched the ground before he was into action, noting the carnage around him. All he could hear was gunfire, and he had only one answer to the cacophony: William.

Laura's desperate action saved him from certain death. He threw himself under the tractor's wheels, wary that it was still running, while the cogs in his mind turned. Peeking around the large rear wheels, he noted the gunfire was directed away from them. Laura, rolling in the dirt with the bullet embedded in her hip, groaning in pain, stoked an anger within him he hadn't felt in a long time.

Knowing what he needed to do, he ducked out and grabbed Laura's arms, dragging her behind the tractor. Jiro had disappeared, leaving his men to face the music.

Connor leaned Laura against a wheel as a masked man ran at them wielding a katana and screaming in Japanese. Connor covered Laura, but the man tumbled forward at the last second, sprawling in the dirt. Connor, sighing in relief, knew who to thank for that one. Though the Honourable Ones were professionals, skilled in the art of ancient and modern warfare, nothing could remove the fear a lone sniper presented on the battlefield. It created a fear deep enough to shake even the most unmovable of hostile forces. Today, that fear was caused by one man: Janus. The Latvian was positioned in the stealth chopper flown by Chapman, swinging around the battlefield. The elite force that Kenji and Jiro had brought together remained steadfast despite the clash between both sides, not giving an inch. Evans grabbed the Uzi strapped to the dead man on the ground near them.

This is getting out of hand. We are running out of time… Connor thought.

* * *

"Keep moving, fellas. The sooner we get to the commander, the sooner we all get paid. First round of Toohey's is on me when we get back home," Will yelled. A few of his men admonished him for suggesting the beverage, offering better options over the internal coms. William smiled. He was in his element, as he and his men raced toward their commander's position.

"I've got Connor in my sights, Will. Situated behind a tractor parked on the northeast side of the clearing," Chapman reported. Janus continued to pick off any strays close to Connor's position.

"Good, lets finish this now," William acknowledged, signalling for his men to push forward.

* * *

Evans, unaware of William's imminent arrival, tagged another of the masked men who dared to push toward the tractor. He glanced over at Laura, her hip bleeding profusely as she pushed a piece of ripped fabric from Connor's shirt onto the wound. As much as Evans wanted to pursue Jiro and find Kenji, he owed it to Laura to keep her safe until help arrived. He was sure she would do the same for him.

"Don't be a fool, Connor. Leave me here, I can protect myself," she said, coughing.

He peeled back the bloodied rag, seeing the wound still seeping. Without medical attention, he guessed she would soon pass out from blood loss. And until she got that attention, they wouldn't know how much damage the bullet had done.

"I won't leave you, although we didn't start this together. We are in this together now, whether you like it or not," he replied in frustration. He was breathing heavily, a mixture of fear and adrenaline pounding through him.

"I should be okay," she said, grimacing with pain as she attempted to move. "On second thought, maybe not. Pass me a weapon to cover you. I take it you have a plan this time?"

Evans grinned, tasting blood as it ran down the side of his head.

"A flesh wound," he said. "You're telling me you have a plan?" Connor's tone was incredulous.

"Yeah, I shoot, and you run," she said. Her face was whiter than before. Evans knew they were running out of time.

"We need to level the playing field," he said. "We can use the jet on the far side of the clearing for better cover. One entrance in and out. We just have to get there first."

He spied the camouflaged nettings protecting key areas around the clearing, attached to metal poles that raised and stretched the nettings tight. Connor began to understand how the Honourable Ones had remained undetected for so long. Connor had to give Jiro and his men credit. They had made the area almost invisible from the air. Now, though, Jiro had made a mistake. With the tractor parked on the material, the netting couldn't hide their island sanctuary, giving Connor and his team above complete access to the clearing.

He knew what needed to be done. He looked at Laura, "I won't leave you for long, but there's something I need to do. You sure you'll be safe here?"

She nodded. "Just come back to me," she replied. Her green eyes seemed to say something else.

He grabbed the other submachine beside Laura. He checked the magazine and, without looking back at her, moved out of cover. His target was the vehicle depot, and the ATV parked inside. He ran as hard as he could, feet thudding hard on the grass. A change of plans arose when two masked men emerged from the garage, likely from the facility below. Almost out of luck, Connor threw himself into the door, hoping it wouldn't be locked.

Evans didn't hesitate when the man sitting before the radio console, and he rose quickly to his feet. Kicking the door shut behind him, he slammed the butt of gun into the man's face. Though Connor was quick, the masked soldier was quicker, drawing his pistol. Connor slapped the operator's arm away, a wild shot flying into the log roof. He threw the man to the ground and grabbed the microphone, dialling the knobs to a specific frequency.

"Connor to Sky One, Connor to Sky One, do you copy?"

Silence was his answer. Evans knew he only had seconds before the soldiers from the garage burst inside his hiding place,

"Connor to Sky One, do you copy?" he called again. No response. About to try a third time, Chapman's voice came through.

"Sky one copies. Sorry, Boss, a bit of a situation up here. Where do you need me?"

Connor figured Southgate would have split his force to reach him. The only problem was, William had no idea where he was.

Evans didn't get a chance to reply as the door burst open, one of the masked soldiers appearing. Evans raised the operator's pistol, and double tapped the intruder.

Evans hoped the pistol had the full seven rounds in its clip as dropped the next man to come through the door. He wasn't sure how many men were in the area, but it didn't matter. All that mattered right now was finding the ambassador and stopping Ikeda from escaping.

He peered through the open door, now pockmarked with bullet holes. The firefight still raged around him. He spied Jiro moving toward the brick building. Seconds later, Connor witnessed the clearing around him come alive.

The camouflaged netting, that had been placed across the clearing during the day, was still active from opposing corners of the clearing keeping the fight hidden from above. If he didn't find a way to bring it down, Chapman and Janus would be blocked from landing or providing aerial support further helping William and his boys. Their primary target was the camouflaged netting, his was Jiro.

Jiro appeared from the building and ran into the garage next to it, out of Connor's view. Evans swapped the pistol for the submachine gun and aimed at the spot where he expected Jiro to drive out. A barrage of gunfire battered the door, forcing him back inside, missing his chance to catch Jiro. The man sped out of the garage and, turning in a wide arc, raced into the darkened forest. Connor saw the flickering headlights as it bounced over the dirt trails and into the distance. He felt a mixture of frustration and personal anguish as the man who would lead him to Kenji escaped their grasp.

An explosion rocked the forest, lighting up the clearing, and gunfire could be heard from the tree line. Evans raised his gun, as two of William's team appeared from the forest. He called out to them. Recognizing his voice, one of the soldiers approached. Evans couldn't remember his name, but the man informed him that the rest of the team were making steady progress and would soon have the area surrounded.

Evans asked for the soldier's radio. He had much to report. He started with Will.

"Will, this is Connor. Haul arse to the cargo containers near the buildings, I need confirmation on their contents, they could come in handy."

"Roger boss don't wait up on me now," came Will's response.

He shifted his attention back to his task,

"Sky One, this is Connor. I need a ride, over," Evans said.

"Sky One copies," Chapman responded. "Get to a position where I can set down, Boss." Connor couldn't see, due to the encroaching netting overhead, as Chapman flew a large circle around the ongoing battle, Southgate's task-force slowly encircling Jiro's forces.

* * *

Will and two of his men, kept firing from their position as they steadily moved to the containers Connor had mentioned. It wasn't like Connor to change orders unless something had come up. His sudden interest in the containers were either a good or a bad thing. Either way Will did as he was ordered progressing slowly as he took a moment to glance above and see Chapman swing around above.

After disposing of two of the Honourable One's men guarding them, he looked at the front of the nearest container. The paint was faded and peeling, it had seen its fair share of sun and water judging by its outward appearance, but what was inside was the greatest mystery. Will noted the padlock on the front and shot it off in a single burst of gunfire.

He ordered both of his men to heave the doors open and as they opened, he clicked on the flashlight on the underside of his gun barrel shining it into its dark interior. The light dancing over miltary hardware he didn't expect to see in the middle of the island.

Keying his mic, he knew Connor would want to hear about this.

Chapter 32

A frustrated Kelly heard Evans call over the team frequency. Whilst she was safe on the *Serenity*, she knew William and his men were putting their lives on the line to get to the ambassador and rescue Connor.

The incoming live feed from Chapman's helicopter as it circled the battle below highlighted the presence of an aircraft that sounded awfully like the government jet they were after, partially hidden under the camouflaged netting. Kelly had already run the serial numbers and passed them onto the soldiers' minicomputers and was waiting for confirmation.

The action below surely attracted the attention of the local police, but they were likely bought off by Kenji. Kelly had ordered two soldiers to block off the road and tell local law enforcement they were performing military exercises in the area. It was a half-baked excuse, but Kelly hoped it would buy them enough time to get the job done and get out. As part of the operation, Evans had requested William's soldiers' guns be loaded with foreign ammunition, Southgate issuing orders for his men to drop their own weapons and use the enemies, if need be.

Chapman's voice sounded over the intercom.

"Kelly, you're going to want to see this."

"What do you have for me?" she asked. She unfolded her legs from their usually crossed position, and now tapped one knee impatiently.

Chapman had sent the newly recharged drone overhead, toggling it to autopilot to provide a steady stream of data helping the soldiers below pinpoint enemy positions. The drone also served as a secondary live feed to the team onboard the *Serenity*. One of Kelly's team sat in front of it, keeping an eye on any reinforcements from other areas of the island.

Kelly saw the fleeing ATV follow the dirt trails through the jungle, kicking up dirt.

"Switch to thermal, see if you can get a read on the driver," she asked the female at the drone console.

Kelly pushed a button. "William, where are we on the ambassador and Connor? I need a reason why we are blowing up an island off the coast of Japan, or I will have some serious diplomatic issues on my hands once Daniels catches wind of this."

"No current location on the ambassador," said William. "We haven't seen anyone leave except for the lone jeep. We will keep looking. "Be advised, we have switched off the netting extension. Kenji's forces have taken heavy casualties, I repeat, heavy casualties. Drone marks no more than six left standing, over, can you confirm?" he asked.

Kelly confirmed from the drone operator beside her that there were few men left to contend with, the gunfire on the island tapering off to near silence. The chopper blades of Chapman were the only disturbance in the quiet clearing.

With the stretched netting's progress halted, Chapman took the opportunity to land. With the last of Kenji's forces surrendering, Connor climbed aboard, accepting a rifle thrown at him by one of the soldiers. Before he stepped inside, he instructed his men to attend to Laura behind the tractor, hoping deep down she was alright.

Chapman immediately rose back to his previous altitude, throwing Evans into the side of the helicopter during the manoeuvre. Evans cursed, reaching for a clip to hook into the back of his pants.

"Kelly," Evans radioed, "I need a read on the leader of these forces - Jiro. Chapman and I are giving chase. Once Will and his boys have locked down the site and found the ambassador, I need them to haul ass to my position. This isn't over yet."

Kelly tracked them, as the drone operator next to her locked onto Jiro's face to begin the facial recognition scan through Interpol's databases.

"Target is currently heading northeast deeper into the jungle. Rough estimates show he could be taking any of a dozen of the local passes for hikers or off roaders. Either way, the man is heading for the coast and not further inland."

"That's good news," Evans said over the comms. "I was told a campground is situated within the crater. We can't risk any harm to the populace on the island. If the ATV is heading out to the coast, we can take Jiro where there is no one around to get in the way."

"Who's your source on that?" Kelly questioned. This was news to her.

"It's a long story," Evans replied, his tone enough for Kelly not to push back. There would be time enough later.

Kelly tapped a few keys on the keyboard and the camera on the underbelly of the helicopter displayed a panoramic image, as the helicopter blazed over the jungle in pursuit of Jiro.

Chapman saw the flashing lights first, calling out to Evans, who was too busy tracing the bouncing lights of the ATV below to notice. Two heavily armed military helicopters were coming at them fast. They looked like Apaches, likely equipped with heat-seeking missiles, something Chapman knew they wouldn't be able to escape. Smoke erupted from one of them as they thundered closer, and his eyes widened in fear.

"Incoming missiles, Boss. Hold onto something, this is going to get bumpy real fast," Chapman said. He pushed the helicopter into a nosedive, and Evans was thrown around the back, items normally tucked away flying around with him as he was rocked back and forth.

The missile trailed them as Chapman wrestled with the small helicopter's controls, the dials spinning counterclockwise as they dropped. Evans, gritting his teeth, pulled himself into the co-pilot's seat.

"Now might be a good time to pop the flares on this baby, don't you think?" Evans said, as Chapman looked at him, speechless.

"This model doesn't have the flares; the Robinson was modified to carry them instead," he replied, his demeanour more erratic than ever before. Evans looked at him like he had said something crazy, a thin smile creeping across his face.

"Good thing I'm the one that thinks of such things," Evans said, flipping a switch Chapman couldn't see, jettisoning flares out behind them as the missile exploded metres from the tail rotor. The blast buffeted the little helicopter, the concussion wave pushing them forward before Chapman levelled them out.

Another backblast erupted from the second helicopter as Chapman performed further evasive manoeuvres to dodge away from its fiery wake. Evans ejected more flares, and the second missile missed its mark as well.

Chapman guessed another would soon be on the way. He turned to Evans.

"We can't go on like this forever. We need to take these guys out. I only have the mini guns. We're out of missiles. I used them to help Will when we first broke through."

"You've never let me down yet, Chapman, let's see your piloting skills at full throttle."

Chapman nodded, steeling himself to fly even lower before the next missile caught them

Evans keyed their comms, speaking to William on the ground.

"Are they ready?" he asked.

Chapman banked hard and continued their run low over the trees.

"On my go, Chapman, pull up hard," Evans said.

As expected, the military choppers gave chase in single file, following Chapman's trajectory, matching his altitude.

"Pull up now!" Evans shouted. Chapman pulled the nose up as far as it would go, pinning both men to their seats.

Evans triggered the comms. "Give them hell Will," he said.

Several backblasts fired out of the shipping containers positioned around the government jet, arcing toward the helicopters who, despite dropping flares, were too slow to pull away. Both took successive hits, exploding in the sky and raining debris on the jungles below.

"What the hell?" was all Chapman could say as he looked over his shoulder at the balls of flame. Blackened and charred hulls dropped to the jungle. "How did you—'

Evans chuckled. "When I was dragged toward the jet, I noticed soldiers near the containers. When I was pinned down behind the tractor, I managed to get a look into one. Why SAM turrets are located here is anyone's guess, but I bet they never thought they would be used against their own."

With the sky now empty, they resumed tracking Jiro's ATV as it continued through the jungle, close to the coastline. Onboard the *Serenity*, Kelly instructed the drone operator to relay the direction and speed of the jeep, allowing Chapman to stalk it from above, like a vulture waiting for a kill.

Jiro's ATV bounced out of the jungle and onto the asphalt coastal roads. The crashing waves far below made him look like an ant clinging to the side of the steep, jagged cliff faces. Evans climbed back into the rear of the helicopter, examining the mess left after Chapman's evasive manoeuvres.

He grabbed a rifle from a hook on one of the overhead racks. The wind whipped around him as they accelerated.

"Get me closer," he said into the headset. Chapman replied by pulling the chopper closer to the cliffs, the ATV continuing along the roads. Looking down the thermal sights of the rifle, Evans considered leaving the man to his own devices. The state of the roads combined with Jiro's speed had the potential send the man careening over the edge. He might not even have to pull the trigger. Wind buffeted the chopper as Evans tried to line up the shot.

"Sorry, Boss, the wind is something else. It is coming off the surf and pushing me into the cliffs. I can't hug them too close, otherwise we'll end up smeared all over the cliff face," Chapman said.

Not the greatest of images, Evans thought. He trusted in Chapman's judgement

"Do the best you can, just keep him in our vision," Evans replied, shouting over the wind.

Connor wished Janus was here to take the shot. The sniper made it look easy. It looked near impossible where he was sitting, and an assault rifle wasn't going to cut it. As he looked down the optic, he knew he need to make the decision.

"I can't take the shot. We will only end up pancaked against the cliff. Chapman, pull back. We will regroup and track him through the drone."

Chapman looked over his shoulder, making sure he had heard Evans correctly.

"Are you sure, Boss? He is right there," Chapman pointed as the jeep continued to fly along the coast road at breakneck speed.

Evans acknowledged he was certain. He was exhausted at getting so close, but not being able to make the shot without putting Chapman at risk.

"*Serenity*, this is Connor. Keep a firm lock on the ATV with the drone. We are heading back," he said

Kelly keyed the intercom, mystified,

"Are you sure, Connor? You had him."

"We won't let him get away. We will get another shot. If he thinks lost him, Jiro might lead us straight to the head honcho himself."

* * *

Kelly tried to understand Connor's reasoning but couldn't figure why their commander had let Jiro go. It wasn't practical in the slightest, given how much William's boys had sacrificed to make it possible. Already, they were unsure of where Kenji was now, as well as the location of the bombs. It seemed that Evans was trying for a hail Mary and Kelly hoped it would pay off. She glanced up at the digital timer on the main screen. *Six hours remaining.*

Part Four:
For Honour and Glory

Chapter 33

The *Serenity* remained at anchor off the coast of the Izu Islands, as the beating blades of the helicopter signalled its return to the helipad at its bow. Evans sat silently in the rear of the chopper, clutching the assault rifle tightly, taking several deep breaths to control his own emotions.

"You alright, Boss?" Chapman asked, keeping his attention on the controls as he descended to the helipad.

Evans didn't reply, leaving Chapman to draw his own conclusions. He trusted Connor, no matter what. The call had been made. Whether he agreed with it was another thing entirely. Chapman knew the man would be deeply conflicted, but he wasn't sure how he could help.

"I just need to wrap my head around the situation, is all," said Evans. "We have less than six hours left on the clock."

Evans looked out at the churning ocean. In the distance, the sun painted a watercolour of oranges and pinks as it slowly sunk in the sky, revealing dark grey clouds. He pulled open the rear door as one of the crew approached the whipping blades, which grabbed at his clothes with invisible hands.

"Has anyone else returned yet?" Evans asked as the crewman shook his head. Evans thanked him as the man prised the gun from his grip. He'd forgotten he was still holding it. The heat of the day rose from the asphalt underfoot into his dive shoes as he entered the interior of the yacht, heading to the Hub.

Rather than risk shooting Jiro, he had made the executive decision to allow the man to live. Instead of returning to the clearing, Evans had decided he was needed back onboard the *Serenity* to plan their next move. Kelly had contacted the local police, deterring them from approaching the scene until they had cleaned up the area.

Evans entered the Hub to applause from his crew for a job well done. Yet he felt he had nothing to celebrate. Not yet anyway. Chapman had taken off again to assist with the retrieval of the ambassador, who had been found safe and sound. William had found him imprisoned in the third cabin on the farm, along with several young children, and two adults. They had yet to break into the facility, but Connor doubted the missiles would be there. Kenji was an elusive military genius, one Connor had not yet bested. By the time Connor and his team had arrived, they would have been shipped off again.

Chapman would bring the ambassador back to the yacht along with Laura, who was going to debrief him on the way back. William's medics had checked her over and found that the bullet had passed cleanly through her leg. Connor believed she would be doing paperwork for some time before returning to the field. It would keep her out of harm's way, but he couldn't imagine it would hold her down for long. She had an attitude and a mind that needed to be out in the field.

Several minutes later, the senior members of Darke Company sat around the conference table. Evans went around the room, listening to every situational report. With Davidson now safe, a burden had been removed from Connor's shoulders. He was glad that Daniels would leave him be. The relieved politician had been told the good news about Davidson before Connor had arrived

Evans was the most attentive to Kurt's report. Kenji had returned to the mainland, the former CIA operative trailing him outside of Tokyo. Local reports had begun pouring in about military action on the island.

Tori had already liaised with the Japanese consulate on the actions on Aogishima Island. Though tight lipped on the matter, they were surprised to hear of Kenji's actions, and of the private security force located there. Evans knew Kenji would be more dangerous than ever, backed into a corner without his security force. It was sheer luck that - wherever the missiles were - they hadn't been set off. Kelly added that Daniels would likely be in contact on the matter of discretion during their search and rescue operation, especially as missiles and gunfire were meant to be kept to a minimum. Evans had asked that information to be omitted during their conversation about the ambassador earlier.

Connor remained seated after the meeting finished, asking Kelly and Chapman to remain behind.

"We need to be smart on the next step of the operation. Kenji will be reckless now. Losing his ace in the hole will no doubt have repercussions. Chapman, reach out to Kurt. Whatever he needs, get it for him, no matter the cost. Once you've done that, take Janus and finish this." Chapman nodded, clapping him on the shoulder and squeezing it as he left the room.

Kelly sat in front of Evans, her curious eyes looking at his, trying to figure out what was going on in his mind.

"Kelly, I need you to take over for a bit. I fell through the cracks on this one when chasing down Jiro. I couldn't take the shot.

Kelly shifted closer and clutched his hand, looking at him. "Nothing can ever prepare you for what happens in the field, Connor, we all know that. You may have missed the shot, but we won the battle, and will soon win the war. You must remember you can't control everything that goes on, but you can trust that we are with you every step of the way. No man is an island, just you remember that" she said, her calm voice allowing him to work through what she was saying.

"Thanks Kelly, I needed to hear that."

A voice over the intercom called him down to the medical bay. "Duty calls," he said, withdrawing his hand. Connor didn't see Kelly's eyes mist over as she watched him go.

Connor left the room in better spirits than before, and took the stairs down to the middle level, striding toward the medical bay, a part of the yacht he generally didn't visit. Double swing doors marked the entry point, and it gave Connor the chills, feeling like he was stepping into a morgue. The combination of the clinical finish of the white floor and tile, along with the smell of bleach, assailed his senses. Inside the room, medical instruments lay on a stainless-steel table near one of several beds. The female doctor was bent over a bed, speaking to Laura, who was sitting up on the clean, white sheets.

The doctor gave him a look, that told him that his visit would have to be brief before would interrupt him to continue her work.

"You held your own out there today," Evans said, once the doctor had disappeared into her office. He looked at the caked blood and dirt smeared across her normally unblemished face.

"You didn't do so bad yourself, cowboy. I saw your moves out there. Some would think you like this kind of thing," she said, with a smile that made her eyes shine.

Evans pulled up a chair and sat down, cupping his hands around his face, feeling the residue of the day clinging to it. He had not yet changed from his torn clothes. Laura's own clothing had been removed, and wore a plain hospital garment

"Sometimes you have no choice. You just do what you need to do out there. It becomes second nature; at least that what my father used to tell me." He felt raw emotion gripp his heart then. Laura sensed the change in his normal demeanour, leaning forward, then biting her tongue at the pain radiating from her hip.

"Your father must mean a lot to you," she replied, choosing her words carefully. "He must be really proud of what you do."

Evans stood up, eyes bloodshot as he looked down at her wound. "I'm sure he would be, wherever he is," he replied.

Laura caught the hint and didn't push him, instead changing the topic.

"Did you get Ikeda?" she asked, fire burning in her emerald, green eyes.

Evans shook his head, ashamed, "I didn't take the shot when I had the chance. Hesitation in the field gets not just you, but your friends killed. I haven't locked up like this in a while."

Laura looked at him, the burning fire in her eyes cooling.

"It happens to the best of us. We can't control how we react to every situation out there," she said, tilting her head. "We can only control how we pick ourselves back up again if we fall."

Evans smiled. He was glad she understood the shame he felt. Even in her condition, she wanted to make him feel better.

"You've got a heck of a setup here. How you've managed to pull this to-gether, I'll never understand," she said.

Evans grinned as he heard the awe in her voice.

"Now that's a secret you'll never know." His response ensured she wouldn't pry further.

"I do have one further question, if you can indulge me," she said. Evans saw a spark of mischief in her eyes. "Can I get some food in this place? I am starving."

Evans was silent for a moment, keeping her in suspense before nodding. He saw her eyes go wide with delight.

"Well, I am dying for some chocolate cake. I have a serious craving for it, and maybe something oriental. I haven't had noodles in so long."

Evans clicked a button beside her bed, which lit up with the words *Room Service*. Laura's eyes were still shining, glad that food would soon be on its way.

"I think I will leave you be," said Connor. "Ambassador Davidson will be arriving shortly, and I best clean myself up before he does."

Laura waved her hand for him to come closer, planting a light kiss on his lips as he did, before leaning back.

"Thank you for saving me," she said. "Again, that is," she added.

"Our goal is to save lives, not end them, unless we have no other choice in the matter," he replied, getting an inkling where the conversation was heading. "And, before you ask, it's always been that way, ever since the organisation was formed."

"As I said to you before, I had never heard of you or your team before this all went down. Why do you keep yourselves in the shadows?" she asked.

"Most of my team have families, and anonymity prevents anyone we go after from making it personal and getting to us that way," he replied.

"Do you just protect Australia from its enemies or are you loyal to just anyone?" the question catching him off guard. Laura had honed straight in on the dilemma he had always faced.

"I have no greater sense of loyalty than to the country I call home, but my team aren't all Australian born. They come from various nationalities, if you haven't worked it out yet, leading to their own loyalties. There are no divisions among my team, and we respect on another's differences. You have met most of them by now and would've seen that in action."

Laura said nothing, waiting for him to continue.

"In answer to the second part of your question," he said, "we work for whoever pays us most of the time. In saying that, we don't take jobs that go against our own principles. We don't work for warlords, dictators, or anyone that doesn't care about justice."

Laura nodded thoughtfully. "Are you saying that not all world governments care about justice?" she asked, drawing him into a debatable topic.

"Maybe not. There are two sides to every coin," he replied, "but I apply discretion when accepting such missions. It's not just my decision, but that of my team."

Laura smiled, taking his hand. She contemplated his words, analysing them. "Curiosity is part of my nature," she said. "I'm sure I am not the only one who has been involved in all of this and felt the same

"So, what happens next?" Laura asked.

"I have a theory - several actually - on where Kenji might be, but all of them have pros and cons."

"What do you mean?" she asked.

Evans held up a finger, disappearing into a storage room. He rummaged around before returning to her bedside with a small laptop. "Don't tell Kelly, but this is her spare. What she doesn't know won't bother her, I'm sure."

Booting up the laptop, he logged into Kelly's recent plot charts for where Kenji may have moved the missiles. Many of them lay offshore among the numerous island chains around the East China Sea. Two were situated on the Japanese mainland.

As Evans began his breakdown of each plot position, a knock interrupted him. Tori's head poked around the polished silver door.

"Sorry to interrupt, Connor. Just thought you should know the ambassador is back onboard and waiting to chat with you… when you have a minute, of course." She flashed a smile at him.

Evans gave Tori a disapproving look but thanked her as she ducked back out the door.

"We can discuss this later," said Laura. "Best go back to saving the world, *Commander Evans*." Laura had evidently caught the interaction between him and Tori.

Evans closed the laptop and headed for the door, where he nearly collided with one of the kitchen crew, carrying a small notepad.

"Careful in there, she's ravenous," he said. "Write quickly or she might take your hand off." He smiled broadly at the confused expression on the young woman's face, before she walked inside.

Chapter 34

With the ambassador onboard, they could focus solely on Kenji and the bombs he planned to unleash. Evans had his team racing to locate them. With Kurt in pursuit of Kenji now, it was only a matter of time.

He bumped into Kelly as he raced toward the interrogation room. She clutched her tablet to her chest, like a student with textbooks, as he made to sidestep her.

"Whoa, there should be a speed limit on how fast you can walk here," she said, narrowly missing falling into him.

"Sorry, Kell, I have so a lot going on in my mind right now. I take it you're looking for me?"

She nodded. "Yes. I figured you were with Laura, so I thought I would give you some time with her before catching you on your way to the ambassador." She spoke in a hurry, her cheeks reddening as she mentioned Laura.

"We may have a huge problem," she continued. "William is still on the island looking over the underground facility. His men have rounded up several scientists and someone we believe is Shinigami. But that's not all. He plugged me into the facility's communications array. While you were busy, I tracked the frequency of the transmissions that went out several hours prior to our island assault. One transmission sought clearance for the 'assets' to be moved from Tokyo."

"No clues for guessing what the assets are. Good work, Kelly," Connor said appreciatively.

"Also, the drone you ordered to track Jiro has pinpointed the south end of the island. Seems Ikeda may never have left," said Kelly.

"Tell the operator to recon the location for Janus and Chapman. Where is Jiro holed up exactly

Kelly opened her laptop, pivoting it on her palm, showing two photos.

"The photo on the left was a year ago. Notice the construction and logging teams in the area. They match what you found on the servers. I found a payment to a local Japanese company. It didn't detail what it was for, but the picture on the right will fill you in."

Connor shifted his gaze from the clearing on the south-eastern part of the island to the fully constructed facility, with cement silos and oil tanks.

"I'll let you have a crack at who's responsible for the construction on the island?" Kelly said.

Connor looked between the two photos, "Let Chapman know as soon as possible."

Kelly nodded, not finished. "One more thing. It wasn't the only payment sent via a Swiss bank account."

Connor raised an eyebrow, waiting.

"On the mainland, Kenji recently acquired a port terminal from a rival company via a shell company located in Kobe. They have a private berth there, if you catch my drift?"

"*Wash away the sins*. Jesus, of course. Kelly, you are a genius. Run it by the team. Let Kurt know about the port, and that Kenji is likely making a play for it. Let's nail him there."

Leaving Kelly to relay the information to the rest of the team, Evans headed for the cabin that Davidson was waiting in, knocking on the door. The older man's voice permitted him entry.

The ambassador had cleaned himself up, and had his wounds attended to by the medical team. His only obvious injuries were a bruise under his left eye and a laceration on his right cheek. They were the only bruises Connor could see. The ambassador's suit jacket was thrown aside, his tie loosened, and his white shirt sleeves rolled up to the elbow, revealing the site of a blood test. His team would be testing for any form or blood poisoning or neurotoxin.

The ambassador rose to his full height as Evans walked into the room. "Whoever you are, I demand you release me right now," he said with all the authority he could muster.

"Listen, Ambassador, you can't pretend you have authority here. You're under my charge, so what I say, goes."

Davidson's expression was wary but alert. "There is no need to worry about who we are," said Evans. "Just know you are safe. You are under our protection, and that of the Australian government."

The ambassador's expression changed from wary to confused. "You work for our government?"

Evans shook his head, "Not exactly. But that's beside the point. We were tasked with finding and rescuing you. Soon, you'll be back in your beloved Japan continuing your previous assignment or returning on the first chartered flight to Australia."

Davidson sat back down on the edge of the cabin's inset bed, leaning forward and rubbing his eyes. "Who tasked you to find me?"

Evans grabbed a chair near a small desk in the room and sat on it, leaning forward. "George Daniels," he replied.

Davidson smiled thinly. "Sounds about right. The big man will probably gloat about finding me, too. Has this hit the media yet?"

Evans shook his head. "Not yet. Media suppression has been active since you went missing, though I doubt what we had to do to find you failed to make the news."

Davidson gave him an incredulous look. Evans waved his hand to disregard the comment.

"Though you don't know me and my team, Ambassador, I need to know one thing. What reason would someone have to kidnap you?"

Davidson had likely had more than enough time to think about that throughout his ordeal.

"I ensure the dialogue between Japan and Australia remains peaceful, so we see eye to eye on global affairs. Japan's strategic location for us is what Cuba was to the Soviets in '62. I was meant to attend the quasi-dialogue summit in Tokyo. On the agenda was the discussion around nuclear warfare and its place in Pacific region.

Evans thought about what Yates had said earlier, the ambassador only confirming what the stubborn American had suggested. "Someone saw fit to prevent you from attending, someone from the very country you are working alongside. What do you know of Toyotami Industries?"

Davidson nodded. "One of our biggest critics for the summit. The CEO believed it would remove domestic opportunities, allowing for the rise of American weapons in the Japanese military. The very idea was preposterous, but Toyotami wouldn't back down. He said he would fight tooth and nail for this not to occur."

"I met Hiroto Toyotami," said Evans. "He struck me as more of a traditionalist. He didn't sound like he opposed the idea but was undecided."

Davidson sat up straight, his eyebrows raised. "I was referring to the son, Kenji, not the father. Kenji struck me as someone that would do whatever it took to get his way. I planned to present my objections to the summit over Kenji being allowed to dissuade his own government in the matter."

"Well, it appears we share a common enemy. He not only took a swing at you, Ambassador, but had a go at me and my team as well. Fortunately for you, I won't let that type of thing slide easily." Despite Connor's even tone, the malice underlying his words was obvious.

"In an attempt to prove Japan's strength, and but also its advances in technology, we believe Kenji Toyotami is going to unleash a doomsday device on parts of the Pacific," said Evans. "This will pave the way for his private army - the Honourable Ones - who took you hostage, to create a new version of the Japanese empire first attempted a in 1942."

The look of shock on Davidson's face was the confirmation Evans needed. The very real prospect that something other than a nuclear device could cause untold destruction was terrifying. *If the ambassador was not aware of these weapons, then how many others were blind to such things?*

* * *

The rotor blades spooled up, whipping the air into a frenzy as Chapman prepped the helicopter for another take-off. Janus walked calmly out of the interior of the yacht, breathing in the cool night air. He carefully placed his rifle in the back as Chapman continued his preflight checks. He had bags under his eyes from that day's sustained level of concentration.

"Boss says we have an easy catch tonight," said Chapman. Janus ignored his quip and climbed into the front of the chopper. Chapman shrugged, glad he didn't have to make small talk, his own weariness sapping his normal ability to fill the silence. Chapman knew Janus was focusing before the mission and said nothing further as they lifted off from the tarmac, looping around toward the southeast part of the distant island.

"Sky One, this is *Serenity*, we have you less than a kilometre from land. The compound is located toward the southeast, nestled among the rocks. The past few hours have shown little movement. Four buildings, two storage sheds, and three vehicles are stationed there, including the ATV that Kenji's henchman, Jiro Ikeda, escaped on."

Janus moved from the front of the chopper to the rear while the intercom sounded in their headphones. He unzipped his rifle case, pulling the sniper rifle from its bag, looking across at the empty bench where Evans had been seated earlier. With the chopper's interior empty, Janus was free to lay his rifle at his feet and close his eyes, taking a few deep breaths before picking it up and holding it loosely on his lap.

Chapman kept his eyes fixed on the distance, the incoming storm lighting up the sky.

"Kelly, got scans on anyone inside the buildings yet?"

Kelly signalled the drone operator. "Scans indicate ten men holed up in the buildings."

"Not as many as we thought, but given the fear of god Evans put in Jiro, can you blame them?" Chapman replied.

Janus grunted in the rear of the helicopter, hefting his rifle, before saying, "Leave them to me. Kelly, is the only option for elimination from the air? Can we not get boots on the ground? Are Will's boys still available for this?"

"Negative, Will's boys are currently working with authorities. It's you or nothing."

"Makes sense. Last I checked my kill count on these missions was higher than all of Will's boys put together."

Janus didn't hear Kelly gag at his comment. She was incapable of pulling a trigger, working behind the scenes to avoid such an unscrupulous task.

"Seems the only entrance is the road Jiro took," said Chapman. "Appears there may have been another road at one point. I'd say Mother Nature took care of that for us: a landslide appears to have taken it out."

Janus slammed home the magazine and racked the rifle's chamber. "Civilians onsite?"

There was a delay before Kelly replied. "Nothing on scans. Thermal shows all holding weapons. Most of the civilian populace is located on the other end of the island. It's at your discretion, Janus, you know the drill." Janus Kelly didn't have to tell hm twice.

Chapman interrupted the conversation,

"Have to cut the chatter now, Kelly. Janus, you ready?"

Janus looked down his thermal sights, making some last-minute adjustments. He just needed to pick his targets, and the rest would follow. He hoped the rain would hold off long enough for him to eliminate their target.

"Preparing to silence engine, blades going quiet," Chapman said, as he flipped a switch over his head. The rotor blades' scream died, leaving behind a solemn quiet.

Janus clipped himself in, then slid open the rear door. *It's a bloody long way down*, he thought.

"Keep her steady, Chapman, I need time to recon the area and pick my targets," he said.

Chapman didn't reply, once more respecting the man's focus as he observed the compound a few hundred metres to their west. He held her steady, a slight headwind buffeting them, but nothing to worry about at.

Janus looked through his sight as he kneeled, the dark night turning to a fuzzy white and grey. He clicked a small device on the side of the sniper rifle, relaying a high-definition live feed to Kelly and the team on the *Serenity*. "Kelly, are you getting this?"

"Clear as can be," Kelly replied. Evans stood behind her, arms crossed, a neutral expression on his face.

"I see the three vehicles," said Janus. "All ground based. I see signs of movement below. I count two well-armed personnel walking along the waterline. No other sign of movement nearby. Will proceed on your go, *Serenity*."

Suddenly, a surge of updraft caught them, surprising Chapman as he struggled to right the helicopter. The wash off the blades made Janus fall backward against the bench.

"Jesus, Chapman, you have one job. Make sure the chopper's steady. Don't make me wring your bloody neck. Only one person is supposed to die tonight."

Chapman didn't reply, gritting his teeth as the craft steadied.

With the chopper in position, allowing full access to the compound below, he put his eye back to the scope, and swept it once more through the world of white and grey.

Evans saw it first.

"Janus, shift your focus right to the second warehouse, see if you can zoom in closer to the roller door."

Janus followed the directions, setting his sights on the roller door as a beam of light appeared underneath it. The door rolled open, then the light vanished. The compound was illuminated by several smaller lights that weren't bright enough to mess with Janus's optic.

"Hold right there," came Evan's voice, sharp in his ear.

Janus immediately saw what Evans saw. Nestled in the warehouse were four torpedo trolleys, empty of cargo. Enough evidence that the bombs may have been there at some point.

"Find Jiro," said Evans, "and eliminate him. That's an order."

Janus shifted his focus, scanning each building methodically with surgeon-like precision.

"Got him," said Evans. "Target is northeast of current location in a two-storey building near the cranes of the compound."

A few drops of rain spattered Janus's reticule, and he wiped it clean with his shirt sleeve. In seconds, the rain got heavier. He shifted his zoom, the reticule covering the distance before settling on the two-storey building. Shifting position slightly, he noted the crane. "First or second building?" he asked.

"Second," said Evans, "dead centre. Appears to be standing still, maybe on a phone call. Who can tell—" The rifle thumped back into Janus 'shoulder before he could finish.

Though suppressed, it could be heard through the intercom like a muffled thump, as the bullet coursed through the air and the thin metal of the building's upper level. Burning a hole through the steel, it ripped into the soft flesh at the base of Jiro Ikeda's skull, killing him instantly. The bullet slicing through the metal like paper leaving a small 'o' ring no more than a few millimetres to tell the story of Jiro's death. The guards on the waterline moved quickly. Their shouts alerted all within the compound, and spotlights flashed on, illuminating the compound like a football stadium on game day. The crowd of men looked like ants through Janus's scope. He thought of himself as the kid who burns ants with a magnifying glass from far above them. He could see the fear on one of the guard's faces as he gesticulated toward a shipping container that Janus had only just noticed himself.

"Chapman, shift right. I don't like the look of one of that shipping container toward the rear." Chapman did as he was asked. No sooner than he shifted, the fake shipping container dropped its sides, the presence of the Surface to Air Missile turret caught them both off-guard.

Janus didn't speak, instead taking aim and dropping the man giving the orders. He then tracked another hostile running hard toward the exposed SAM turret. Yet to be activated, and Janus wanted it to stay that way. His gun belched fire again, and he smiled in grim satisfaction. With the lights illuminating the compound, it made it easy for Janus to pursue further wanton destruction. He sighted something that would help him do just that. A fuel tank, no doubt for trawlers, or fishing craft. He aimed and shot once more, and the fireworks began. The initial explosion sent a towering fireball into the sky. He closed his eyes, careful not to lose too much night vision, the rain coming down harder as he leaned back into the cabin, so the water didn't run into his eyes. He saw the chain reaction below, as nearby barrels of oil exploded. In the chaos, most of the guards were maimed or killed, some barrels spiralled into the sky like bottle rockets before exploding, sending oil over much of the compound, literally adding fuel to the fire.

"Mission accomplished," Janus said. A booming explosion rocked the helicopter. The concussive shockwave was a prelude to a mushroom cloud of smoke and fire which rained razor-sharp metal and flaming oil onto the terrified men below. They were either impaled or suffered third degree burns. The fire and destruction danced in Janus's eyes, sending a sinister smile across his features

Janus continued to watch in the off chance someone managed to get away as the vehicles were caught up the explosion. A tyre from an ATV smashed into one of the fleeing soldiers. *If there was ever a way to go, that wasn't it*, Janus thought. Keying his mic, he told Chapman their mission was finished.

Chapman piloted the helicopter away, unperturbed. He looked away as the explosive crescendo of the fiery opera that Janus had conducted with his beloved instrument of destruction reached its zenith in an almighty explosion, leveling the compound, and incinerating all within it.

* * *

The phone line cut out as Kenji was receiving updates about the operation on their island sanctuary. When he heard what had caused the outage, he was at a loss as to who would so brazenly attack him before his mind settled on his confrontation with Mr Harding, the Australian businessman. He had severely underestimated the man. Harding wasn't a businessman - that much was now clear - but Kenji needed to find out who he worked for and what he wanted. This was the second time Harding had got lucky. Ikeda had described inspecting a luxury yacht with an Australian captain. Normally that wouldn't strike him as odd, except Ikeda's description matched what he remembered of Harding. This Australian was messing things up, and he was getting closer. Too close for Kenji's liking.

Ikeda's role in this was over. It was a small loss, but not a crippling one in his master plan. *Four hours remained.*

He sighed, dialling a number for his driver to meet him around the front of his villa, as he stood among the glass shards and scattered bodies of his private security. Not only had Mr Harding attacked his beloved company, but also conducted a raid on his villa in Tokyo, the only logical conclusion given his appearance at the tower earlier. It wasn't in his nature to forgive nor forget, and Kenji silently vowed that Mr Harding would pay.

Chapter 35

Connor exhaled loudly as he stood outside the conference room. He was weary; they had been working around the clock and his sleep deprived body craved rest. He had witnessed the success of Janus and Chapman's mission long before they arrived back onboard the yacht. He had watched the carnage on one of the ship's wall-mounted monitors, the large fireball still burning long after they returned, illuminating the grey storm clouds that did little to cool its raging heat.

"Nice and quiet was the memo, wasn't it?" he asked them both once they were back onboard.

"Figured Ikeda needed a bit of fanfare after the drama he caused inland with our boys," Janus replied, with a casual shrug.

Chapman, with his boyish good looks and satisfied grin, clutched his helmet to his side like a hotshot aviator. Evans figured Chapman cut a better pilot look than Tom Cruise in Top Gun. Janus, as usual, treated everyone to his customary stony-faced grimace.

"I think celebratory drinks are in order," Chapman said, the grin still glued to his face. Janus shook his head and walked the other direction.

Evans shook his head in wonderment at his remarkable team, before entering the conference room into a flurry of activity from Kelly, who had pulled everyone she could together

"Connor, there is more at play here than we originally thought. With the discovery of the torpedo trolleys, it would be safe to say the bombs are out there somewhere already, and it's only a matter of time before they're used," Kelly said, ambushing him no sooner then he entered the room.

"Time, we do not have. Where could they possibly be? Better yet where is Kenji?" he replied, adding more questions than answers to Kelly's own.

They had all seen the same news reports from the mainland. Soon, the world would know of Toyotami Industries' illegal, anti-competitive deals, and its attempts to trick the Japanese government into doing its bidding. To add fuel to that fire, the police investigation into the recent training operations on Aogishima Island had reached the same news agencies. Questions were already being asked concerning the power and influence the company had at its fingertips courtesy of those underhand deals.

Evans had been waiting on news from Kurt from the mainland, but since the mission on the island and the removal of Ikeda, no one had heard from their covert operative. He instructed Kelly to home in on Kurt and his movements, pinpointing his location somewhere near the Japanese port of Kobe.

Seconds later, the voice of Kurt came through the room's speakers. His voice was rapid and breathless as he relayed the events since Evans and the rest of the team had reached Aogishima Island. Kurt explained what had played out on the mainland, including the police investigation into the background of Toyotami Industries. This investigation may have prompted Hiroto Toyotami to intervene.

A meeting between father and son had been set up. Kurt had tailed Kenji's limousine to a secluded location on the outskirts of Tokyo.

From there, he had seen Kenji do something he had never seen coming. Drawing a pistol from inside his suit jacket after a heated debate, Kenji shot his father dead in cold blood. Kurt had figured the meeting was supposed to repair the relationship between the two, but he was dead wrong. Hiding in the darkness, he had watched two men emerge from the shadows and remove Hiroto's body, place it in a body bag, and load it into the back of a van. With his father's blood not yet dry, Kenji had left, Kurt tailing him to the nearby port of Kobe, and Toyotami Industries' private berth.

"How did you tail Kenji?" Kelly asked.

"I still have my skills from when I was undercover in the Yakuza. Still, it doesn't take a genius to know how to break into a car," Kurt replied, his breath returning to normal.

"Are there currently any ships in the shell company's berth at Kobe?" Evans asked.

Kelly started typing on her laptop. Seconds later, they had their answer. "There is one ship currently located in the berth. I will have to probe deeper, but the scheduling shows the ship isn't scheduled to leave until tomorrow."

"Plenty of time for Kenji to smuggle the bombs onboard," Kurt said.

"Kurt, I need you to get on that ship. We need to be certain the bombs are onboard. There are two ways this can go down. I want to be sure we have both covered."

"You got it," Kurt replied, before adding, "Boss, how would he get them on without anyone seeing? Japanese border patrol and immigration would've scanned every load coming in and out of the port. Meticulous is all they know."

William, usually quiet in team meetings, spoke up.

"I don't think he would've paid them off. Scrap metal, that's how he is likely doing it."

Everyone looked at him before turning to Kelly, the resident know-it-all, for confirmation. She nodded.

"It's possible, especially if the bombs' outer shells are made of steel or anything metallic. They could be hidden among scrap metal, thereby passing detection."

Tori leaned back in her chair. "Kenji is smuggling the bombs inside containers again. But this time he is more prepared, he has them surrounded by scrap metal to throw the metal detectors. No doubt the manifest list scrap metal too, so they can hide the weight of the bomb."

"Don't forget it's his private berth, so it's possible money he's bribed dock workers or even immigration officials to look the other way," Evans added.

"Well then, seems we have a mastermind on our hands. Now we know how far this man will go to start the next world war," Kelly said.

"I hope you have a better plan than the last few, Boss. I'm getting tired of pulling your arse out of the fire," Tori added, winking at him referring to their previous escape in North Korea which felt like an age ago.

Connor smiled at his team, "I have one or two in mind. Right now, I'm sure Kurt has already read my mind on the first plan."

"Sure have, Boss," came his reply.

"What about the second, Connor?" Kelly asked.

"I'm still working on that." Evans grinned sheepishly. Kenji's unpredictability had him on edge. Right now, they still had no way of tracking where the bombs were.

Chapter 36

Though Kurt had yet to meet the Toyotami son in person, he had to admit he ran a tight ship. Getting into the terminal had been easy. The hard part had been getting near the private berth. The place was a hive of activity. With all his skill, he only just evaded patrol patterns that left a gap of seconds when he could avoid detection. He crouched low behind wooden boxes stamped and branded with the Toyotami Industries logo. He peered inside the nearest. It was empty.

Returning his attention to the activity at the berth, he admired the ship as it loomed large and ominous in the darkness. Watching the dockworkers going between the ship, he could see that they were not as lazy as the workers he normally dealt with. Quite the opposite, in fact. The workers seemed to patrol as well, moving at a pace that meant at any one time, several pairs of eyes were focused on the freighter's gangway. They appeared to be loading a mixture of food, alcohol, and other goods on the ship with peak efficiency, container after container swinging onboard via the large cranes near the berth. The noise of the cranes as the containers thudded against the deck would hide any sound Kurt might make if he had to dispose of the guards, but it wouldn't help him board the ship, given the amount of activity around the only entrance.

Kurt's gaze flickered from the berth to the port itself, alive with twinkling lights and activity. Dockworkers and machines worked around the clock to keep the economy flowing. Though he didn't know much about the commodities that left the port, Kurt knew it serviced an international market, judging by the many countries' flags flying on the ships at berth.

A voice full of authority drew his attention back to the activity around the freighter as a man in a white suit strutted toward the berth. It was Kenji, who had disappeared as Kurt sat outside the terminal making the call to Evans. Kurt couldn't imagine what kind of person could kill their own kin. Kenji waved his hands wildly at a man standing with a smoke in his hand near one of the buildings. Kenji's rage could be felt from Kurt's position, as the worker tossed his cigarette on the ground and ground it into the dirt before moving away to pick up a box. As he did, two of the men near Kenji dropped what they were carrying and closed in on the oblivious dockworker, grabbing both of his hands, and holding him. Kenji delivered two successive punches into the man's stomach, sending him onto his knees.

Kurt could sense what was about to happen but couldn't steel himself quickly enough. The man held up his hands to plead his case, but Kenji ignored him, pulled out a suppressed pistol and shot the worker point blank in the head. The man's head jerked back as he fell into the water with a splash. It wasn't the random act of violence that surprised Kurt, rather the fact that the men who had assisted Kenji went back to work as though nothing had happened. To Kurt, they appeared to be robots, fearful of Kenji. A tingling sense like someone watching him set the hairs on his neck on end and put him on edge. He watched Kenji point in his general direction, as though he saw through Kurt's hiding place.

Three of the dockworkers approached his position. He watched them come, unsure if they were armed. As they meandered around the berth, their demeanour suggested he may not have been spotted after all. He relaxed for a moment.

Kurt knew he would only have one chance to get on the freighter before the workers got too close. He slid into the empty container nearest him and pulled it shut as the voices approached. He lay perfectly still, hoping that there was no need for them to check its contents. He heard one of the men utter a few Japanese curse words as the lid knocked slightly. He held his breath. This was it. If he was caught, he could fight the few closest to him, but not all of them.

He heard movement on top of the lid before a hammering sound began. A nail burst through the lid, and then another, throwing sawdust into his eyes, making them water.

His misfortune continued as a piece of sawdust he accidentally inhaled made him want to cough. Doing his best to stifle the feeling, his throat burned as the box shuddered and jolted around him. Kurt heard voices outside the container before he had to brace herself as the box tilted violently. His mind reeled at what was going on outside, but he quelled his fear by telling himself he was likely on a dolly trolley being wheeled around to be placed onboard.

A short time later, he was deposited on something hard and, as he held his breath, he heard the sound of clinking chains. The chains were pulled around the sides of the box, and then he was airborne. The crate swayed in the air as he was hoisted onto the deck. Kurt could only hope he was not placed in a stack. He would be trapped, and the crate would become his coffin. The thought of it made him want to lash out in fear. He gritted his teeth and reminded himself that he was a professional, that the fear would pass soon enough.

Kurt had noted that the dockworkers didn't possess weaponry, but he was certain once he left his hiding place all bets would be off. The men onboard would shoot him on sight, no questions asked.

Outside the box, under the watchful gaze of Kenji, the last of the crates and shipping containers were being loaded onboard. Unlike the one Kurt occupied, not all were empty, most consisting of broken weaponry and other items that would pass muster should the freighter be inspected.

Remaining silent, he waited and listened to the commotion outside as the thudding continued, the yelling of various workers either guiding in the containers or demanding crates be moved to make room for more. Then he heard it; the steady thrumming building up below him, a steadiness that reminded him of turbines. Before his posting in Tokyo with the CIA, Kurt had completed a mission hiding on an oil freighter bound for the Middle East. He heard the same rhythm now, then a loud hissing, and finally, the reverberating horn telling him the freighter was about to head out: destination unknown.

* * *

Evans sat beside Kelly in the Hub, one leg bouncing so much it made Kelly stop what she was doing and look at him with concern.

"It's not like you to be nervous before a mission. Quite the opposite, in fact," she said.

Evans ran his hand through his hair. It had grown longer over the past few weeks and was desperately in need of a cut. "Just a lot on my mind."

"Like what?" Kelly asked.

"My father used to remind me if I ever led men or women, never to ask someone to do something I wouldn't do myself," he said, quietly.

"We both know if you could trade places with Kurt, you would, but you need to let him do his thing, and you do yours," she said.

She clenched her jaw before looking away and resuming her typing. He was about to ask what was on her mind when Tori came up behind him.

"William and his men are ready to go. Seems all they needed was a quick wash and they are ready to get back at it. I'll never understand men."

"Touché, Tori," he said, thinking of Laura in the medical bay. "Let's hope we get another update from Kurt soon," he said, returning his attention to the central monitor. Kelly hit a button on her console's keyboard and a blip appeared on the screen, zooming in on the port of Kobe. The satellite image clearly displayed Kurt's location through the tracking chip implanted in his leg, and it showed him moving out from the port.

* * *

Onboard the Japanese freighter, Kurt began counting to one thousand, a technique he normally employed for one of two reasons. Firstly, to calm his rapid heartbeats and keep a clear head while on operations The second was to ensure ample time was spent preparing for whatever came next. In this case, he was waiting for the noise around his crate to die down, returning to the steady rhythm of the ship's turbines. He had been sitting in a foetal position for what felt like hours. He he shuffled around to a position that allowed him to push the lid off. As he placed his hand on the pine lid, he hoped that they hadn't thought to stack anything on top of his crate, but as he pushed, he felt it give slightly. It was then he remembered the nails. He pulled a small knife from his boot and slid it under the lid. Praying no one was around, he jerked the knife upwards with force, the sound of cracking wood echoing off the steel hull.

After a minute, the only noise was a distant clanking of chains and the groaning of the hull as he rose to his full height from his hidden position, the box lid resting on his back in case he needed to crouch once more. He waited a few minutes more before climbing out fully. He replaced the lid and looked around. He was surrounded by dozens of crates like his own. Wanting to know what else might be onboard, he pulled a small flashlight from his pocket and clicked it on before gripping it with his teeth, using his free hands to pry open one of the containers. Once more the sound echoed around him before he slid back the box lid and sighed. Empty. The next was the same, and the one after that. On the fourth try, he encountered packing peanuts, and he groped around in the foam until he pulled an assault rifle from within, quickly followed by four more. As he examined each, he realised they were all broken in some way. He threw them back in the box, confused, wondering what they were for.

Kurt heard a quiet buzz, then several light bulbs suddenly dispelled the darkness, catching him off guard. He swung around, watching as the room began to resemble a honeycomb of crates and containers, making him appreciate the length of the ship and its cargo. Male Japanese voices muttered nearby, maybe arguing, as Kurt looked for a new place to hide. His previous hideaway now ruined by the splintered wood, as well as the others nearby left him without many options. Without thinking, he threw the lever on a nearby metal shipping container and dragged it open. Knowing he couldn't lock himself in, he slid inside and pulled the door toward him, leaving enough of a gap for him to hear and see.

Tapping his earpiece, he tried hailing the team, getting only static. Either the comms were jammed, or the signal stopped by the thick metal hull. Either way, he was on his own until he could find some way to communicate with the team. Looking around in the semi-darkness of the container, he remembered he had left the flashlight and knife on top of one of the crates near his hiding place.

The voices were drifting away when a rogue wave hit the side of the ship, sending him forward and then backward inside the container. The clattering sound of his knife and flashlight skittering along the floor was like nails on a chalkboard to him. The voices became more alert and urgent, followed quickly by running footsteps heading his way. He pressed himself against the door and waited for the first voice to come near, letting him pass before the second arrived. Then he threw open the door into the second of the two men, the large metal door slamming into him with full force.

The ship rolled in the water, adding weight to his punches as they fought. The metal door had broken bone, and Kurt followed up with a punch to the mid-section of the first man, then another directly in his face. His right fist breaking the man's nose and blood began to gush freely. Before the man could defend himself, Kurt followed up with a knee that sent the man back into a crate, his head bouncing off the edge hard. He collapsed, out cold. Kurt, like Janus, liked to remain in the shadows where possible.

After patting down both men, he concluded they were civilians.

A feeling of guilt crept into his mind as he looked at their prone forms. They carried nothing lethal. One of them had an inhaler in his overalls, but that was all Kurt could find on either. These men were only doing their jobs, unaware of the dire circumstances they were involved in. He felt no pride in what he had done to them. They were innocent in all of this, hired by Kenji who cared nothing if they lived or died.

Moving quickly, he dragged their unconscious forms into the shipping container. He jogged in the direction they had come from, finding a stairway connected to an overhanging gantry that ran the length of the ship. Kurt climbed the stairs by clutching both rails as the ship rode the swell.

Outside, the rainstorm had turned into a raging force, waves cresting high over its metal decking.

Kurt imagined the ship tossing like a ragdoll in the surf. The team back onboard *Serenity*, despite its advanced engines, were just as helpless up against Mother Nature.

Reaching the gantry, he spun the handle on a door, and pushed it open. Immediately, the static connection in his ear resolved itself into a familiar voice. "Kurt, this is Kelly. Do you read?"

Kurt peered outside into the night. Wind and rain lashed the freighter as it rode the ever-growing swell that sent waves crashing over the deck. Lightning crackled through the sky. He backed up and closed the door, struggling to hear Kelly's voice.

"I copy. I am aboard the freighter. I cannot confirm heading at this time." He desperately wanted to shout, but his voice would likely draw attention throughout the ship.

"Have you located the bombs yet?" Evans's voice was barely decipherable.

"I'm struggling to hear you guys. Negative, *Serenity* on the bombs. Still getting my bearings. This ship is huge and I'm not sure where to start. There must be over two hundred containers on this thing, and a million crates." Kurt was thrown forward, bracing himself against the wall.

"*Serenity* copies, we just need confirmation, Kurt. Once that occurs, we can send in the cavalry." came Evans's reply.

Kurt hazarded another look outside as a large bolt zigzagged through the sky, followed three seconds later by an almighty crack of thunder. He hadn't expected it, despite counting and he felt himself leap into the air for a second. The weather would make things difficult but might keep most people away from the slippery and wild deck topside, giving him more opportunities to search.

He studied the deck and the towering containers, and wondered where Kenji might have stashed the bombs, when another lightning strike flashed. The flash lit up a figure braving the conditions on the main deck, ensuring the containers there were securely tied down. Desperate to get away from the storm, the absent-minded seaman turned toward Kurt's hiding place, blocking his exit onto the deck above.

Chapter 37

A hand reached out for Kurt. He reflexively avoided it before another followed through. This time, he deflected it into the steel hull, the man crying out as his hand broke. Kurt used the man's forward motion to pull him forward and send him stumbling down the stairs. The man caught himself on the way down. Certain now that Kurt was no ordinary stowaway, he reached behind his back, pulling a wicked-looking blade from a scabbard, then ran up the stairs at Kurt. At the top, the man swung hard, making Kurt leap up the stairs toward the topside door to escape the vicious arc of the blade.

Aware of how narrow the space was, Kurt grabbed the injured man's arm and pulled him forward with all his strength, stepping outside, and slamming the door hard against the seaman's arm. The dropped blade skittered along the deck before being swallowed by the monstrous sea. Kurt threw the door open and kicked the hapless man, sending him tumbling down the metal steps. Kurt didn't need to see the outcome; the sickening crunch at the bottom confirmed the man's fate.

Steeling himself for what was next, he made the decision to move topside. The wind whipped his jacket and the rain lashed his face as he struggled to keep his balance on the slippery surface. The whole ship rocked in such a manner that it reminded him of a child's toy in a bathtub, at the mercy of a greater force. Kurt stumbled and fell toward another railing, this one leading to one of the mighty cranes on the upper deck.

Placing a hand over his eyes to shield them from the rain, the lightning lit up one end of the vessel allowing him to see the bridge. Time was of the essence, but he had yet to search more than a quarter of the ship. Looking back at the door he'd come from, he took a chance and raced for it. Throwing it open and descending back down into the lit cargo hold, Kurt had one thing on his mind: he needed to find someone to talk to, and fast.

Sliding down one of the railings to save time, he sidestepped the body of the man at the bottom. Struck with yet another moral quandary, he opted to grab the least damaged arm and drag the sailor behind one of the containers. Satisfied his conscience was now clear, he made his way along the full length of the freighter, knowing at some point he would arrive at the stern. As he neared the middle section of the freighter, he paused, again hearing voices. Kurt moved closer, peering around a faded red container to see what awaited him.

Two Japanese soldiers sat at a small metal table, one with a well-known Japanese beer in his hand. He looked a bit green.. The other was shuffling playing cards, his mask on the chair beside him. Kurt could only see the back of his head. The man with the beer was either about to be seasick or had consumed too much alcohol, much to his colleague's amusement. A comment made by the sober soldier caused the other go behind one of the containers near Kurt. Kurt noted the drunken man's mask hanging over the corner of his chair.

As the drunken soldier rose, he stumbled and moved toward Kurt's location instead. Kurt just managed to duck back into the shadows, where he contemplated his next move. Unlike the two civilians, Kurt had noticed several things wrong with the picture before him. The man bending over in the corner was ranked private, the other shuffling cards was his superior. In any military branch, gambling, and consumption of alcohol on were serious offences if caught, though he doubted anyone would care on a freighter such as this. The second issue was the assault rifles beside them, hanging over the back of their plastic and steel chairs. The third was simple enough: where were the bombs? If these were Kenji's men, that's what they would be guarding, and the masks were a giveaway. Deciding the answers would come soon enough, Kurt moved toward the drunken soldier and silenced him without remorse. The other soldier was so intent on shuffling the cards, he didn't sense Kurt coming until it was too late.

Kurt throttled him as the soldier's cards spilled from his hand, across the small table and onto the floor. The soldier's legs kicked out in spasm, knocking both the table and chair as Kurt dragged him away from both to ensure he couldn't use either as a weapon, and held him as tightly as he could.

"Unlike your friend, you may yet live. Tell me where I can find the bombs that were smuggled onto this freighter," he hissed in Japanese.

The choked soldier tried to get a view of his captor, but Kurt pulled harder, ensuring he couldn't see who had caught them by surprise.

"You have five seconds to comply before I break your neck. Tell me where the bombs are," he hissed. The man still didn't say anything at first, but his defiance waned as Kurt started counting. The man pleaded with Kurt, insisting he didn't know about any bombs. If they were anywhere onboard, they might be located toward the stern. The soldier said they had been ordered to keep any of the regular crew away from a section of the ship. Kurt had to wonder if Kenji's idea was to sail to a preconceived spot, drop the bombs via crane and sail away, making it look like the freighter was caught in a freak accident as it was swept up by the ensuing tidal wave. On a night like tonight, it wouldn't be such a bad plan.

He applied greater pressure to the soldier's windpipe, knocking him out. Returning to the overturned table and chairs, he took an automatic rifle, slinging it over his back. He was already equipped with his customary silenced pistol, now he added the knife holstered on the soldier's thigh, putting it on his own to replace the one he had lost earlier. With no time to waste, he moved quickly and quietly in the only direction he had left to explore.

Despite the soldier's warning, he was yet to encounter any other personnel on board, making him wonder if the meagre crew and two soldiers Kurt had disposed of were all they had. The idea seemed absurd, but so did a bomb that created a tsunami underwater, and that was real enough, or so he thought.

Reaching a door, he looked through the small porthole inset in the steel. He could see movement, but the window was caked and grimy from encrusted sea salt. He breathed and wiped it with his sleeve, clearing it just enough to see what was unfolding on the other side, taking his breath away.

* * *

Kenji stood in front of the submersible pool, its water boiling from the swell that raged around the ship. It was a unique modification he had made to the freighter, one that he took pride in. The room itself was mostly empty, stacked with only a few boxes and three containers. The containers were there to ensure the transfer went smoothly.

Two men took hold of a container's handles and pulled them down and outwards. He smiled malevolently at what lay inside. The bomb lay on the trolley before him. It was shaped like a torpedo, except the fins had been placed on either side to carve through the water like dorsal fins on a dolphin or shark, and one end housed a standard torpedo propellor. The original plans had allowed for a drop bomb, but in the off chance that was unavailable, he needed to ensure a backup was implemented, in this case, an underwater drop.

To anyone on the outside of the ship, the freighter was just another vessel in the shipping lanes of the Pacific, nothing out of the ordinary, even down to the cargo onboard. It was the perfect plan, and - despite the few delays he had encountered - he was certain he would not see the meddling Mr Harding, the American businessman, Harry Yates, or even Ambassador Joshua Davidson. The loss of his second in charge, Jiro, was a small matter now. He had prolonged this long enough. He watched as the missile was pushed out of the container and lined up with a hatch far above them. Following his orders, and despite the heavy weather, a lever was thrown, and the cargo hatch above began opening. It looked like a cavernous mouth from below. A crane on deck was ready and waiting. One of the masked men near Kenji pulled out a walkie talkie and spoke into it.

Far above them, the crane came to life and lowered its cable into the depths. Elations coursed through Kenji. He had achieved everything he had set out to do.

The masked man with the radio stopped the crane operator just before the cable hook reached the bomb, everything rocking wildly in the confined space. Rain poured through the gap like a waterfall. Seawater sloshed over the deck and onto the men down below. Not one person in the room cared. All their attention was on the bomb.

History was about to be rewritten. It was a shame, Kenji reflected, that his foolish father hadn't lived to see his son's greatest achievement.

Chapter 38

Kurt ducked down behind the door, keying his earpiece.

"*Serenity*, this is Kurt," he said, his breath trembling as he processed the fact that the bombs were very real and were almost in motion. Kurt was certain that Kenji's diabolical nature meant there would be no kill switch.

"Go ahead Kurt," came Evans's reply.

"I have visual on the bomb, not bombs. It's located within the cargo hold of the ship that I tracked from the berth. The bomb is to be dropped not by air, but through a submersible pool in the bottom of the ship. Are you enroute?"

* * *

Evans looked at Kelly, their worst fears realised. It was time.

"Kurt, William is three minutes out. Standby. If there is any way you can delay Kenji, you have my express permission to do so," Evans said, adrenaline pumping. He knew there was little he could do for Kurt until William arrived. He just hoped he wouldn't be too late.

Tori had been feverishly flicking through the shipping manifests as quickly as her hands could manage. What she saw made no sense so far. There was a discrepancy in the Toyotami Industries manifests she couldn't put her finger on. Turning to Kelly, she rolled her chair closer, coming to a stop just by her left shoulder.

"I've been flicking through the shipping manifests. They all check out with other reports, except for this one, and—" she scrolled with the mouse, "this one, where there seem to be duplicate manifests."

Kelly scanned the two cargo manifests, and as her eyes moved further and further down, her jaw tightened. She turned toward Evans.

"We have a major problem. I mean a *major* problem. Kenji doesn't have one bomb; he has another one hidden in the shipping lanes somewhere."

Evans infallible mind hadn't considered the possibility of another bomb., Kenji's brazen actions were beginning to fall on them like dominoes. "Two bombs?" The revelation had them stunned. "Where is the second freighter?"

"According to the manifest, if its correct, the second bomb is currently tracking south," said Kelly.

"You don't think Kenji is in bed with the Chinese, do you?" Tori asked.

"I doubt it. The man removes anything from the equation that doesn't work for him. Textbook psychopath, though China would stand to gain from such a devastation of Taiwan's coastal defences."

"You with me on this?" Evans asked Janus beside him.

Janus nodded. Leaving Kelly to trace the freighter, both men strode to the door. They were already kitted out in black combat attire, and they broke into a trot to the elevator, taking it to the helipad on the back of the yacht.

Evans plugged in his earpiece as they grabbed their helmets from a bench before bracing themselves for the wild weather that was set to lash them.

"Bloody hell. Couldn't have picked a better night for hell to break loose," was Janus's response when he saw the rain spattering the glass door. "It was better watching it on the screens in the climate-controlled room downstairs."

Evans ignored the comment as Laura appeared on crutches, aided by Harry Yates.

"I often wondered how we got down there," he said, eyeing the elevator.

"Cool it Yates, we have a situation here. There's a second bomb out there. I need your assistance on this," Evans said, then switched his attention to Laura, who nodded, a silent understanding between them.

Chapman's voice interrupted them.

"Hey, Boss, it's getting pretty wild out here, we have to go now," he said. There was no fear in his voice, although any sane pilot knew it was almost certain death to be caught in these hurricane-like winds. Connor glanced again at Laura, her green eyes appraising his own before he walked out into the storm. The message had been loud and clear from her. *You come back to me.*

Chapter 39

Two Robinson chopper plunged through the rain and wind that surged high in the atmosphere, each with separate targets. Thin tendrils of darkness seemed to cup themselves around the aircraft as William in his team's chopper kept watch through the drizzle that coated the windscreen. A fork of lightning lit up the huge swell beneath them, the water moving in a way that gave it a life of its own. They had left the *Serenity* as soon as Evan's call had come through. Despite his objections to the weather outside, Evans had pushed ahead for the team to infiltrate the freighter and rescue Kurt, hoping both bombs were on the same freighter.

All in day's work, William thought, as turbulence rocked the chopper. He watched the pilot grip the joystick harder in front of him until his knuckles were white.

William glanced behind him, watching his team check their weapons and pull on their helmets, checking the night vision googles. The team, usually full of conversation, said little, as they all knew what they were about to do. No one relished the thought of dropping from a chopper onto the slippery deck of a ship being beaten black and blue by the savagery of the waves. They knew that if they didn't do it, no one else would. Not only that, but innocent lives were at stake.

* * *

Evans and Janus sat in the rear of their helicopter alongside three of William's team, who waited silently like their colleagues. A grim mood hovered over all within the cabin. Evans liked working alongside these men. He had come to respect their lack of complaint and total focus when on an operation. He looked at Janus beside him, the sniper out of his usual element, struggling to pull tight one of the straps that kept his Kevlar vest pulled tight across his chest. Noticing Evans staring at him with a lopsided grin on his face, he reddened in the already red interior of the helicopter as it thundered along. Chapman feathered the throttle. Unlike William's helicopter ride, his was calmer and more controlled.

"Think you can give me a hand?" Janus asked, and Evans pulled the strap tight.

"When we get to the second freighter," said Evans, "the boys here will move toward the bridge and take control of the ship. You and I will head toward the cargo hold. If Kurtis right, there should be a submersible pool located at the keel, and that's where we will find our target."

Evans had to yell to be heard over the blades as they neared the freighter.

Once their operation on Aogishima had been completed, Evans had kept close to his chest the realisation that Kenji had tried to hoodwink them. He ordered the helmsman to navigate the ship toward the Philippine Sea once all his team had returned. He figured that once the first freighter at Kobe set sail, he wanted to ensure his team were positioned to intercept any change of plans from him or from Kenji.

The time remaining for the choppers to intercept was a different matter entirely. He knew he couldn't reach Kurt's freighter. That would be up to William and his team. He and Janus were heading toward a second freighter. According to the shipping manifest Tori had pulled up, it was heading for America. Its contents were listed as scrap metal. He would put money on the fact the Americans didn't know was coming.

"Heads up, Connor. Freighter in sight dead ahead," Chapman said through their helmet comms.

The storm outpaced them, a jagged fork of lightning lighting up the ship as they approached. The freighter was huge, three hundred metres long, rising and falling with the mammoth waves that beat against it. The bow cleaved through the ocean, rising to meet the swell, seeming to float in the air before hammering down into the surf, the four hundred-thousand-ton ship sending a mixture of spray and foam through the air and back into the already roiling water.

"I'm going to perform an overpass, Boss. See if I can find a safe place to drop you. The freighter is all over the shop right now. You're liable to be squashed like a bug if I place you where those containers are sliding."

No sooner than the words left his mouth, Evans looked out the rain-smeared window as one of the cables holding the containers snapped, and two of them rolled off the freighter into the ocean. The remaining containers slid around the deck like a giant, and extremely heavy, game of Tetris. As Chapman flew a wide arc around the freighter, Evans made out the white letters gleaming on the back: *Kitori Maru*.

* * *

Unknown to Connor, William was dealing with the same situation as his team entered the airspace around the second freighter, *Akagi Maru*. The containers were sliding all over the deck, and a safe landing was well and truly out of the window.

"Alright, boys and girls," William said, his usual chatty self-coming to the fore, "it's about to get rough. Hold on." He gritted his teeth as the pilot thundered around the bridge in a loop, skilfully moving closer to the stern. Tiny pinpricks of light sparkled from the bridge through numerous windows, making it feel as though they were hovering near an apartment complex.

William pulled open the door, rain lashing his face as the wind tore at his skin like sandpaper. Throwing down the heavy cable, he gestured with his hands, before sliding down the rope, the rest of the team following suit. As the last of them landed heavily on the slippery deck, they moved quickly to the bridge door. One of his men spun the outside wheel to unlock it, pulling it open as William stepped in first, submachine gun held ready. A crew member stepped out. Instinctively, William brought a fist across the sailor's face, the oblivious man hitting the doorway frame and falling back inside with a thud.

Checking the room was empty, he turned to his team.

"Keep focused, people. I need two teams, one to go high, and one to go low. Head amidships, that's where you are likely to find the bomb and Kurt. Once we take control of the bridge, we can ensure the authorities know what's going on."

The first team, consisting of three of Will's men, moved toward the upper staircase and climbed it slowly, wary of the rocking of the ship. If Kenji's forces appeared now, they would be terribly exposed.

William headed with the rest down the lower staircase, not encountering any resistance. At one point, a heating pipe alongside him popped a rivet, sending an explosion of steam into the passageway, making him duck underneath its hissing spray.

Reaching a doorway on his left, William gestured with his weapon as one of the men spun the wheel and pulled it back. He pointed his gun at the open doorway, waiting for gunfire to follow. Instead, several Japanese crew members were tied to their bunks, gagged. The team moved in, pulling down the gags. One of the crewmembers started babbling about the explosives onboard. William tried to slow him down, as his Japanese was patchy. He asked loudly if anyone spoke English, and one of the men came forward. The man told him there were explosives placed along the sides of the ship to trigger when it went down, ensuring no evidence was left behind. These men were the original crew, locked up once they were out to sea. The freighter was now under the control of Kenji and Ikeda's' men. The man couldn't confirm numbers for William.

Thanking him, he keyed his earpiece and told Chapman about the men onboard. It was news to him. William knew it was a risk saving the lives of the innocent crew, meaning Chapman would have to make a return trip. If the bomb was released, there was no way he could rescue William and his men in time.

Chapman radioed that he was hovering above them, and one of William's men accompanied the freed sailors to the deck to load them onboard. That left William with one of the more experienced members of his squad. They moved into the hold, seeing stacks of containers within.

"Kelly, it's William. I need Kurt's tracking device location relayed to my wrist computer. Can you make it happen?" A few keystrokes later, and Kelly complied, Kurt's location showing him nearby. They moved quickly toward his location.

Turning a corner, they ran into two soldiers in black armour. Spotting William, they ducked behind containers as bullets whizzed by them, before they returned fire.

William's colleague grunted as a bullet skimmed his tattooed arm, drawing a small trickle of blood. The hostiles continued to lay down fire as Will keyed his mic again.

"Kurt, it's Will. Can you move back to my position?"

"Seems like my rescuers need rescuing. Is that how it is?" Kurt replied.

"If that's what you want to call it, yes. Move, dammit," William hissed.

Moments later, as William reloaded his weapon and moved out to fire, shots rang out and both enemies fell from their hiding spots, landing heavily on the ground. Kurt appeared around the corner, blowing the top of his pistols as though in a Western.

"It's about time you showed up. Kenji is inside, and they have spent the last twenty minutes ensuring the bomb is ready to be dropped. The crane is centred as we speak," he said, concern etched on his face.

"Priority one is the bomb, and two is Kenji. You ready?" William asked, Kurt -pistols still held ready - nodding. They jogged along a corridor, down a set of stairs, and back to the door Kurt had been crouched behind.

William looked through the grimy porthole. Barely making out Kenji, he saw their target looking at the dangling bomb as it was moved into position above the submersible pool. William signalled to his man who spun the wheel on the door and pulled it open. Kurt moved in front of William as they entered the large space. William levelled his gun at the back of Kenji's head, as the man turned and looked at them. It was then William knew something was wrong.

Chapter 40

Connor and Janus accompanied the soldiers through the passageways, stepping over the two bodies of the hostiles that had confronted them earlier. Reaching the same junction the others had on the *Akagi Maru*, Evans headed to the bridge with two of the soldiers.

Janus went below to secure the bomb within the hold. With a silent understanding between them, they had parted ways, not realising that neither of them might see each other again.

Evans climbed fifteen flights to the top of the bridge, moving slowly due to constantly looking up, wary that anyone waiting above would likely see him before he saw them. When they reached the top, the amount of equipment he wore, coupled with clutching the weapon while looking up meant he was in a world of pain, but he pushed that down. He stood to the side of the doorway leading to the bridge, listening. Hearing nothing, he signalled one of his men to prepare a flashbang. He slung the assault rifle over his shoulder, swapping it out for a pump-action shotgun. Rather than lethal rounds, he opted for beanbag rounds to breach and clear. As he spun the door's wheel with one hand, he pulled it open and let the soldier beside him throw the flashbang inside, closing the door as the dazzling flash seeped through the sides of the door. Opening it again, Evans moved in first, sending two beanbags into two of the dazed crew on the ground. Another popped up to attack him and was dropped by one of the men moving closely behind. The room was clear. A chart room led off the bridge, but a quick scan showed there was no one inside. It didn't make sense. Keying his mic, he tried to hail Janus.

"Janus, this is Connor, bridge is clear, no sign of Kenji. How are you holding up on your end?"

There was no response. Evans tried again; once more, radio silence. The knot in his stomach tightened. Something hadn't gone to plan. He told both men with him to hold the bridge. He was going it alone as he headed back down the stairs, leaping onto the landings as quickly as his legs could carry him.

He kept trying to hail Janus as he ran down to the lower levels, stepping over several bodies of dead or concussed soldiers. As he rounded the corner, instinct made him pull back, A glimpse of a soldier confirmed his worst fear. He shot the man in the chest and then the head, concussing him.

Janus's voice came through his earpiece.

"Connor, it's a trap, get out of the—"

The transmission ended, but Connor had heard all he needed. The mission was just beginning.

Taking another set of stairs, he paused to examine a diagram on the wall. Tracing his route with his finger, he found amidships, where the submersible pool should be located, moving further down to an open door. He kept close to the wall as he crept nearer, careful to not reveal his shadow under the lighting above. He could hear voices on the other side, one of them Janus's as the normally silent man roared out in pain. Evans stepped into the open doorway and was mortified.

Janus was being held hostage, and the two men that had gone with him were kneeling on the floor with guns pointed at the backs of their heads. The situation was nothing like Evans had expected. He pointed his shotgun at the man in the suit, whose hair was wet, and whose normally crisp attire was drenched, with dirt marks all over it.

The reason for Janus's pain was the long samurai sword Kenji held in his hand. He had run it slowly along Janus's arm vertically for what looked like the fifth time, making Evans wonder how quickly his friend had been captured.

"You, Mr Harding, are beginning to be a thorn in my side. Or should I call you by your actual name, Commander Connor Evans?"

Evans couldn't hide his surprise at his identity being uncovered. He doubted Janus would have given up the information. Either Kenji had been working his angle the whole time, or Jiro had got Connor's name to him before Janus finished him off.

"Ever since you stepped foot into my father's company with that smug look on your face and that offer you knew he couldn't refuse, I knew you were not serious. Our company has been failing for years, and out of the blue you arrive, offering money to side with us. You should know, Commander," Kenji said with venom in his tone, "that we Japanese have honour, and that honour is the reason why we are both feared and respected throughout the world."

Evans could see the delusion in the man's eyes. He licked his salty lips before replying.

"No, Kenji, your father believed in honour before you put a bullet in his skull. Where was the honour in that?"

Connor's knowledge of this event saw the Kenji's illusion of grandeur dissipate briefly before returning, the malevolent look etched on his face once more.

"So, you've been tracking me just as I have been tracking you. A worthy opponent at last. In a few short moments, you will join the many beneath our feet that fought and died for such honour. There is no honour in war; the deeds of the many go untold," he said, pointing to the bomb that hung above him. "On my command, this will drop into the ocean and the people of the world will know Japan's might again. The stories of the dead will be heard, and you will be the first to bear witness to it."

Evans looked past Kenji for a way to save Janus. He was tired of grandiose speeches by tyrants and leaders. Silence was a greater speech than this empty rhetoric. The room was stacked full of crates and five soldiers stood around Kenji. Connor's own men were under guard. The odds were stacked against him.

William's voice interrupted his thoughts. "Connor, Kenji is not on this freighter. Repeat, not on this freighter. The man we captured is a decoy. Kenji must've known we were coming. We have the bomb onboard, but not Kenji."

Evans didn't need telling that the sneering features before him belonged to the genuine Kenji. The situation was hopeless for him. It was him against several armed masked men. Connor held up one hand and dropped to his knees in the hope that Janus would be set free, or at least saved from harm. The nearest masked sneered and slapped Evans hard across the face, reaching for the gun he had placed on the deck.

"Now you will watch your friend die. Honour dies on the battlefield—" Kenji said, as an explosion rocked the ship toward the bow. Kenji stumbled forward and hit the railing around the submersible pool as everyone fell forward or sideways.

Janus had fallen forward, grasping his bleeding arm. The cuts weren't deep, but given the razor-sharp edge of the samurai blade, his flesh was like a blade of grass against it. Evans scrambled forward toward his inured friend as his two captured men wrestled with two of the masked soldiers to get back their weapons.

Evans tore off a piece of his shirt and wrapped it around Janus's arm, pulling it tight. Kenji roared and grabbed Evans by the neck, dragging him to his feet. As Kenji choked him, Evans used the man's weight against him, throwing him over his shoulder. Kenji landed squarely on the deck, writhing in pain as his back hit the hard metal.

"What the hell was that" Janus said, gritting his teeth, his thick Latvian accent returning due to the pain that wracked the big man's body.

Another explosion rocked the freighter as the bomb bounced in its cradle above them, swinging precariously like a wrecking ball. Evans knew any control of the bomb would come from the crane above, but he would need to get there first. He wasn't sure how Kenji planned to drop it, but he figured a radio message to the crane operator would be enough.

A chorus of voices sounded in his earpiece, so he removed it, leaving it dangling across his chest as Kenji rose to his feet, and headed for the door, opting to run away. *Where is the honour in that?* Evans thought, as he hoisted Janus to his feet. The two soldiers beside him threw themselves behind crates and opened fire on the last of Kenji's masked men were hiding behind another.

Another explosion rocked the ship.

"This place is breaking apart, we need to get topside now," Evans yelled as they raced out of the room together.

The freighter tilted, sending them both sprawling to the ground. Kenji slipped on one of the stairs, then raced onwards.

Janus scrambled to his feet first, clutching at his wounded arm as he ran up the stairs with Connor close behind. A clanging sound began as he heard his men shouting below. Plugging his earpiece back in, Connor heard one of his men shout that the bomb was rocking dangerously, and they wanted to be far away from it when it went. If the ship was rigged to blow, it might set off the bomb.

Connor watched Janus slide to the side of the corridor, yelling back at Evans as a barrel rolled down the passageway, hitting the wall at the other end with a deafening clang. They continued, leaping up the stairs two at a time, giving chase to the man who had threatened millions. Connor looked down at his wrist computer. *Less than an hour left.*

* * *

William kept trying to hail Evans with no luck. With the crew removed from the *Akagi Maru*, they had rounded up everyone else on board, including Kenji's men. He knew the only way to stop the weapon was to blow the ship up on the surface. William had already checked in with Kelly, who informed him their position was clear of busy shipping lanes and far enough from land for the bomb to be detonated safely.

The *Akagi Maru*'s bomb, unlike its counterpart, was locked firmly on the missile trolley, and pushed back into its container. With nothing more that could be done, he raced topside to the hovering helicopter, dancing wildly among a grey and black skyline like cracked glass.

The thundering rotor blades of the chopper beat the rain around him into stinging needles as an explosion rocked the bow of the ship. William wasn't sure how long they had set the plastic C4 explosive for as he sprinted toward the bow of the ship. He clipped onto the flailing rope hanging from the waiting chopper, as Chapman threw a lever to winch in the rope. William flew into the air, grabbed the chopper's landing skids, and climbed into the cabin.

Another series of explosions rocked the *Akagi Maru*, as William hauled the door shut. The dim glow of the interior didn't hide the dripping bodies within. William smiled at his men.

"At least we get one hell of a fireworks display to watch, so it's not all bad," he said, as the freighter exploded.

The chopper flew away from the ship, which separated into two halves as the stern of the ship rose and then sank. The bow plunged backwards into the raging waters, leaving no trace that the heavy freighter had ever been there, the Pacific Ocean claiming another victim.

One of his team asked the single question that occupied William's mind. *Where is Evans?*

"So far, nothing," William said. "Kelly has been trying to raise him for a while, but it seems both Janus and Evans are MIA. Kurt is flying toward them now. The storm isn't letting up, so it's possible we just have poor signal and can't get through."

"How far to their location?" Kurt asked as he hugged a thermal blanket around him, shivering slightly as he wore thin clothing compared to the heavier outfits of the other men onboard.

"About forty minutes. By the time we get there, it will be far too late."

Chapter 41

Janus and Evans kept the pressure on Kenji as they raced toward the bridge. Connor warned his men ahead to hole up and prepare to meet Kenji as he ran through to them.

Climbing fifteen flights didn't feel so bad with his adrenaline still pumping as he reached the top deck. Evans barged through the door and saw both of his men lying on the floor, blood pooling around their bodies.

Kenji stood with a pistol in one hand, and the short sword he'd used on Janus in the other.

"Seems like your trap didn't work, Commander," Kenji said. His eyes were like two black coals staring directly at Connor. The swaying of the freighter was starting to make Evans feel giddy, despite his experienced sea legs. Janus leaned against the stairwell, clutching at his arm, blood pooling on the deck underneath him.

"Take a look at your friend, Commander. If you keep chasing me, you will allow too much blood to leave your friend's body, and still his heart. Is that what you want? Is catching me the only way to prevent your world from falling apart?" Kenji turned his head, looking out of the rain drizzled windows. "To me, it looks like you are willing to sacrifice your friends for a cause not of their own."

Despite Kenji's cutting words, Evans was prepared to do what it took to prevent him wiping out innocents. His team knew this. Deep down, though, he questioned his own morals. *Just how far would I go?* The loud, thumping blades announced a helicopter's arrival, making Evans think William had come to save the day. It was the opposite.

It was a heavy haulage helicopter and, as Evans and Janus watched, they saw the crane operator pull the bomb from the cargo hold, swaying erratically. Evans had to wonder how the operator even got it out of the hold without blowing them all sky high.

"You see, Commander, it's always best to have a Plan B," Kenji said, as a large cargo net fell from below the chopper to the deck, two man sliding down ropes from winches on either side to clipped them onto the net. The bomb was lowered into the net as the helicopter battled the elements to move away from the rocking ship.

"You see, Commander, I'm always prepared. You should be, too

Without warning, Kenji raised his pistol and shot Janus twice, once in the shoulder and once in the stomach, sending him reeling backward and down the stairwell with a loud crash. Even before Janus had hit the ground Kenji had made his move. He threw open the only other door in the room, the one that led to the top of the bridge.

Evans made the only choice he could in that situation. He jumped down the stairwell and kneeled beside his friend, holding Janus as he gasped.

"Leave me, you've got to stop him. Kill the bastard and end all of this," Janus said. Evans saw blood flowing from underneath his shoulder. The Kevlar vest Janus wore had stopped the worst of the shot aimed at his stomach. Kenji's aim had been true when he aimed at the shoulder, making Evans think the second was more for good measure. The vest had not protected his friend's shoulder. Connor examined the wound. He could see it wasn't a kill shot, but he knew that internal trauma wasn't something that could be seen by the naked eye. Evans had seen men in such a situation die if not quickly treated.

Chapman spoke from his earpiece. "Boss, the whole ship is about to explode, you need to get out of there now." The voice sounded distant as Janus lay bleeding on the deck. Connor only had to look around to see he had failed his team. The bodies of two of his men lay up on the bridge, and his oldest friend had been badly hurt in his pursuit of the radicalised psychopath. The only person unscathed was Evans himself.

A klaxon alarm blared above him. The main console lit up, indicating the ship was taking on water. Evans climbed to his feet and saw through the window that the chopper had completed the removal of the bomb before the explosions began to separate the ship. Not prepared to leave his friend behind, hoisted Janus to his feet as he cried out in pain.

"Chapman, multiple casualties onboard. Janus has been shot, two men are missing down below, and two of the bridge team didn't make it," he stated, feeling a wave of emotions overtaking him, sapping his strength.

"I grabbed both of Janus's men from the deck already, Connor, rest assured they are safe and sound. Was that other helicopter one of ours?" "Negative. They managed to remove the bomb from the freighter before it sinks. All that's left is Kenji. We won't be able to catch it now. I failed us," Connor said, cursing his stupidity.

"Not on my watch, Boss. From up here I can see someone clutching the railing on top—"

"Sounds like Kenji was left behind, despite his best efforts to plan his escape," Connor said, his emotions changing as he sensed an opportunity.

"I need you to get the boys on the chopper to take care of Janus. I will deal with Kenji myself. This has gone on too long," Connor said, as he threw open the door and climbed the short staircase. He pushed the hatch open as the rain cascaded down, wary1 that Kenji might be waiting for him to emerge.

Kenji clutched one hand on the rail as the ship bucked violently. Connor climbed out of the bridge carefully.

"It's over. You've lost, Commander. The world you know is finished…" Kenji yelled through the heavy rain, struggling to be heard over the crashing waves.

In his peripheral vision, Evans saw Chapman swing around to the bridge to assist Janus. Unbelievably, the badly injured big man was hauling himself out of the hatch close behind him as Chapman fought to keep the chopper level with the rising and falling railing.

Kenji used the swaying motion, coupled with yet another explosion on the freighter below, to throw himself at Connor.

Focused on Janus behind him, Connor was unprepared for the crazed man leaping at him. He dodged the swinging short blade as it clanged against the rail, barely missing slicing off his ear. His own rage built at the atrocities the man had committed so far in the name of restoring the Japanese empire. He ducked away, kneeling, and pulled his combat knife from his boot. The two men stood toe to toe as - out of the corner of his eye - Connor saw one of Will's soldiers drop to the roof, aiming his gun at Kenji.

"No! He is mine," Evans spat, the whites of his eyes ablaze in the darkness as he stared at the dark pits on Kenji's face.

Kenji clutched to the railing for dear life after his attack. He still had his short blade and pistol in his waistband of his suit pants.

The ship lurched violently once more, and the pistol flew out of his pants and over the railing.

"It will be a fitting end to see your legacy end here. It's a well-known fact that the captain always goes down with his ship," Connor said. Kenji, enraged, threw himself at Connor once more. Janus, meanwhile, was being airlifted to the turbulent chopper, as Chapman struggled against the head-winds coming off the roof of the bridge.

Kenji leapt at him again, trying to find an opening to silence Connor once and for all.

Connor fended off his slashes with his knife, hoping to tire the man and throw him off balance, ducking under one slash as he lost his footing on the slippery surface.

The ship tilted forward, becoming almost vertical. The latest explosion had begun to split the freighter down the middle, and a large crunching sound could be heard as the weight of the water brought the two halves of the ship together again.

Chapman had to pull away from his position as the spinning turbines of the keel rose out of the water, briefly turning them into air turbines, the chopper receiving an updraft that had everyone inside clinging to their seats for their lives.

Evans and Kenji took calculated swings at one another as they balanced like gymnasts on the slippery surface. With the churning waves battering its metal hull, the ship fell forward in its death throes. Both men fell, clutch-ing the wire cables that ran along the railing to the multiple antennae on top. Fortunately for Kenji, his blade was longer than Evans's combat knife.

Connor watched as the extended reach allowed Kenji to swing at the cables, trying to sever them and send Connor into the spinning propellors below.

"Why won't you die already?" Kenji said. Veins popped in his head and neck as he swung wildly at Evans.

Connor inched away, but his gloved hand was beginning to burn as he clutched at the cable.

A wild swing from Kenji saw his blade clatter off the metal surroundings of the cable. They didn't separate, but loosened as Evans felt his weight pull it down.

Torn between holding on with one hand and fending off Kenji's wild swings, Evans did the only thing he could.

Twirling the knife around in his hand, he threw it as hard as he could, lodging it into Kenji's neck. The blade dropped from Kenji's limp hand as his eyes went wide in shock.

With one final look at Evans, he fell toward the spinning blades below, Connor turning away from the sickening display.

"That's for Australia," he said, before a jolt above returned him to reality.

"Chapman, get me the hell out of here now!" he called. The cable loosened and gave way, detaching from the metal post. He gripped onto it as he collided with the dark red hull. Trying to gain footing on the hull was like trying to run on ice, as his feet couldn't find any grip.. Connor struggled to maintain a grip on the wire, his gloved hands not finding traction on the thin cables.

He began to slip toward the spinning propellors below. One of his gloves began to give way, the Velcro just holding out, as the whooshing blades of Chapman's chopper came closer. Connor shook his head to clear the sea spray and rain in his eyes. With one eye open, he watched Chapman apply a delicate balance of pedal and throttle to turn the nose of the chopper around, lining it up with the hull at an almost ninety-degree angle, peering through the rain that poured down the windshield.

Over the thunderous sound, he could hear Chapman saying someone was going to jump out to him. Then his earpiece was soaked through, and he couldn't hear anything but the thunder around him.

* * *

Inside the chopper, Janus, despite his injuries, argued with the two soldiers to allow him to rescue Connor. He clipped on the harness, knowing full well that his right side would not be strong enough to hold Evans's weight. He would have to on his weaker left side.

He edged out of the chopper and kicked out, instructing Chapman to lower him down quickly. He shot down toward his friend and commander as Connor's grip gave out and he fell.

Evans had never believed the stories people say about their lives flashing before their eyes. As he fell toward the abyss, he refused to believe it was an angel coming toward him as his plunge was suddenly halted. Something strong gripped his arm and pulled him upwards.

The winchman drew back the cable with Janus clutching onto Evans with his one good side, cursing up a storm as the pain flared up again. Chapman managed to keep the helicopter steady enough for the two soldiers to help Janus bring their commander back onboard, slamming shut the exterior door as the helicopter pulled away.

Connor felt a level of fatigue he'd never felt before as one of the soldiers fussed over him in the dim battle lights inside. No one bothered to look back as the sea claimed another soul and reefed another vessel. Sucking it down into its depths with nothing more than a gurgle as the surface swell continued to writhe.

Janus looked at both men inside with him as he sat back on one of the benches. Chapman piloted the chopper away. Connor grabbed one of the headsets, his own helmet lost somewhere on the bottom of the Pacific in the now sinking *Akagi Maru*. He asked Chapman to tune into a frequency he knew well and waited.

After Janus signed off on the call, Kurt came over the intercom. "I didn't think you still carried that kind of weight," he said as Janus pulled the headset off, sighing.

"We won't know yet whether we managed to save at least one country. Only time will tell," Connor murmured. Somewhere in the Pacific, there was still a bomb loose. Connor hoped he wasn't too late as he felt thin tendrils of darkness grasp at his vision.

Chapter 42

Connor Evans felt the warmth before he saw the light. He opened his eyes slowly. His head pounded, and his body felt like it had been beaten black and blue. He tried to get up before pain arced up his back and he fell back down. Turning his head, he saw his clothing laid out on a chair beside him. The simple contents of the room reminded him of a setup he had only seen once before. The modesty and lack of decoration made him think he was on a naval ship.

There was a knock at the door. He called out for the person to enter.

Special Agent Laura Goddard stood resplendent in dress whites complete with black heels as she strode over to the bed. She sat down gingerly.

"How are you feeling?"

"Like someone took a hammer and tongs to my body. What happened to me?" Connor replied, closing his eyes to the streaming white light through the porthole.

She smiled He had never noticed how much warmth that smile brought to him.

"I think you have way too many people to thank for getting you off that ship, but at some point, according to Janus, you fell, and he was there to catch you. He has been calling himself your guardian angel all morning and, quite frankly, it's starting to rub people the wrong way."

Connor started to laugh, thinking of the big man giving himself titles. He broke into a coughing fit which hurt more than he'd expected. He didn't remember taking such a beating, thinking he was mostly unscathed, but then again adrenaline hides many things.

It was then that the situation dawned on him. "Hold on, the bomb? Did we—"

She placed one hand on his exposed arm on the white cotton sheets,

"It's finished. You did it, Commander Evans. You and your team saved many peoples' lives, a high honour among those who know. Unfortunately, only you and your team will ever know. The government asked me to debrief you when you woke and to promise not to tell a soul," Laura said.

She said the first part was in a serious tone, but toward the end, a dimple appeared at the side of her mouth. "So, we've all got to promise never to utter a word to anyone about it," she finished.

He made a sign across his chest. "Cross my heart. Just one thing, how did we stop the helicopter from dropping the bomb?"

Laura went to respond, but another knock at the door interrupted her. Two men entered. The first, like Laura, wore dress whites, and as he approached, Connor saw the insignia marking him as an admiral. The other man didn't need any introduction. Janus sported a black eye, and his arm and shoulder were wrapped in a sling, but he still wore his customary frown.

Janus noticed Laura's hand on Connor's arm and gave him a. Laura withdrew it instantly, her cheeks turning red as she put her head down.

"Forgive me for not introducing myself sooner, Commander Evans. We figured we would let you sleep it off. I am Admiral Marcus Sheehan. I want to thank you for protecting my country from the unnamed psycho who threatened to flood our island paradise." His New Zealander accent, light and energetic, made Connor's own Australian accent sound deeper and thicker.

"We were out in the waters performing military manoeuvres when the call came through. I must say, I was a bit surprised to hear from a frequency I haven't heard from in a while, but I guess some of us never forget the old times, do we?" Admiral Sheehan said.

He took a step closer to Evans, making him feel like he should be standing to attention and saluting. The natural routine of any soldier kicked in and he raised his hand closer to his forehead as the admiral lowered himself gently onto the bed,

"Your man Chapman and I go way back, Commander. But you and I do, too." Connor's eyebrows raised at that. He looked at his friend, but Janus seemed just as surprised.

The man's silvery grey hair on either side shone as the sunlight poured through the porthole.

"Actually, Commander, your father and I go way back. We both attended separate military schools, but we met one day in a bar while coming together for the annual war games in the Pacific. We were inseparable after that, and we remained friends for many years, even now."

The man lowered his eyes, and he picked a thread from his cotton pants, "Your father would be proud of you, and I will make sure he hears about this."

Evans could feel raw emotion threatening to boil over inside, and he lifted the sheet to wipe one of his eyes as he nodded his thanks to the admiral. The two men understood what was meant in the moment.

"Welcome to the *HMNZS Te Mana*, Commander Evans. Take your time to recover, get your sea legs, and when you are ready, we will take you ashore."

As the admiral left, closing the door behind him, Janus moved to the side of the bed and threw himself down on Evan's legs, drawing a gasp of pain as Connor kicked like a child to get him off.

"Jesus, you weigh a ton. When we get back onboard, you clown, we are going to ask Kurt to give you a rundown of how he stays lean and mean," Evans warned. Janus's response was nothing short of withering.

"Maybe so. But can you imagine two of him walking around?" he grumbled.

Evans conceded that Janus had him there.

"You're right, one of him is more than enough. So, where is everyone else?"

"After you made the call, the admiral fired off a missile at the hostile's helicopter disintegrated it into little bits and pieces. From there, the admiral rounded up Chapman and everyone onboard this cruiser. Once here Will's men got their wounds checked out. I was sent to the medical bay, and you were given this beautiful cabin to sleep in." Janus rubbed his face, seeming to think of something else, before he looked at Connor with the most serious look he'd ever given him.

"I had a bunch of pretty nurses to look after me. So it was worth it in the end, to not see your smug face for a while"

Janus rose, looking at Laura and Evans, sensing the spark between them. "Two more things. Maybe you should ask Agent Goddard here about how the news is reporting our latest venture. The other thing is Harry Yates. He wants to talk to you when you are better."

"Where is he now?" Connor replied, still more interested in the first part of Janus's comment.

"Probably at some bar on land, spruiking his craft. I can get the guys to fetch him, or you can go ashore and see him yourself. Last thing. Remember all that data you scraped off the servers from Toyotami Industries? Well, it seems they've gone bust. Their whole operation has been shut down. It's a good thing you happened to pull all their weapon schematics off their servers before it did. Might come in handy in the future."

With that last comment, Janus left the room, unfazed by the emotion in the room. Evans, on the other hand, didn't know what to say to that, figuring that Kurt might be able to look at it back on *Serenity*. The weapons whiz would be excited to get his hands on schematics to build some prototypes.

He looked at Laura, who had shifted closer to him.

"You aren't going to tell the government about my operation now because of that new information, are you?" Connor said, with a lopsided grin.

"Some things are best kept a secret, don't you think, *Commander Evans?*" she said at barely a whisper. She bent down to him, and their lips touched.

* * *

A few days later, Evans felt more alive than he ever had before. Wearing a tan linen polo with Bermuda shorts, he climbed the steps of a small bar and restaurant in Devonport across from the yards of the New Zealand Navy.

Pulling down his sunglasses, he spotted the man trying to come onto the female bartender. Evans came up behind him and placed a hand on his shoulder. The man squirmed under his grip, as Connor sat on a barstool beside him.

"You should know by now, Mr Yates, to steer clear of things that are bad for you, and I'm not just referring to alcohol," Connor said, as Harry looked straight into his eyes. The American was surprised at Connor's sudden appearance.

"How do you know she is bad for me?" he asked. Evans smiled and pointed back down toward the bar to a man built like a tank, with a balding head and tribal tattoos on the side of his face.

Evans shook his head at the man, as the brute glared at Yates. The American gawked.

"How did you know that?" he said in awe, focusing his attention on Connor, away from the brooding gaze of the Māori man. Evans tapped his hands on the counter to get the woman's attention.

"It doesn't matter what I know. It's what you know, Harry. You see, our little jaunt around the Pacific made me realise that your harebrained scheme to acquire the bomb for yourself suggests that you shouldn't be turned loose on the world just yet."

Yates looked perplexed as Evans continued.

"What I am saying is, how about we do business together, you and I?"

"You and I go into business? What will I get from it?"

Evans tutted loudly as the woman came over and he ordered a bourbon on the rocks. "You Americans, always wondering what's in it for you."

He took a swig of the bourbon and smacked his lips together. "I want your contacts in the military, your government contacts, and whatever other connections you have."

Yates looked at him like he had gone mad.

"Are you serious? They aren't just my contacts, they are my father's too, and no amount of money can buy that loyalty," he hissed, starting to ball his hands.

Evans pulled his wallet from his shorts pocket and slid a slip of paper over to Yates. Before the man reached for it, he threw back the glass of bourbon and placed it on top, holding it there.

Leaning in close, he whispered "For what it's worth, Mr Yates, it was a pleasure seeing you again. I am sure at some point we will meet again, sooner than you think."

Evans left Harry with a smile, rising and putting out his hand, which Harry took rather limply, before exiting the premises.

Connor placed his sunglasses back on his face and inhaled the air of Devonport Harbour, looking out towards the berthed ship he had climbed off earlier that day. Sighing, he checked both ways before he crossed the road and walked past two cars, knocking on the passenger window of the third: a black sedan with Auckland plates.

"Fifty dollars," Evans said to the driver of the vehicle, as he peered in.

"You're on," came the reply.

Evans looked at his watch and tapped it, just as Yates sprinted out of the bar, looking in both directions. Connor started to laugh.

Chapman was sat in the driver's seat shaking his head as he reached for his wallet.

Evans leaned on the roof. The heat of the day couldn't sap his good spirits as he looked out over the busy city and port, wondering what adventure waited for them next.